"I don't care what you have to say."

Trace pointed to the door. "You can show yourself out."

"Trace, please?"

"No."

"The least you can do  what I've got to say?"

"And why should I do that?" he asked. "Because we parted on amicable terms? Because you're a decent person? Because you always have everyone else's well-being in mind?" Delainey's stare narrowed and he laughed because they both knew none of those reasons were true. "My point exactly. You have no leverage with me. The minute I saw that fake smile you pasted on for my benefit, I knew you came with something in mind."

"Fine," she said with a dark glower. "You've caught me. I need your help."

"Sucks to be you."

"Is that all you've got for me after everything we'd been through?" she countered, her eyes glazing a little. "At one time, you loved me."

"A long time ago." He stared, unable to believe she'd thrown that card down. "A *very* long time ago."

Dear Reader,

I love writing complicated love stories—ones with twisted, gnarled attachments and entanglements—and that's exactly what you'll find with Trace and Delainey. Difficult choices, painful pasts, and yet the heart wants the heart wants, right? That's how I felt about these two lovers, both strong and stubborn at the same time, neither willing to admit that they were wrong, but the love they share refuses to die. How romantic!

But this story isn't only about two lovers, it's about the sphere of influence surrounding them as they struggle through the complicated mess that is their life, which includes family, friends and career. Life isn't always pretty, but the joy is that much sweeter when you search for it.

I hope you enjoy Trace and Delainey's love story; I certainly enjoyed writing it.

Hearing from readers is a special joy. Please feel free to drop me a line via email through my website, at www.kimberlyvanmeter.com, or through snail mail, at Kimberly Van Meter, P.O. Box 2210, Oakdale, CA 95361.

Kimberly Van Meter

KIMBERLY
VAN METER

—

A Real Live Hero

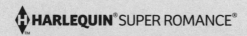
HARLEQUIN® SUPER ROMANCE®

Recycling programs
for this product may
not exist in your area.

ISBN-13: 978-0-373-60835-5

A REAL LIVE HERO

Printed in U.S.A.

ABOUT THE AUTHOR

Kimberly Van Meter wrote her first book at sixteen and finally achieved publication in December 2006. She writes for the Harlequin Superromance and Harlequin Romantic Suspense lines. She and her husband of seventeen years have three children, three cats and always a houseful of friends, family and fun.

Books by Kimberly Van Meter

HARLEQUIN SUPERROMANCE

HARLEQUIN ROMANTIC SUSPENSE

*Home in Emmett's Mill
**Mama Jo's Boys
***Family in Paradise
‡The Sinclairs of Alaska
§Native Country

Other titles by this author available in ebook format.

A writer relies on many research tools to aid the task of creating a completely fictitious world, and while the internet has become an invaluable tool in that endeavor, talking to knowledgeable people cannot be beat.

To that end, I'd like to thank Hollywood producers Jeff Mercer and Christina Villegas for answering my many questions about producing a reality show on location in Alaska.
Any mistakes are my own and no reflection of their true talents!

And to my son, Jaidyn...I am so proud of the young man you're turning into.
I know you'll go far no matter where you go or what you do in life.

CHAPTER ONE

"Tough break on *Vertical Blind*."

Delainey Clarke glanced up at the sympathetic voice and offered a tight smile in response, but hurried all that much more quickly down the brightly lit hallway, hoping she could reach her small cubicle of an office and hide.

She managed to slip inside and dropped the fake smile the minute she was safely behind the closed door.

Tough break? More like death knell. *Vertical Blind* had been her last chance at making her mark at the network as an associate producer, and it had bombed so badly her boss had not only passed on picking up the pilot but had given her newest idea the sardonic brow, as if to ask, "Are you kidding me?" which did not bode well for her future.

Hollywood was a rough town—no, actually, it wasn't a town at all because that would imply that it was inhabited by people. Hollywood was a shark tank, and she was definitely feeling more like chum than a predator at the top of the food chain. What was she going to do? At this rate, she needed more than just a hit, she needed an award-winning, knock-it-out-of-the-park hit in order to restore her status around the network before someone else came along and booted her from her tiny, cramped office.

Suddenly, the back of her head connected with the door as someone tried to enter, and she stumbled away, rubbing the back of her skull with a scowl as Hannah Yaley walked in looking day-spa fresh and plainly perplexed.

"Delainey...were you leaning against the door?" she asked.

Speaking of sharks. Delainey smiled for Hannah's benefit, though why she even bothered, Delainey wasn't sure. They didn't like each other, but for the sake of appearances they played the same passive games as everyone else in this fake town. "What can I do for you, Hannah?" she asked, smoothing the tiny wrinkles from her slim skirt and wondering how Hannah always managed to look as if she'd just collected her clothes from the dry cleaners. "Congratulations on the ratings of *Hubba Hubba,*" she added with false cheer while gagging on the inside. Reality shows were cheap to produce and easy to make a good impression on within the right demographic, but shooting a reality show about the wild shenanigans of college coeds during spring break was like shooting fish in a barrel. *Hubba Hubba* had beaten out every other show in its demographic, making Hannah Yaley the new network darling. And Hannah hated Delainey.

"Thank you, we're very proud of our team," Hannah murmured with put-on modesty. Then her expression crumpled appropriately as she added, "I was so bummed to hear about *Vertical Blind*. I had such high hopes."

Sure you did. "Well, I should've known… A drama about rock climbing was a logistic nightmare, not to mention expensive, and if you don't get the right time slot…" She let the rest of the excuses trail, knowing she sounded like a pathetic loser and preferring to act as if the failure was simply an unfortunate casualty of the business and no real tragedy to her personally.

God, if only that were true. Hannah nodded in complete understanding, but her eyes glittered with undisguised mirth as she said, "Well, I just wanted to pop in and see how you were doing. I was worried you might've taken this recent failure a little hard. But I should've known you'd handle it with grace. You are such an inspiration, Delainey. If I were you, I'd probably end up sobbing in a corner, sucking down vodka and cranberry until I died of alcohol poisoning."

She emitted a sharp laugh at her own joke, and Delainey gave her a brittle smile in return.

"Yes, well, where I'm from, giving up isn't an option."

"Oh, that's right, you're from Alaska...." Hannah shuddered delicately. "Must be murder on the skin. But then, it's not as if there's much opportunity to show much skin when you're bundled in a parka, right?"

Delainey affected a surprised expression as she glanced at the wall clock. "Damn, I have an appointment to get to," she said, grabbing her purse. "Thanks for checking up on me. It means a lot that you care."

Hannah's expression was mildly frosty as she replied, "Of course. We girls have to stick together in this boys' club."

"Absolutely," Delainey agreed, yet wished she could roll her eyes so hard she saw her brain. Just once, she'd like to call Hannah on all her fake bullshit, but Hannah was the favored one right now and Delainey was already getting appraising glances from the other producers, the vultures. She shouldered her purse and followed Hannah out into the hall. "Anyway, good chatting with you. On to bigger and better, right?"

Hannah's expression was patronizing as she said, "That a girl. Such spirit..." before walking away—and if Delainey wasn't mistaken, her shoulders were shaking with suppressed laughter.

Argh! Delainey wished she had a real appointment to dash off to. That might lift her spirits at least a little bit, but as it was, her calendar was depressingly free of appointments. No one was interested in taking a meeting with Delainey Clarke.

Not even the public access channels.

When she'd first arrived in California, she'd been hungry for a new life. Everything had been new and exciting, and she'd been eager to learn the rules of Hollywood's brutal social game. But the bloom had certainly worn off the rose at this point. *You're just depressed over* Vertical Blind, she told herself, trying to prop up her ego and heal her bruised feelings. *This is the nature of the business that you love.*

Did she love it? Not at the moment.

Delainey detoured to her favorite coffee shop, and even though she knew she shouldn't spend the money on such a frivolous purchase, she really didn't think she could face the rest of the day without something sugary and caffeinated.

She needed a hit. *God, please.* She'd come too far to fail now. She'd do anything to succeed. *Just send me something I can work with...*

TRACE SINCLAIR FOUGHT the urge to bat the microphone out of his face as he cast the reporter at the other end a dark look. "I've already given a statement," he said curtly, pushing his way past the throng of reporters all clamoring for an exclusive that he'd already said repeatedly he wasn't going to give. Damn nuisances. He was just doing his job. Why didn't they pester someone who was interested in flapping their jaws about themselves?

"Is it true you're the best tracker in the state of Alaska?"

"How did you know where to find Clarissa Errington?"

"Were the conditions a hindrance to your tracking skills?"

"How close to death was the governor's daughter when you rescued her from the mountain?"

"Please, Mr. Sinclair, don't you know you're a hero? Wouldn't you like to tell your side of the story?"

"No."

"Mr. Sinclair!"

Trace climbed into his truck and gladly put the horde behind him, finally able to breathe. But before he could fully relax, his cell phone rang. He peered at the evil piece of technology that he abhorred and restrained himself from chucking it into a snowbank when he saw his boss's number pop up on the screen. He bit back a muttered curse and answered the phone.

"Yeah?"

"Would it kill you to grant an interview or two? It's really good publicity for the Search and Rescue program, and we could use a little good press, if you know what I mean."

"It's not my job to pander to the press. It's my job to find people. End of story. I don't remember reading anything in my job description that said one word about granting interviews that no one's going to care about when the next big story hits."

"No one cares about lost tourists—but everyone cares about a lost thirteen-year-old girl who just happens to be the governor's daughter. It might not be your thing, but it's big news, and you will give the press a story."

"If I said 'bite me,' would you fire me?" he asked.

"No, because that's exactly what you'd want me to do so you could get out of talking to the press. C'mon, Trace…take one for the team. We need this."

Trace swore and shook his head, knowing Peter would badger him almost as incessantly as the press, and frankly, it would be harder to avoid his boss than the reporters. "One interview," he said. "And I mean—one."

"I guess if that's all I can get out of you," grumbled Peter, adding a sharp, "But it'd better be a good interview. Plug the program several times and make sure you mention how you couldn't have found the girl without your support crew."

"Yeah, sure," Trace said. "Gotta go. Set up the interview and let me know when and where. I'll show up with bells on."

"Sure you will," Peter said, not believing him for a second. "If you don't show up…"

"I will," he assured Peter, sighing. "I promise."

"Good." Peter clicked off and Trace tossed his phone onto the seat, freshly irritated. He didn't understand what the big fascination was with him doing his job. Nobody got this fired up about the mailman delivering the mail. Why should anyone care about what he did? In a perfect world, everyone minded their own damn business and left each other alone.

He hated reporters.

He hated the limelight.

And he most definitely hated toeing the line for someone else's agenda.

The only thing that made this situation tolerable was the fact that Clarissa Errington hadn't been frozen solid by the time he'd found her.

He swallowed the sour lump in his throat.

Clarissa had cried with relief when she'd seen him appear from the dense forest, his orange vest blazoned with Search and Rescue in bold black lettering, and she had stumbled into his arms, terrified and sobbing, so cold she could barely hold on to him.

It wasn't that he was flippant about saving a child's life; it was that he simply didn't want accolades for doing his job. He wasn't a hero, and he hated when anyone used that term to describe him.

He was no hero. He was just a guy trying to make a living doing the only thing he'd ever been good at.

What was so interesting about that?

He needed a beer. Maybe two or three. Was it considered bad form to show up to an interview drunk? Celebrities did it, so why couldn't he? That ought to quash any more of that hero talk that kept getting tossed around.

Peter would likely blow his top if he walked in three sheets to the wind, and Trace didn't want an earful from Peter's wife, Cindy, who'd blame him for causing Peter's blood pressure to skyrocket.

Nope, he realized. Stone-cold sober was the only way available to him.

Just get it over with and be done with it, he told himself.

Twenty minutes of his life and then he could put the nuisance behind him. After that, everything could return to normal and the rest of the world would find something else to chew on while he went back to doing his job—quietly and without microphones being shoved in his face.

CHAPTER TWO

DELAINEY SETTLED INTO her leather-backed chair, ready to throw everything she had into this pitch meeting, having spent a week brainstorming for the most interesting and stellar idea for a new show in the hopes that the gods of television were smiling down on her and would grant her a boon.

Her nerves buzzed from too much caffeine, but she was operating on too little sleep and couldn't chance that she might doze off at the most inopportune time. Calm down, she told herself sternly, working hard to breathe slowly and steadily to still her shaking fingers. *This is only the single most important meeting of your life, so why stress?* Ugh.

Frank Pilcher, head of programming, sat at the head of the long conference table, looking as austere and foreboding as ever, and no matter how many times Delainey tried smiling and putting on her best face, he rarely appreciated her efforts. In short, that man terrified her— more so now than ever because that baleful stare seemed centered on her more than anyone else. Or maybe she was just being paranoid....

"*Vertical Blind* has, in the history of this network, lost more money in the first six weeks than any new show given the green light from this company in the past five years. What have you got for us to lose money on this time, Ms. Clarke?"

Oh. Maybe she wasn't being paranoid. Was it possible to slide down in her chair and slink from the room on the power of her own mortification? A shaky smile fit itself to her lips and she opened her day planner with all her notes and ideas, but her eyesight had begun to swim.

"Well?"

"Uh, yes, well, *Vertical Blind* did not perform as well as we had hoped," Delainey admitted, clearing her voice when a small shake betrayed her. "But, I have been studying the demographic test groups and have found that—"

"Conversely, Ms. Yaley, your show, *Hubba Hubba,* is blowing all projections out of the water," Frank said, cutting Delainey off in mid-sentence, causing her cheeks to flare with heat as she had no choice but to sit and nod in response to Frank's assessment. "The kids seem to like watching one train wreck after another ad nauseum."

"Yes, sir. We are very pleased with the momentum of *Hubba Hubba*," Hannah said with a smile. "The show easily snags the seventeen to twenty-five age bracket, and already we're getting calls from quality advertisers eager to place their product in the commercial slots. Overall, I'd call *Hubba Hubba* a smashing success, one the network can be proud of."

"It's lucrative for sure, but something to be proud of? I wouldn't go that far," Frank said, surprising both Hannah and Delainey. "Although *Vertical Blind* dropped like a stone, the concept was, at least, less inane than *Hubba Hubba*."

Hannah lost her smug smile and nodded, unsure of how to respond, not that it mattered because Frank had moved on. "There was a time when we made quality programming. We need to find a way to do that as well as continue to make money. Thus far, we've missed that mark. I want to hear ideas that do both. And I don't want to hear any more ideas about shows that follow young, drunken idiots around all summer," he warned the group with a dark glare. "I want to hear something people can really get behind and care about, and not because it's filled with debauchery or alcohol-soaked shenanigans."

Hannah pretended to study her notes, as if she'd actually jotted something down that might fit the criteria, but Delainey knew for a fact that since *Hubba Hubba* was a hit, Hannah had been looking for several different ways to copy its success, relying mainly on the same format and concept.

Which left the floor open for Delainey to take the stage and show Frank what she could do. "Actually, as I was saying, I think I may have some ideas you might like," she started, flipping the pages until she came to the circled ideas. "I was thinking there aren't any cooking shows aimed at teens—"

"Teenagers don't cook," Ira West interrupted drily. "I should know. I have two at home who barely know how to operate the toaster."

"Right, scratch that," she said, drawing a line through the idea and moving to the next. "So, America loves an underdog. I was thinking of something along the lines of—"

"Alaska!" Frank snapped his fingers with a wide smile that looked wholly unnatural on his face, and her hopes plummeted when she realized he hadn't been listening to a word she'd been saying. "We need that guy who saved the little girl from the mountains.... What was his name? It's been all over the news. Fascinating stuff. He's a tracker. I didn't even know that people still did that."

Tracker? In Alaska...? She stared in confusion, hating that she'd spent all that time scribbling notes on pitches she'd never get to present when she should've been watching the damn news instead. She looked around the table, and confused expressions mirrored hers until Ira ventured, "I think his name is something like Trick? Trent? It's a weird name, I remember that much...."

Suddenly, Delainey's lips felt numb. Could it be? No way. It wasn't possible. But...he was the only tracker in Alaska who might've had the skills to rescue that girl.... What the hell... she'd take the chance and hope she was right. "Might it have been Trace Sinclair?" she supplied in a small voice, hoping to God that fate wouldn't be that cruelly interested in watching her squirm like a gutted worm on a hook.

Much to her chagrin, Frank snapped his fingers with open glee. "That's it. Trace Sinclair. That's a name with charisma. And his job is interesting, too. Sort of a throwback to the old ways. Is he an Indian of some sort? Maybe his skills were passed down from his ancestors.... Wouldn't that make a good story?"

"He's not a Native Yupik. He's as white as you and I," she murmured, hardly able to believe they were discussing Trace Sinclair around the war room table. "But he's the best tracker in the state of Alaska, or so I've heard."

Hannah turned slightly hostile as she asked, "And how do you know so much about this man?"

That was privileged information and she was not about to spill her private details, but when she saw the avid interest in Frank's eyes as well as the envious looks around the table for having valuable information, she immediately sat a little straighter and smiled more brightly as she answered without hesitation. "Oh, Trace and I grew up together in Homer. We're great friends. He and I chat all the time—when he's not out saving lives, of course," she proclaimed, hoping she wasn't struck down by lightning for blatantly lying through her teeth. It wasn't that she didn't know him—oh, Delainey knew Trace better than anyone on this planet—but she'd definitely lied about their close ties.

Truth was, Trace probably wouldn't spit on her if she were on fire.

But no one else had to know that, least of all anyone at this table.

"So if you're such close pals, how come you didn't know who Mr. Pilcher was referencing?" Hannah asked, suspicious.

"Honestly, sometimes I forget that what Trace does is so exciting. And my mind was focused on all the great ideas I'd planned to pitch today," she said, trying to steer the conversation back to her advantage.

Frank waved everyone else into silence as he pinned Delainey with an expectant look. "Schedule a meeting with this man," he said. "I want to meet him."

A flush of fear crept up her neck as she faked an airy laugh. "Oh, Mr. Pilcher, I hate to be the bearer of bad news, but Trace is way too busy for a trip to California, even if it were to meet someone as important as you. But the next time I chat with him I'll let him know you're a fan."

"I think he'll want to hear what I have to say," Frank said. "I think the next big thing is going to be the heroes of Search and Rescue, like your friend, Trace. Imagine this…cameras following Trace—is he good-looking?" Frank paused for Delainey to answer.

"Very," she admitted. "The camera would love him. The female fan mail would be astronomical."

Frank liked her answer. "Excellent. The cameras follow Trace as he tracks people in the Alaskan wilderness, saving lives. We could play up the dramatic element—will he or won't he save them? You have to watch to find out! This could be big."

"I'd be happy to go to Alaska to talk to this

Trace Sinclair. I could be on the first flight out tonight," Hannah offered.

Hannah alone with Trace? Delainey knew she had no room to be territorial, but the idea of Hannah putting her moves on Trace made her want to howl. "I'll go," Delainey said quickly. "I know the area and he and I are already friends, so it makes sense for me to go."

Frank agreed. "Delainey has a point," he said, causing Hannah to deflate somewhat—and that made Delainey happy.

Emboldened, Delainey added, "I can almost guarantee that I can get Trace to agree to shoot a pilot, Mr. Pilcher. I doubt Trace would even talk to anyone else."

"Is he a difficult sort of fellow?" Frank asked.

"Not difficult," she hedged, praying for forgiveness. "But I know we'd have a better chance of success if someone he felt comfortable with brokered the deal."

Frank agreed with Delainey's completely fictitious logic, and she wanted to fall face-first onto the table. Maybe she should've gone into screenwriting instead of producing. Seems she had a flair for making stuff up. Good grief, what was she getting herself into? Frank looked pleased with himself as he announced, "It's a done deal then. Delainey will go to Alaska and talk to this Trace Sinclair immediately. The story is hot right now and I want to hook into the momentum."

Just talk to Trace? Maybe that was doable. She knew for a fact Trace wouldn't agree to a pilot, but Frank didn't know that and surely he wouldn't fault her for failing, right? But just as Delainey's despair had begun to lift, Frank added, "Don't come back without a signed contract in your hand."

Oh, hell. There went her career. She managed a nod as if her mission were completely possible, and she scooped up her day planner, phone and other miscellaneous items before scurrying from the war room, her heart beating hard enough to make a bruise.

What had she done? Had she just promised to deliver Trace Sinclair—a notoriously private individual—to the head of programming when she had less than zero chance of success?

She was sunk.

She might as well have promised Mr. Pilcher to deliver a unicorn while she was promising the moon. *Go back and tell him the truth—that Trace Sinclair probably hated you for breaking his heart and splitting when he'd needed you the most.*

Delainey swallowed, not quite sure if she was choking down a ball of shame or regret. Either way it didn't feel good, and she wondered if she was on the cusp of a nervous breakdown.

She was on the brink of losing everything. She'd left Homer to make a name for herself in Hollywood as the next Nora Ephron, and thus far all she'd managed to do was scare off every talent in the area as the kiss of death. No one wanted to work with her, and she was dangerously close to losing her condo. Sure, she'd overpaid in the first place, but she'd assumed once she started making the big bucks, the mortgage would be a snap. Well, the big bucks had yet to pour in, and Delainey was suffocating under that monster payment. But she loved her condo. It had represented her new beginning, a bold, fresh start after wrenching herself out of a lifestyle that had nearly sucked her in under the guise of love.

She couldn't lose her condo.

She couldn't lose her job.

Bottom line: if Trace Sinclair stood between her and success, she'd truss him like a Christmas turkey and deliver the man with a bow perched on top of his blond head.

Watch out, Alaska. I'm coming home.

CHAPTER THREE

TRACE WAS AN early riser by habit, but this morning he buried his splitting head beneath his pillow, with a groan, to escape the sunlight slanting in from his bedroom window and stabbing him in the eye.

God, he would never drink like that again. *Ever.*

Damn reporter. He knew it wouldn't be a good idea to start talking about himself and what he did for a living, because invariably someone with a nose for research would turn up his sister's case and his role in it. Simone's death was always a juicy story, no matter that it was nearly a decade old. And just when Trace had started to relax, the woman peppered him with questions from the past.

"When you were searching for thirteen-year-old Clarissa Errington, were you worried you might have a repeat of what happened with your youngest sister, Simone Sinclair?"

That one question had frozen Trace's lips and he'd simply stared at the woman, immediately filled with disgust. "I'm not here to talk about the past," he said, shooting a glare at Peter for putting him in this predicament. Peter looked chagrined but motioned for him to continue. "We can talk about the Errington case and that's it," he practically growled, but the woman was a bulldog and didn't let it go.

"Tell me how it felt to save young Errington and how it contrasted with not being able to save your sister. Are you in this business because of your sister? Did that one tragedy—"

"This interview is over." He ripped off the mic clipped to his shirt and tossed it to the ground. The reporter looked aghast and shocked, which only went to prove that she didn't have the sense God gave a goose. He sent Peter a stony look, and Peter dropped his head in his hand in frustration. The last thing Trace saw before he left was Peter talking to the reporter. Whether Peter was trying to smooth things over or trying to stand up for Trace was unknown, and Trace didn't care. It was time for that beer.

One beer had turned into two, then three and then he lost count.

And now he was paying for his indulgence.

He made his way into the kitchen and made a pot of coffee, then gulped down three aspirins with a swallow of water while he waited. Trace bent over the sink and splashed his face several times with ice-cold water. The frigid shock chased away the grogginess but made his head want to explode. Just as he was about to pour a blessed cup of the strong, dark brew, he was stalled by a polite but firm knock on his door. What the…? Very few knew where he lived and even fewer visited. And those who would, rarely bothered because he was never home.

He stalked to the door and jerked it open, ready to scare off whoever had the misfortune of knocking on his door today, but when he found who was standing on his doorstep, for a moment all he could do was stare in total shock as awareness rippled through him like an unpleasant virus bent on destroying him from the inside out.

"Hello, Trace."

An attractive but entirely too thin platinum blonde stood smiling at him with white gleaming teeth. Was this some kind of joke? Some kind of sick prank? She looked different but he'd recognize those green eyes anywhere— Hell, he'd stared into them enough times to sear them into memory forever. "What are you doing here?" His voice was flat, emotionless and entirely unwelcoming, but she didn't seem to notice. She started to speak, but he interrupted her. "Forget it, I changed my mind. I don't care." And then he slammed the door in her face.

Delainey Clarke had balls of steel to show up on his doorstep. Balls of ever-lovin' steel.

"C'mon, Trace, don't be rude," she said from behind the door. "I need to talk to you."

"There's nothing you could say that I would want to hear," he called out, going to his coffeepot and pouring himself a cup. He lifted the cup to his lips and heard the door opening. She'd always been a pushy broad, which probably worked in her favor in California. He turned with a scowl, but she didn't seem to mind that he wasn't exactly ushering her in with open arms. "Don't you understand what a slammed door means? It means *you're not wanted*," he said, emphasizing the words.

"Once you hear what I have to say, you're going to thank me," she assured him with a bright, completely fake smile that he could see right away was part of her gimmick.

"I don't care what you have to say," he disagreed, pointing to the door. "You can show yourself out, the same way you showed yourself in. And lose my address."

"Trace, please?"

"No."

The sudden tightening of her jaw nearly made him laugh. Delainey had never been much of a poker player. Everything she felt and thought ran across her face like a ticker tape. "Why do you have to be such a jerk all of the time?" she asked, crossing her arms. "The least you can do is just humor me and listen to what I've got to say."

"And why should I do that?" he asked, almost conversationally. "Because we parted on amicable terms? Because you're a decent person? Because you always have everyone else's well-being in mind?" Delainey's stare narrowed and he laughed because they both knew none of those reasons were true. "My point exactly. You have no leverage with me. I don't care what you're selling. And trust me, the minute I saw that fake smile you pasted on for my benefit, I knew you came with something in mind."

"Fine," she said with a dark glower. "You've caught me. I need your help, and if there was anyone else on this planet I could ask I would. But of all the dumb bad luck, you're the only one I can ask."

"Sucks to be you."

"Is that all you've got for me after everything we've been through?" she countered, her eyes glazing a little. "At one time, you loved me."

"A long time ago." He stared, unable to believe she threw that card down. "A *very* long time ago."

She held his stare and after a long moment said, "Listen, I suppose you have no reason to care any longer, but I'm on the verge of losing everything if I don't succeed in convincing you to become the next star of the network I work for." At his incredulous expression, she pushed forward in a rush. "You don't understand. This could be good for both of us. I'm not asking you to do something for me without being compensated. Trust me, the money is good. And if the pilot gets picked up, it could mean even more money with endorsements and commercial deals, and I could help you navigate the tricky contract—"

"You mean you would help me negotiate a legal document?" he mocked, and she stopped her spiel. He gave her a patronizing look. "I wouldn't trust you to negotiate my cell phone bill."

"I could lose everything if I don't land this deal," she said, her eyes filling for real this time. "Please help me, Trace. All you have to do is agree to film the pilot, and anything after that we can renegotiate. I need this. My last three shows have tanked and no one wants to hear my pitches anymore. I'm like the black plague of Hollywood."

Trace sipped his coffee, unable to believe her nerve and unwilling to believe her tears. "I'm sure you'll figure something out. You're a resourceful girl."

"Damn you, Trace," she muttered, wiping at the moisture leaking from her eyes. "I never realized how much of an unfeeling bastard you are."

His mouth twisted in a wry smile. "Funny, I thought the same thing about you when you threw my offer of marriage in my face right about the time when my entire world was crumbling. I guess what they say about karma is true."

"That's not fair and not even the same," she said hotly. "Are you such a weak individual that you'd dredge up the past to hurt me now?"

"I'm not dredging up anything. I'm stating facts. And I wasn't the one who brought up the past first. You tried to guilt me into dancing to your tune by bringing up our history. But, honey, what you don't realize is that for me, the past is simply that and I have no interest in revisiting it." He walked away with a wave. "Sorry for the wasted trip. I hope your plane doesn't drop into the ocean on your way back to California."

He heard her gasp and then the front door slammed again as she bolted. He hoped that was the last time he saw Delainey Clarke ever again.

And he'd mistakenly thought his crippling hangover was the worst way to start his day....

RUDE. OBNOXIOUS. Petty. Selfish—a litany of un-flattering words skipped across Delainey's brain as she drove back into town. And after she'd ex-hausted all the mean words she could think of to describe the man she'd once fancied herself madly in love with, she tried feverishly to think of a way to salvage the situation.

Perhaps she could find another tracker who might be willing to step into the limelight.... But even as she entertained the idea, she dis-carded it. That curmudgeon Pilcher wanted Trace—no substitutes would suffice—and if she didn't deliver the man, her tiny cubicle of an office was going to get a new resident and she'd be out on the street.

How could Trace be so cold to her after ev-erything they'd been through? They'd been high school sweethearts and his sister, Miranda, had been her best friend. At one time, they'd been thick as thieves. And now? Well, she was sur-prised at how much it stung that he couldn't stand the sight of her. For the briefest moment, she toyed with the memory of Trace, his dark blond hair a tousled mess, and his eyes warm with adoration as he stared down at her, his touch as gentle as a summer breeze. Trace had always been the quiet type, but with her he'd opened up. They'd spent hours, fingers twined together, planning an imaginary future that, now as she recalled the details, had been plainly impossible given her dreams and goals.

"We'll have two kids—twins!—and they'll be the cutest kids on the planet, of course," she'd chattered happily one day their senior year while they were lying side by side on his parents' roof, staring up at the summer sky. "And you'll, of course, be the best dad in the world because you're so patient and kind and super smart. I'll work in California and come home on the weekends, or maybe you could do something in California and we could get a cute apartment together. I can't wait to live someplace where you can wear shorts and a T-shirt nearly all year long. I'm tired of all the snow and freezing my tail off."

Trace had laughed at her impassioned declaration and then had distracted her by sealing his mouth to hers, and his tactic had worked... for a time.

But in the end, Delainey had had no intentions of staying in Homer, no matter who was doing the asking. Sadness tugged at her heartstrings for the loss of something special, but she didn't see the sense in crying for the past when there was nothing that could be done about changing it. Besides, her future wasn't in Homer. She belonged in warm, sunny California, where the beaches were dotted with surfers and bikini-clad girls. Already she felt the Alaskan chill seeping into her bones, trying to take up permanent residence in her marrow. No, she may have been born in Alaska to a fisherman's family, but Delainey was meant for bigger things, which is why Trace was going to help her get what she needed, whether he wanted to or not.

So how was she supposed to encourage Trace to do something he plainly didn't want to do?

Hollywood was filled with difficult people; she'd just have to find a way to work around Trace. And if she couldn't do that, she'd find a way to *compel* him to sign on the dotted line.

She detoured from her route and headed for the Search and Rescue office. Perhaps if she couldn't get Trace to see things her way, his boss could.

There was more than one way to skin a cat—and she was desperate enough to try anything.

CHAPTER FOUR

DELAINEY HAD BRIEFLY considered going straight
to Trace's boss to plead her case to someone in
actual authority, but after taking a critical look
at her travel-wrinkled clothing and the dark circles under her eyes that no amount of expensive,
high-end concealer could completely hide, she
knew she had to freshen up first. For that matter, now that she gave it some more thought, she
probably should've done that before attempting
to persuade Trace to join Team Delainey after
such a protracted hiatus, but she'd been running on pure adrenaline and hadn't wanted to
stop to think.

Sometimes thinking was bad. She needed action, not bouts of quiet pondering.

However, since her first plan had blown up
in her face in spectacular fashion, she had to
adjust her tactics.

She gripped her suitcase handle and blew out
a determined breath as she stared at the small
house where she grew up. If only she'd had it
in the budget to spring for a hotel. The network

usually paid for those things, but Hannah had to open her big fat mouth—that woman was the devil—and Pilcher hadn't approved the hotel voucher. Delainey couldn't help but worry that Pilcher was punishing her for the failure of *Vertical Blind,* which made her only all the more desperate to close this deal.

Which meant, for the time being, sucking up her aversion and distaste at the idea of going home and making the best of it.

Oh, God, if only she didn't hate this place. Everything looked the same—same worn and faded shutters that never saw a fresh coat of paint ever, same stench of fish everywhere—same bleak sense of poverty clinging to every plank.

Panic overwhelmed her good sense, and she entertained the option of putting a hotel stay on her personal credit card. But she was already maxed out, and her savings account was, frankly, anemic at this point. So there was no option but the one staring at her.

Delainey purposefully lowered her shoulders and lifted her chin. She was stronger than this. One trip home was not going to derail her. She'd faced down bigger threats than her sad past. No problem.

She opened the door, wincing as it screeched on its hinges. The sound, to her ears, was a loud announcement to everyone in town that Delainey Clarke had returned with her tail between her legs. She jerked her hand away and nearly turned on her heel with a "Screw it" on her lips when she heard her brother's surprised voice.

"Laney?"

"Thad?" She stared at her younger brother, unsure of her welcome. He looked different, older. Life as an Alaskan fisherman was a hard one, and it'd started taking its toll on her brother. There were faint crow's-feet bracketing his gray eyes from squinting into the harsh sunlight reflecting from the water, and his arm was in a cast. "Surprise..." she said with a tremulous smile.

"Damn, girl, you are a sight for sore eyes," Thad said, breaking into a grin and quickly folding her into a hug. She tried not to wrinkle her nose at the subtle scent of fish clinging to his clothing, but it brought back a wash of unpleasant memories and she had to stop herself from stiffening. Thankfully, Thad hadn't noticed. "Man, I never thought I'd see the day..."

That made two of them. Delainey shrugged and smiled. "I had some business to do in the area and thought it was time for a visit."

At that, his expression was mildly reproachful as he said, "Yeah, it's been a long time. Too long. I know you and Pops didn't exactly part on good terms, but eight years is a long time between visits."

Guilt tugged at her. He was right but the idea of coming home before she'd achieved her goals had been an effective deterrent to visiting, even though at one time she and her brother had been close. She supposed it was her fault they'd drifted apart. "Did you get the Christmas card I sent?" she asked.

"Yeah. It was real sweet. That gas gift card was nice, too. Pretty extravagant, too, but I suppose when you're pulling down the cash like you are…" Thad's misplaced pride only made Delainey feel that much more like a fraud, but she had to shelve those feelings for now. Besides, if she managed to land Trace, her worries would be over. Finally.

"What happened to your arm?" she asked.

He lifted his arm to glance at it then answered with a shrug. "Slipped on fish guts and landed wrong. Pretty stupid way to break an arm. No glory at all," he said. She smiled. Her brother hadn't changed much. He was pretty much still the man-boy she'd left behind, and for that she was grateful. Thad reached for her suitcase and took it before she could protest. "I'll put this in your room. How long are you staying?"

"Not long," she answered, wandering the

living room, wondering when her father and brother became better housecleaners. She'd expected an inch or so of dust on every surface, but everything was surprisingly clean. "If you're not on the boat, who's working with Pops?"

"He's got a few guys he picked up for short-time work. My cast is supposed to come off within the next two weeks, and then I'll be right as rain. It's a good thing I was here when you arrived. Pops is sure gonna be shocked when he sees you." The slight nervousness in Thad's voice didn't surprise Delainey. The homecoming wasn't likely to be filled with a joyous hug and reminiscing. "Hey, Laney, there's something I need to tell you."

She nodded, half listening, and went to the kitchen. Again, the cleanliness shocked her. Her father had never been one to lift a finger when it came to domestic stuff and surely hadn't expected Thad to pick up the slack, either. All of the household responsibilities had fallen on her shoulders, no matter that she'd been only nine when her mother had died. She couldn't count the times she'd slaved in that kitchen, wishing and hoping for a different life. She hated fish, and when her father had put little store in her doing anything more than cooking, cleaning and eventually marrying a man from good fishermen stock and settling down, she'd burned with a desperate desire to bolt at the first chance. Delainey roused herself from her mental walkabout just in time to catch Thad's awkward conversation.

"Laney…if you give her a chance you might really like her. She's good for Pops, you know? I mean, she's real sweet and Pops isn't the easiest to get along with—"

"Wait… What are you talking about?"

"Brenda."

"Who is Brenda?" she asked, confused.

"Didn't you hear me? Brenda is Pops's woman now. She's real nice, so don't go and say anything that'll hurt her feelings."

"Pops is dating?" The idea had never occurred to her, but now that she looked at her old house she saw it through different lenses. There was definitely a woman's touch, aside from the obvious cleanliness. Silk flowers were sitting in a vase on the windowsill and she could actually see through the glass of the window, when before it was crusted with years of mud and hard-water residue.

"He's more than dating. He married her."

"Married?" Her father was married? "I couldn't even get a phone call?"

"Well, Brenda wanted to tell you, but Pops… You know how he can get. He's still hurt over the way things went down when you split. And you haven't much tried to fix things since, so he figured you didn't need to know."

"He wants *me* to fix things?" She tried not to be insulted, but her blood pressure rose just the same. "He's the one who said he never wanted to see me again."

"You know he just says that stuff. He doesn't mean it."

"No, I don't know that, Thad," she retorted stiffly. "Where I come from, people mean what they say and say what they mean." Not exactly. No one in Hollywood spoke from his or her heart. Because no one had one. Being fluent in doublespeak was a requirement, and Delainey had been woefully unprepared when she'd first landed on the scene as a young producer with stars in her eyes. She hated thinking of her young self; so embarrassingly naive. "So he went and got married. Good for him. Is she deaf, dumb and blind?" She'd have to be to voluntarily put up with Harlan Clarke.

"Not generally, but I've been told I have an exceedingly cheery disposition, if that counts for anything," a voice from behind her answered, and Delainey whirled to find a short, chubby woman with apple cheeks and a frizz of dull blondish curls on her head, carrying two grocery bags. Thad rushed to help and the woman unloaded her bags, eyes sparkling with curiosity and knowing. "I've waited a long time to meet you, but I must say, I never expected you to be so much like your father."

"I'm nothing like my father," Delainey said, stiffening. "You must be Brenda." At Brenda's nod, Delainey offered a stilted apology but wanted to sink through the floor. "I didn't realize you were here. I'm sorry for that comment."

"Oh, honey, don't worry yourself about that. From what my friends tell me, stepmothers and their stepdaughters are bound to share words at some point or another, so I figure we'll just get that out of the way right quick so we can get on with being friends."

Who was this woman? Delainey looked to Thad, almost for help, but Thad was already on Team Brenda and hoping Delainey would join the team, as well. Unfortunately, Delainey wasn't interested in being on anyone's team aside from her own. "I didn't realize my father had remarried," she said. "Congratulations."

"Boy, I bet that cut like a razor coming out of your mouth," Brenda observed almost cheerfully. "Darlin', we've got a lot of catching up to do. Are you staying for dinner? I'm making your daddy's favorite, spaghetti with meatballs."

Delainey looked to Thad with a frown, and he supplied an explanation. "Since Brenda came around, he can't get enough of her cooking.

Loves her spaghetti and meatballs. It's pretty good. You'll like it."

"My, how things change when you miss a few years," Delainey muttered under her breath, feeling much like Alice when she tumbled down the rabbit hole. "Anything else? Perhaps Pops has suddenly taken a liking to classical music, too?"

"Goodness no, your daddy has a fondness for folk country and always will, bless his soul. I like some George Strait myself, but the bluegrass took some getting used to." Brenda moved past Delainey and started making herself at home—well, Delainey supposed it was her home now, too. But she was discomfited to realize she felt some bristling sense that Brenda was poaching on her turf when Delainey hadn't been around in eight years. "Are you too tired to help out? I know that flight can be a doozy. If you're not too tired, I could always use an extra hand in the kitchen."

"I don't cook," Delainey said flatly. She hadn't cooked in years, almost refused to after she left Alaska. Cooking was domestic. She wasn't a housewife. She was a businesswoman who held dinner meetings, if she ate dinner at all. She eyed the pasta. Too many carbs. "I'd planned to stay here, in my old room, but I didn't realize… If it's too much trouble, I can get a hotel room."

"Thad has told me all about his successful sister living the glitz-and-glamour life in Hollywood, but there's no sense in spending good money when you have family to take you in. Now, go wash your face and spritz off and we'll gab like old hens in a henhouse before your daddy gets home. I'm sure we have lots in common."

"I can't," she said, sharp enough to earn a pleading look from Thad, but she couldn't act as if it was completely normal to cook a family meal with her new stepmother—a woman she'd never even known existed until five minutes ago—when it was bad enough that she knew her father wasn't going to exactly do a cartwheel when he saw his ungrateful, selfish daughter showing her mug around town again. Delainey rubbed at her forehead and knew she couldn't stay here. No. No. No. "Actually, I think it would be better if I stayed at a hotel. I wouldn't want to disrupt the house. Besides, as much as I know you're trying to smooth things over between me and my dad, our issues run deeper than you can imagine. It's going to take more than sitting around the dinner table stuffing our faces with carbs to change what went wrong between us. I'm sorry."

Brenda pursed her lips and narrowed her gaze. "Suit yourself, dear. But remember, regret is a terrible companion. It's like a house-guest who never leaves."

"I don't have any regrets."

"Sure you do. We all do, but yours are plainer than most, I can tell you that."

"You don't know me and I don't appreciate you foisting your brand of country wisdom on me." She looked to her brother. "Could you please get my luggage? I'll find a place to stay elsewhere."

"Come on, Laney…" But when Thad saw her mind was made up, he dragged her suitcase from the room and handed it to her as she waited by the door, eager to get away. "If you'd just give her a chance," he said in a low voice that only she could hear.

"I'm not here to make friends, Thad. I just needed a place to sleep. I should've known that coming home wasn't going to be that place." At his crestfallen expression, she softened minutely. Thad was a good kid and had always been kindhearted. She caressed the scruff on his cheek and said, "I'll call you when I get settled and we'll go to lunch. I promise. In the meantime, take care of that arm."

She'd just slammed the trunk closed when the sound of her father's old truck rumbled down the street. *Perfect timing,* she wanted to mutter. Another five minutes and she'd have been gone. If she'd been thinking straight, she never would've presumed she could stomach staying with her father. She didn't care if she ran through her savings account like water through a sieve; she wasn't sleeping one night under the same roof as that man…and his new wife. Hand on the door handle, she contemplated leaving without a word uttered, but a part of her wanted him to acknowledge her—perhaps only so she could refuse the gesture. But when he stopped for the barest moment and gave her a once-over then kept walking, she balled her fists and wanted to scream. Delainey fought the urge to follow him straight into the house to give him what was coming to him. But she didn't confront him. No, instead she stood like a statue, staring and doing nothing. *Nice to see you, too. What a jerk.* She climbed into her rental and drove away, not realizing until she was a mile down the road she had tears tracking down her cheeks.

CHAPTER FIVE

TRACE WANTED TO PUNCH something. No, that wasn't the right word. He wanted to *destroy* something. How dare Delainey Clarke show up as if everything was peachy between them. That soul-sucker lost the right to show her mug in his personal space the day she'd thrust his offer of marriage back in his face and left town so fast she broke the sound barrier. And at his bleakest moment! He made it a point not to go there, but seeing Delainey again brought the memory front and center.

"You're the only thing that makes sense in my life," Trace had said, bending on one knee, his voice breaking as he presented the small diamond he'd scrimped and saved to purchase. He didn't make a lot of money but he didn't spend frivolously either, and it had taken a year to save up the cash to make the biggest purchase of his young life. But she was worth it, he'd told himself. Delainey was his heart and soul, and he needed her in his life more than anything. Especially after Simone. "Please do me the honor of being my wife."

Delainey had stared at the ring as if it had sprung fangs and hissed at her and she actually took a step back, distancing herself from it and him. "No," she whispered. Her green eyes had misted and widened and she shook her head, almost in horror. A sick feeling lodged itself in his gut and he felt like a fool kneeling, so he climbed to his feet and snapped the ring box shut. "I can't."

"Why not?" he asked, confused and hurt. "I know you love me and I love you, so what's the problem?"

"The problem? If you don't know, then you don't know me at all. I have a degree in film production. What kind of job am I going to get here with that?"

"You're serious about going off to California?" he asked, incredulous. "My career is here. You've always known that."

"And you've always known that I have big dreams that *aren't* here."

"Yeah, well, what does that have to do with getting married?" he asked, irritated and defensive. He'd always thought her talk of running off to California was kid stuff, not the kind of real-life aspirations that adults followed through with. He'd assumed she'd use her degree to get a job with the local television studio in Anchorage, certainly not something in Hollywood. But even so, he didn't understand why she'd reject everything he was offering based on that reason. "I mean, we could still get married, you know. We'd work something out."

"And if we did, you'd want me to stay here, and I'm not going to stay here. I've been saving up for a plane ticket to California and first month's rent and security deposit for an apartment."

He stared. "You've been planning to leave?"

"Yes. I told you that was my plan after graduating college. I stayed a year past my plan, and I'm not going to stay here another year." Her eyes, so beautiful to Trace, seemed to harden into green chips of stone as she continued. "You never listen to me, Trace. You're a country boy and I'm made to be a city girl. I thought we could make it work, but the fact is I've been realizing that we're not meant to be like I thought we were. I was going to tell you…"

"When?" he demanded to know. "After I'd purchased our first home?"

She graced him with a look. "Sarcasm? Is that necessary? This is hard enough to do without you being mean."

"Forgive me, I just had my dignity stomped into the ground," he replied caustically, tucking the ring box into his jeans when he really wanted to chuck it as far away from him as he could throw it. "So, are you breaking up with me, too?" At her silence, he swore under his breath, unable to believe this was happening. It was like a bad, bad dream. "You have excellent timing," he said, happy to use anger as a shield against the pain that was coming. "Excellent timing. I thought I was at my lowest with my baby sister being murdered, but you showed me I had so much further to fall. Thanks, babe. You're a doll."

"I'm sorry," she said, her face flushing. "I should've told you sooner, but then everything happened with Simone and…"

"And what? You wanted to wait to rip out my heart?"

"I was trying to be considerate."

"Well, thank you for your *consideration*." He scorned the sudden appearance of tears in her eyes, saying as he walked away, "Good luck in California. I never want to see you again."

"Trace…"

But he kept walking. Closing his heart for good.

Trace opened his eyes and realized his fists were clenched so hard his knuckles had whitened and he'd carved little half-moons into his palms. Eight years was a long time, but apparently not long enough. Seeing Delainey again brought all the rage and hurt right back to the surface, spilling over the sides and contaminating everything around it. He hated her. God, he hated her. She'd used him, played him, and then when he hadn't been of any more use to her, she'd left him behind.

So now Delainey needed him for something? She could go hang herself and see if he cared. Whatever trouble she was in, she could just figure out a solution without his help.

And what the hell had she done to her face and hair? She looked as fake as a three-dollar bill with her platinum-blond hair and button nose. Not much of an improvement, if his opinion mattered much. He'd preferred her light brown hair, which had complemented her green eyes, giving her a mysterious air that was almost bewitching. Now, she just looked like every other plastic woman running around trying to be someone she wasn't. And she was way too thin. He could practically count the ribs in her side when before Delainey had always been a little on the soft side—not thick by any means, but soft and feminine with full, rounded hips and nice, healthy breasts. Alaska was a harsh place, and having a little meat on the bones helped insulate against the bitter cold. At her current frail size, Delainey was likely to freeze to death waiting for a latte.

He groaned when he realized he was still spending way too much energy thinking about Delainey, and he knew he needed to occupy his mind with something else before he lost it. He dialed his sister Miranda and tapped his finger with agitation as he waited for her to pick up.

"Hey, Trace," she answered with a smile in her voice. Obviously, she wasn't aware that her former best friend was strolling around town. Should he tell her? He didn't want her to be blindsided as he'd been, right? "You're never going to guess who showed up on my doorstep."

"Churchgoers trying to save your soul?" Miranda guessed, half joking.

"That would've been more welcome than who it actually turned out to be." He waited a half second before continuing, "Delainey Clarke."

"What?" All laughter fled from Miranda's voice, and he could actually imagine his sister sitting straighter in shock. "Are you kidding me?"

"I would never make a joke in such bad taste," he said. "She knocked on my door looking for a favor of all things. Can you imagine?"

"Wow, that's either really brave or really stupid," she said. "So what did she want? Is she dying or something? Or maybe she's started a twelve-step program and she's trying to make amends for something."

"It's work-related, I guess. She wants me to sign on for some show of hers."

"You? Plainly she's forgotten how antisocial you are."

"Yeah, plainly."

"So what are you going to do?"

"What do you think? I told her to get off my property and lose my address," he growled, surprised his sister had to ask. "I don't owe her anything, and I certainly don't feel like handing out any favors after what she did to me and my family."

"Yeah, it sucked," Miranda agreed, but there was something else in her voice that puzzled Trace.

"She abandoned you, too. You were best friends."

"I remember. And trust me, I totally understand why you're not happy to see her again. But aren't you the least bit curious as to what she's been doing for the past eight years?"

"No."

"Oh."

"Should I be?"

"I don't know. I guess I'd be curious. How'd she look?"

"Like someone who spends all day staring at food they're never going to eat."

"Huh?"

"She's too skinny."

"Anything else?"

"Her hair is platinum blond and she definitely had a nose job."

"Wow. That's a lot of change. I wonder why she did all that. She was always a pretty girl without all that stuff."

Pretty didn't accurately describe Delainey Clarke. She'd been gorgeous, at least to Trace. She'd always been embarrassed by the bump on her nose, but Trace had found it endearing—just one more part of her that had made her unique. Now? She looked plastic. "She wore fake eyelashes, too. And her forehead didn't move. She probably had her face shot up with that cow pee that everyone talks about."

"Cow pee? You mean Botox? That's not cow urine. It's the bacteria that causes botulism. And if her forehead didn't move, it's likely she's had it done. Scary stuff. But I'm sure in Los Angeles that's as normal as going to the grocery store to pick up eggs."

"Yeah, well, she can go right back to L.A. and fit in with her people because there's sure as hell no place for her here anymore."

"Is she staying with her dad, I wonder? They didn't part on good terms, either. She burned every bridge on her way out."

"No clue. Harlan's a hard man and always

has been. I can't imagine he'd welcome her with open arms any more than I was willing. But she is his daughter, so who knows."

"You know he never treated her right," Miranda reminded him. "I always felt bad for her."

"Don't. She's like a cat—she always lands on her feet."

"You don't know that. Maybe she's changed. A lot can happen in eight years. People can change."

"You, of all people, are the last person I'd expect to hear say, 'Maybe she's changed.' What's going on with you?"

"Maybe I've grown up," she said, teasing. "Having a kid does change you. And, I don't know, maybe I'm tired of carrying around all this anger for things I can't do anything about. Besides, we need to conserve our energy for the fight on the horizon, which, speaking of, have you managed to drop by our parents' place yet?"

"No." He withheld a sigh and ran a hand through his hair, knowing he was going to catch an earful. "I've been busy."

"Busy doing what? I thought you were taking a breather after the Errington case."

"I am, but just because I'm not out with the Search and Rescue crew doesn't mean I sit around all day."

"Trace, no one would ever accuse you of sitting around and twiddling your thumbs. You're not hardwired to sit still for one blessed second."

Trace couldn't argue that point. "You know that program, the Junior Search and Rescue?"

"Yeah?"

"Well, every chance I get I've been spending it with them. I like the kids. They're eager to learn and it feels good to pass on the skills, seeing as I don't have any kids."

"That's cool. Speaking of kids…it'd be nice if Talen had a cousin or two," Miranda said, dropping a not-so-subtle hint.

"Don't look my way. Talk to Wade. But now that you mention Talen, you ought to have him join the program. I think he'd dig it. He's an outdoorsy kid, so it's right up his alley."

"Good idea. I'll talk to him about it. I worried he might be too young."

"Never too young to start learning how to read your surroundings. Dad had us out there as soon as we could walk."

At the mention of their father, Miranda returned to his least favorite subject.

"Trace, I really need your help. I know it's not your idea of a good time—trust me, it's not mine, either—but Mom's out of control and Dad… Well, he's almost a lost cause, but Mom's in danger. We need to get that house cleaned up before it collapses on her."

Miranda thought their mother had a hoarding problem, but Trace was fairly certain Miranda was exaggerating. How bad could it be? Trace thought the bigger issue was their father's illegal drug operation. But he'd promised he'd take a look and see for himself. "I'll go today," he assured her.

"Should I meet you there?" she asked.

"No. You and Mom tend to spark off one another—"

"Just like you and Dad?" she cut in, knowing him well. "Maybe it'll help to have a buffer."

"With any luck, he won't be around. But even if he is, I'll keep it civil."

"Okay. Let me know how it goes." She hesitated, then added, "And give some thought to what I said about Delainey. You never know... maybe she regrets how things were handled, too."

Trace bit back an irritated sigh. His sister used to be fierce—almost too much of a ballbuster—but now, she was downright tame thanks to that new guy of hers who'd come in and reintroduced joy to her life. Don't get him wrong, it was great and all, but sometimes he missed the ballbuster.

"It's not that I'm not in favor of the kinder, gentler Miranda Sinclair, but you're wasting your breath and your benefit of the doubt. If anything, she's gotten worse. She's a user. So before you go and invite her to lunch or something, remember how she abandoned everyone when they needed her."

"Yeah, I know. You're right," she conceded with a sigh. "If I see her, I'll try not to clip her with my Range Rover."

At that, he laughed. "Exactly. Knowing her, she'd have you arrested and that new boyfriend of yours would have to arrange conjugal visits in jail."

"You're gross," Miranda said, but she was laughing as she hung up.

Trace's smile faded and he tossed his phone to the sofa. Delainey Clarke…why'd she have to come around again? His life had finally settled into a familiar-enough routine that was devoid of too much emotion. He didn't date—he found most women too clingy—and he made his life revolve around work. And he liked it that way.

He saved lives.

Period.

What did Delainey do with her life? She'd been in an all-fire hurry to get out of Alaska so she could be famous. Had it worked out for her? Was she some bigwig in Hollywood now? She'd said she was in a bind. What kind of bind?

Who cared.

Not Trace.

For the past eight years he'd worked at erasing Delainey from his memory. He'd burned pictures, destroyed videos and otherwise removed all evidence he'd ever loved her.

As for the hole she'd left behind?

It'd become such a familiar feeling, he'd barely noticed it any longer.

And if there were times when he couldn't sleep, it wasn't because his mind was torturing him with memories of how much they'd been in love, because he knew that had been a total illusion. No, Delainey had done him a solid by leaving, because he'd rather be alone than spend a lifetime with someone false.

The sooner Delainey split town again, the better. She wasn't good for anyone. Least of all, him.

CHAPTER SIX

TRACE FROZE AND immediately glowered when he saw Delainey chatting up his boss, Peter, and knew right away that she was there to cause trouble. Peter caught sight of him and motioned him into the office, which he was tempted to blatantly ignore but chose instead to meet the situation head-on. Whatever Delainey had up her sleeve he could handle. She couldn't force him to participate in her stupid show, and he felt fairly confident that Peter couldn't make him either without facing some serious legal ramifications.

"Trace, come here a minute," Peter said, smiling from ear to ear. "I've been chatting with your friend—"

"She's not my friend," Trace corrected him, shooting Delainey a dark look for telling his boss anything to the contrary. "And whatever she's selling, I'm not interested in buying."

"Careful, Trace, you might come off as unlikeable," Peter said, a tad nervously, and Trace's senses went on full alert. Something wasn't right.

Peter was practically simpering—not an attractive look on a man closing in on his sixties—and Delainey looked like the Cheshire cat. "Delainey has presented us with an amazing opportunity, and I think we owe it to the department to listen to her offer."

"I already know her offer, and trust me, it comes with hidden strings attached. Besides, I'm not interested and without me, there's no show. Right?" He looked to Delainey for confirmation. She nodded but cast a confident stare Peter's way as if to reassure him—and that made Trace nervous.

"Imagine the publicity," Peter started, and Trace waved away his protests.

"Exactly what I don't want. It was bad enough talking with the reporters. I sure as hell don't want a bunch of cameras in my face 24/7. No one wants to watch me do my job. I can't imagine how that would make for good television, and I would question anyone who thought otherwise."

"Delainey seems to think differently and I think we ought to listen to her judgment. She wouldn't come all the way to Alaska on a harebrained idea, right?" He looked to Delainey to boost his argument, which she was only too happy to do.

"Absolutely, Peter. Although Trace doesn't

seem to appreciate his own value, my boss is positively drooling to get him on paper. And of course, we're happy to make it worth the department's while for the inconvenience."

"I told you my answer is no, and I don't care how you pretty it up."

"Trace, you're being shortsighted," Peter said, trying to assert some authority. "Think of the department."

"I am. Don't you realize she's not interested in true stories but fake drama? Producers like her do everything they can to ramp up the tension and the excitement with creative editing. We could end up looking like idiots."

"I would never do that," Delainey assured Peter. "We want to accurately portray the hardworking men and women of the Search and Rescue. I feel this is an opportunity to highlight a career choice that not many are aware of. Think of all the positive feedback this project could create."

"We don't suffer from an image problem," Trace said, crossing his arms and standing his ground. "We do our job quietly and efficiently—we don't need cameras documenting our every move."

"Trace, I can't believe you are so naive," she said, shocking him. "The squeaky wheel gets the grease and your wheel has been moving so soundlessly, the powers that be have completely forgotten why you're important. Budget cuts are everywhere—even in Hollywood—and I can't imagine a program being so flush that they couldn't use a bump."

"We haven't been flush in years," Peter grumbled. "Everyone's been instructed to tighten their belts and we've had a hiring freeze for three years."

"See?" Delainey said, smiling. "Stop being so stubborn. It's a month of your life and then we're out of your hair."

"I said no."

Delainey sighed as if Trace were being deliberately difficult, and Peter's mouth had firmed to a tight, agitated line.

"We all have to do things for the greater good sometimes," Peter said gruffly. "Even you, Trace Sinclair."

"Of course, as the star of the show, you'd receive a salary—"

"I'm not interested in your money," he ground out.

"Then donate your salary to a worthwhile charity," Delainey continued, unfazed. "Because this is happening."

"Oh? And why is that?"

She smiled and he held her stare, wondering what her ace was. She was too confident, too unruffled. And Peter was nervous as a long-tailed cat in a room filled with rockers. Something didn't feel right. He narrowed his gaze at them both, finally coming to rest on Delainey. "You've greased the wheels to ensure your success. What'd you offer him?" he asked, going straight to the point.

She didn't pretend to misunderstand and answered without a hint of guilt. "Money for a program that's been on the chopping block… something you care about."

Trace swore under his breath, glaring at Peter and feeling betrayed. "You promised me that you'd give me time to try and figure something out."

"Trace, be reasonable. The Junior Search and Rescue program is expensive and the liability is too high right now to take on when the entire department is facing brutal cuts. It was either the junior program or an employee. Times are hard and the state is strapped," Peter said, lifting his shoulders in a helpless gesture.

Damn bureaucrat. He narrowed his gaze at Delainey. "How much money did you offer?"

"Enough to keep the program funded for the next year as well as some equipment donations—provided you agree to sign on the dotted line. Like you said, without you, there's no show. The head of the network wants you and he'll accept no substitute."

Manipulative little she-devil. She'd hog-tied him without so much as breaking a sweat. He smiled thinly. "You sewed that right up, didn't you? Nice and tidy with a little bow, too."

"A girl's gotta eat," she answered with a smile. "I'm just doing my job."

"Everything's about the job, isn't it?" he asked, punching below the belt, but he didn't care. She deserved it.

Delainey ignored his jab and offered her hand. "Is it a deal?"

He stared at her outstretched hand and fought the urge to slap it away. The idea of touching her, particularly to strike a devil's bargain, scalded his good sense. But she had him. She'd struck at the jugular and he had no choice but to stem the bleeding. He hadn't thought she'd sink so low, but she had and she didn't look the least bit apologetic. "I'm curious…how'd you know about the Junior Search and Rescue?" he asked.

"What does it matter?" Peter asked, irritated. "The program needs money and Delainey is here offering it. I don't see the problem."

Delainey graced Peter with an indulgent look, but the one she sent Trace was downright glittering with challenge. "Part of my job is to solve problems, wherever they may arise. I noticed that picture on your wall." She pointed directly behind Trace and Trace mentally swore. "And you seemed to be happy around all those little kids. I asked Peter who the kids were and he said they were the program's first junior volunteers. And then he mentioned that the program was on the chopping block. I saw an opportunity and I took it."

"And we're very grateful you did," Peter added, shooting Trace a meaningful look. "Now is no time for pride, Trace. Think of the bigger picture. Those kids love that program, right?"

Trace jerked a nod, privately fuming at how neatly Delainey had circumvented his refusal.

Delainey smiled. "Problem solved. Provided Trace agrees to our terms."

Well, he supposed she'd won this round, but he didn't have to be gracious about losing. He took a step closer, actually crowding her personal space a little, and she faltered just a tiny bit as she stared up at him. He hoped she saw the burn in his eyes as he said, "You think you've won, but you might want to think twice. I've spent the past eight years cultivating a deep and abiding hatred for you, and now you've just given me an outlet. You might find me a difficult person to *manage*."

She swallowed and in the background Peter sputtered in indignant embarrassment at Trace's harsh words, but Trace didn't back down. And she knew he meant every word. She drew a deep breath and lifted her chin, like a badger staring down a predator that was twice its size, and finally said, "I look forward to working with you, Mr. Sinclair." Her voice didn't shake, but there was the slightest wobble to her bottom lip that gave away her nervousness.

That's right, honey. You're right to be nervous. You just bit off more than you can chew.

And Trace hoped she choked.

"Get everything in writing—every last dime she promised," he called over his shoulder as he left. "Delainey Clarke has a bad habit of making promises she never intends to keep."

DELAINEY STRUGGLED TO keep her expression professional and unaffected by Trace's parting comments, but she felt sliced to ribbons. He hated her? How could he say something so cruel after everything they'd shared? Just because she'd had bigger dreams than their little Alaskan town, suddenly she was the villain? How about the fact that he hadn't been the least bit interested in helping her achieve her goals and had simply tolerated her aspirations as the ramblings of a dreamer?

Before she realized it, she was clenching her fists. It was several seconds before she registered Peter's voice trying to smooth things over, as if he were afraid she'd change her mind after Trace's rude display. As if she could change her mind. She was just as rooted in circumstance as Trace was, not that the jerk cared. "He's got a tough shell but he's a softie at heart," she heard Peter saying, and she absently nodded with a forced smile. "I'm sure he didn't mean what he said about hating you. He's just mad at being pushed against his wishes."

Oh, she had no doubt that Trace meant every word, but there was no sense in throwing a fit over what he'd said. The past was dead and she was here to see a job done. "It'll be fine, Peter," she assured him, snapping up her papers and tucking them into her slim briefcase. "Hollywood is filled with difficult people. Trace Sinclair isn't even a blip on the radar. I'll have my office email the necessary paperwork from legal."

"Of course," Peter said, fidgeting a little as he walked her to the door. "Search and Rescue appreciates the opportunity and the donations. I can assure you, it's a great cause."

"I'm sure it is," she said, smiling. "Now…" she continued, pausing. "Would you be able to recommend a good hotel? My reservations got mixed up and I find myself without a place to stay for the time being."

Peter winced. "Oh. That's terrible. Unfortunately, we're right in the thick of moose season. All the hunters from out of the state come to bag a prize to take home. The hotels book months in advance."

She held her smile but froze inside. Crap. She'd forgotten about moose season. "No worries. I'm sure I'll find something."

"Are you sure?"

"Yes, I'll be fine. Thank you for your assistance in persuading Trace to participate in the show."

Delainey navigated the muddy snow in her heels, careful not to slip as she made her way to her rental, and quickly processed her situation. Great. She had Trace locked in but now she had nowhere to stay.

She blew out a frustrated breath and gripped the steering wheel tightly to rein in the scream building beneath her breastbone. Why couldn't something work out in her favor for once? Was it too much to ask for a little grace?

Her only choice was staring her in the face. Bile rose in her throat until she felt it clawing up her esophagus. Jerking the car into Drive, she pulled onto the main highway and headed east—back to her father's house.

CHAPTER SEVEN

DELAINEY FOUGHT THE welling sense of panic and desperation as she took a moment to collect herself, determined to appear strong and undeterred by this most recent setback. She was Delainey Clarke and she was stronger than any challenge hurled her way. Yes. No. Why hadn't she remembered about the damn moose season?

If only she'd kept in contact with some people then she might've pulled some strings, but she'd cut ties quite brutally so what could she expect? The problem with burning bridges was that they weren't there when you found yourself needing to retrace your steps.

She blew out a breath and climbed from the car, retrieving her luggage and making that walk back to the front door. Now that she knew her father had remarried, she noted more details she'd missed the first time. The house still looked old and worn, but there were small attempts to pretty up the exterior. Delainey's mother had tried, too, with varying success. When her mother had been alive, she'd attempted to grow flowers that were wholly unsuited for the bitter cold of Alaska, but it seemed Brenda had fared much better with hardy peonies. Delainey stared at the small bright patch of color against the faded house siding and wondered how she'd missed them the first time.

She closed her eyes and drew a faint memory of her mother, digging in the hard topsoil, trying desperately to bring some of her native California to life in Alaska, but ultimately crying when her ill-suited choices shriveled and died in the harsh temperatures.

"Why won't anything grow here?" Anna Clarke had muttered under her breath, nearing tears. She sank back on her heels, dirt clinging to her gloves and staining her knees. "This place kills everything with its constant shadows and brutal cold. I hate it here." The last part came out as a hiss, and Delainey had stared with widened eyes as her mother had broken down and sobbed hard for reasons Delainey couldn't fathom.

Delainey wondered why her mother had never left. She'd died in the very place she despised, yet couldn't get away from.

Why was she thinking of that stuff? Wasn't her situation bad enough? She didn't need to dredge up painful memories of the mother she'd barely known. She knocked once and then let herself in, steeling herself against the looks and the questions, just wanting to get some sleep. Jet lag had begun to set in, and she was quickly losing her tentative grip on her sanity.

TRACE FOUND HIMSELF at the Rusty Anchor, needing to blow off some steam. He was still percolating at a pretty hot clip at how neatly Delainey had maneuvered him into a corner, trapping him as easily as an expert hunter on the trail of his quarry. It burned how he'd underestimated her desire to succeed. She'd truss up her grandmother and put her on a spit if she thought it could get her ahead.

"You're looking meaner than a hungry bear tonight," Russ, the bartender, commented with a wry grin as he slid a beer across to Trace. "Who pissed in your cereal tonight?"

Trace offered a grim smile but otherwise remained silent. He didn't want to talk about Delainey. Hell, he didn't want to talk at all, not that Russ or anyone else who knew him would find that odd. Trace had never been what anyone would call a Chatty Cathy. Russ took the hint and moved on, but someone else had noticed him and took a seat beside him. Chanel No. 5 assaulted his nostrils and he knew, without turning, who had sidled up beside him.

"You're a sight for sore eyes," Cindy Sutton

nearly purred, leaning toward him and giving him more than an eyeful of what she was offering. Cindy wasn't hard on the eyes and it'd been a while since Trace had enjoyed the company of a woman. But just as his libido kicked to life, someone else walked into the bar, effectively killing anything that might've risen to the occasion.

Cindy tracked his stare and her mouth gaped open. "Is that? Holy hell... She looks different, but I'd swear that's Delainey Clarke."

"It's her," he answered, swigging his beer, irritated all over again that she'd shown up. Why couldn't she find a nice rock to hibernate under for the duration of her stay in Homer?

"Damn, she looks good," Cindy said with open envy. "Didn't she run off to Hollywood? I bet she's had work done. Is that a new nose? And new boobs? She must have a sugar daddy back in Tinseltown. No one looks that good naturally."

"I prefer a more natural look," he said, throwing Cindy a bone. Cindy smiled, appreciating the sentiment, but her gaze remained centered on Delainey as she navigated the small bar. Delainey stood out like a sore thumb among the hardworking, humble people in the bar, and she knew it based on her tentative expression as she made her way to a small table to sit alone. He looked away, hoping she got the point and left soon. "She's as fake as a stuffed jackalope."

"Yeah, but she looks pretty damn good. I don't think I'd mind having a little touch-up now and then." Cindy sighed and returned to Trace with renewed interest. "So, you were saying about liking natural girls?" she teased and he chuckled.

"If I were good company at the moment, I'd definitely be game to spend some time with you, but I'm not exactly fit for human companionship."

"You always say that," she retorted with a sly grin. "But I seem to remember the key to turning that mood around."

He cast Cindy an appreciative glance but kept his mouth zipped. Try as he might, he couldn't keep his stare from tracking to Delainey sitting off by herself. He wanted to ignore her, but his eyes didn't seem to be having the same conversation with his brain. Cindy caught his stare and called his bluff. "Natural, my ass. You can't keep your eyes off her," she said.

"It's not that," he said, stiffening at the idea of anyone thinking he was regarding Delainey in a sexual manner. He couldn't imagine a less likely bed partner. "She's here on business, not pleasure, and even if she were, I wouldn't be interested."

"Let's say I believe you about not being interested—which I don't—but what kind of business?" Cindy asked, curious.

"The Hollywood variety," Trace answered vaguely. He wasn't ready to announce to the world his part in Delainey's little project. It was embarrassing—and annoying. "She won't be in town for long."

"Hollywood? Oh! That's so exciting. Do you think some big celebrities will be in town? I've always wanted to meet Pierce Brosnan. He's delicious." Trace paused to regard Cindy with mild annoyance and she said, "Wait a minute… didn't you and Delainey have a thing back in the day?" Cindy asked, then snapped her fingers before he could confirm or deny. "Yes, that's right. You and Delainey were high school sweethearts. God, how'd I forget that? She's been gone awhile now. You still have a thing for her?"

"God, no." He made a grimace and sucked back his beer. One thing he'd forgotten about Cindy was that she was a terrible gossip. "There's nothing between me and Delainey, and there never will be again. As soon as she's out of Alaska, the better off I'll feel."

"Ouch. Touchy." Cindy tipped her beer back, then added with open disbelief, "Well, whatever you say. Something tells me you and me hooking up tonight isn't going to happen. Seems you've got someone else on your mind." She cast a purposeful glance Delainey's way and Trace wanted to growl his protests, but Cindy had already hopped from her stool and set her sights on someone else for the night. No hard feelings on her part, but she wasn't about to waste time on a guy who wasn't going to warm her up later that night. Trace could respect that and he half wished he'd taken her up on the offer. Hell, he'd enjoy the look on Delainey's face as he walked by, snuggled up to Cindy, maybe with a hand resting possessively on Cindy's behind for good measure. Would Delainey even care? What did he care if she did?

He finished his beer, irritated with himself and the dumb questions. He signaled for a fresh beer and realized someone else had taken up the stool beside him. His senses went crazy and he knew without turning that Delainey had plopped herself next to him as if they were buds. "What the hell are you doing?" he asked, point-blank. "Dealing with you once a day is plenty. This is my private time."

She looked as if she was trying to be brave, but there was something fragile about her put-on confidence that he couldn't help notice. It didn't lessen his animosity, but it did pique his curiosity. By all accounts she'd accomplished her goal. She'd managed to maneuver him into agreeing to something he had no interest in doing, but the expression on her face was anything but triumphant. "Is this your victory celebration?" he asked sourly as he tipped his beer. "Come to rub it in my face?"

"Get over yourself, Trace. I didn't know you'd be here. I just needed something to wind down. Jet lag is killing me but…I couldn't sleep."

"Hotel bed not as soft as yours at home?"

"I'm not staying in a hotel. I'm staying at my father's place," she answered quietly, lifting her chin as she shrugged. "All the hotels were booked."

Oh, that was sweet justice, he thought. "Guess you forgot about moose season," he said, openly enjoying her unfortunate circumstance. "That sucks. You and your old man were never on good terms. How's that going for you?"

"It's ungentlemanlike to gloat," she said, looking away. "It's going as well as you can expect."

At that he did chuckle and earned a black look, but he didn't care. Served her right. She couldn't come around disrupting people's lives without consequence. "Well, at least your old man cares enough for you to give you a place to bed down. If it were me, you'd be sleeping in a snowbank."

"Do you have to be so mean?" she asked, her eyes suddenly glittering. "Are you going to be this nasty and cruel the entire time I'm here?"

"I'm not the one who started this," he reminded her. "I don't recall being nice and civil as one of the stipulations of your little deal. Or was that in the fine print?"

Delainey grabbed her beer and swiveled off the chair, but as she started to stalk away, she seemed to think better of it and stopped to say, "We broke up eight years ago, Trace. Don't you think it's time to let it go? Grow up, for Christ's sake. So, I managed to talk you into taking a job that will benefit you in the long run as well as do something great for that little department you work for. Sue me. But just remember, as you're sitting there throwing stones at my expense, you weren't completely innocent. You had a choice, too. Don't make me the bad guy just because I took the choice that was right for me."

Trace watched her melt into the crowd, and he was tempted to run after her if only to tell her she was full of crap. She was wrong, he told himself. And plainly she'd rewritten history to suit her purposes.

What the hell was she talking about? Choices? The only choice she'd given him was whether or not to keep the CD collection they'd amassed together.

She hadn't been interested in choices; her mind had been made up and he'd been left behind.

Screw this.

He flicked a few bucks onto the bar and left in disgust.

And he was supposed to work with her every day of production until they wrapped?

God help him. He might just pitch her over a cliff if given the opportunity.

CHAPTER EIGHT

DELAINEY OPENED HER EYES after a fitful night's rest on an old lumpy mattress that had definitely seen better days and wondered what she'd done to deserve such adversity in her life. Milky morning light filtered in through the thick window covering, and she rubbed the grit from her eyeballs. Today, she would fax the signed contract paperwork to the network and then she'd start the process of getting her skeleton crew up here to start shooting. The hardest part would be finding a hotel for them to hole up in for the duration of the shoot. Her mind was already picking at the challenges ahead, even sluggish as she was without her morning espresso to jolt herself alert.

She knew her father was likely long gone, having woken up at the crack of dawn to take the boat out, so at least she would be spared the awkward and uncomfortable recap of last night's reunion. But she could do nothing about the memory.

"There she is," Brenda had announced, smiling as Delainey had opened the front door and walked in. Delainey had forced a tight smile when Brenda added, "I was going to tell you that moose season is upon us and every hotel would be filled to capacity with tourists, but you ran out of here so quickly I didn't get the chance. But we knew you'd figure it out soon enough when you couldn't find a room."

"Yes, well, here I am," Delainey said, her cheeks burning. Her father sat in his recliner, wordlessly watching her with a hard expression, and Delainey had fought the urge to say something terribly immature. "Is the room still available?" she managed to ask with some semblance of civility.

"House hasn't changed," her father answered gruffly.

"A simple yes would suffice," she mumbled, moving past him and pulling her luggage behind her.

"Seems to me that you're hell-bent on changing who you are and where you came from," he remarked, and Brenda shushed him.

"Now, Harlan, give the girl a chance to get settled. Can't you tell she's nearly dead on her feet?" Brenda shook her head, chuckling at her husband's gruff attitude, and Delainey thought the woman was insane for finding anything about Harlan Clarke appealing. He was mean, ill-tempered and rude on his best days. Was it any wonder her mother had been miserable? "Don't pay him no mind. He's happy to have you home for a few days."

Delainey held back a snort while Harlan shot his wife a dark look. *Yeah, right. He was clicking his heels with joy.* "I'll do my best to find suitable accommodations as soon as possible," she said, finished with the conversation. "Good night."

Unfortunately, the walls were incredibly thin and Delainey caught their conversation even as she closed the door behind her.

"Now, why'd you go and say something like that, you old poop? That wasn't nice at all." Brenda had admonished her husband with open disapproval. "She's never going to come around again if you don't start being nicer."

"I don't care what she does," Harlan said, and the recliner squeaked as if he were adjusting his position. "And that woman ain't my daughter. I don't recognize that woman at all. She's a stranger."

"Something tells me that she was a stranger before she got all fancied up. You two have a lot to talk about."

"Like hell we do."

"Oh, Harlan. Now you're just being stubborn. You need your children right now."

"I don't want to talk about it, Brenda. Leave it be."

Delainey frowned. What was Brenda talking about? Was her father sick? Delainey sat on the bed, extreme fatigue pulling at her. Wouldn't Thad have called her if their father were sick? Of course he would've. Perhaps Brenda had a penchant for the dramatic and there was nothing truly wrong with the old goat. An odd pang of worry pierced Delainey's chest, even as she tried to dispel it with reason and logic. Everything was fine and she was exhausted. Delainey fell back on the bed and closed her eyes, so tired that she thought she could sleep the minute her eyelids fluttered shut.

But that's not what happened. In fact, she'd been so tired, she actually *couldn't* sleep. Nervous energy kept her from finding sleep, and before she knew it she was heading to the Rusty Anchor for a nightcap.

And that had turned out equally fabulous, she wanted to groan as she rolled to her side and put her face into the pillow. She'd known that Trace wasn't going to be warm and welcoming, but she hadn't expected him to be so damn mean. Had she really messed him up so badly that now he hated women? Or maybe it was just her?

Delainey rose from the bed on stiff limbs and

made her way to the bathroom to shower. The questions in her head had no answers; there was no point in spending so much time wondering about the whys and what-fors. Trace hated her and he was going to make the next few weeks as miserable as humanly possible. *Deal with it and move on.* She'd handled difficult people before without breaking a sweat. She would just have to treat Trace as she would a hostile, pain-in-the-ass star—smile and nod, then at the end of the day, enjoy a really big glass of wine.

Delainey drew a deep breath, moderately comforted by her plan. But even as she armed herself with the details, her insides trembled and she felt a little sick to her stomach. She didn't want Trace to hate her. Truthfully, sometimes private memories of Trace and his love were the ones that insulated her against the worst moments in her career. She knew he didn't love her any more, but there was a time…a sudden lump rose in her throat. Ugh. Why was she doing this to herself? Masochistic, that's what this was. What good would come of wallowing in the past?

Move on, Delainey—there's work to be done.

"TRACE, I KNOW YOU weren't keen to do this project, but once you get started, I think you'll enjoy—"

"Peter, don't try and sell me on this project. It's a waste of your breath and my time. You and I both know why I'm doing this, and it's pretty much extortion no matter how you try and pretty it up."

"That's harsh, Trace." Peter glowered but didn't deny it. "You've got no head for administration, son. Times are tough. Call it what you will, but if an outside entity such as Hollywood comes waving dollar bills under our nose, by damn we're going to do what we can to make it happen. You think I like cutting programs? Well, I don't. But when I see a relatively easy way to make the budget expand rather than constrict, I take it."

"Yeah, well, I was strong-armed into taking this gig, and I don't feel right about it."

"You have the right to your feelings," Peter said. "Even if they're wrong."

Trace did a double take. "What do you mean by that?"

Peter sighed. "You're a good man and an even better tracker, but you're stubborn as the day is long and sometimes when you dig your heels in about something you're as immobile as an ass pulling against the lead. Why don't you tell me what your beef is with that pretty producer? She seems real nice."

He snorted. "Delainey Clarke is like the first

freeze across the water. It might look solid but it's deceiving, and if you trust it with your weight, you're liable to crash through the thin surface and drown. She's not trustworthy and she's not a nice person. Don't let her pretty face trick you."

"You two have history?"

Trace didn't want to admit it, but he figured if Cindy Sutton remembered his past with Delainey, chances were someone else was going to remember, too, so it was best to just let it out. "Yeah, we've got history. Plenty of it. We were together. I even asked her to marry me—eight years ago before she took off for California and left her boot prints on the backs of every single person in this town she stepped on to get out."

"Guess that was before my time here," Peter said. "Eight years is a long time. Maybe she's changed. Seems harsh to hold her to decisions she made when she was practically a kid."

"She wasn't a kid when she split."

"You forget, anyone ten years or more younger than me I consider a kid. That includes you."

"Trust me when I say that Delainey Clarke hasn't changed. She's just as manipulative and cutthroat as she was when she left. Take my advice and steer clear."

"Maybe I'm old-fashioned, but I think you could be a little nicer to the lady. I don't know your history, but you're going to be working with her. Don't you think things will go a lot more smoothly if you're not constantly sniping at one another?"

"Hey, nowhere in the contract did it state I had to be nice."

"No, but I expected more from you," Peter said, surprising Trace. Peter was, generally speaking, pretty easygoing, but he was taking a firm line on this issue. Somehow Trace's attitude toward Delainey struck against some inner chivalrous code that Trace never knew Peter adhered to. "And frankly, your behavior doesn't reflect well on the department. I'm not saying you have to be buddies, but you need to be professional. That's all I'm asking."

"You're serious about this?"

"Why would I joke about something so important?"

Trace realized Peter truly wasn't joking, and he shook his head at the ridiculousness of the situation. He was being ordered to be nice to the woman who'd trashed his heart at the worst possible time in his life, and yet he was the one being difficult. Hell's bells… But what could he do? Peter was his boss, and for whatever reasons Peter wasn't letting up the pressure. Trace threw his hands up. "Fine, I'll be civil and professional. Should I put that in writing?" he asked caustically.

"No, your word should do. She'll be here today to debrief us on the shooting schedule. You'll get to put your acting skills to the test. I'd better see a reformed man."

"I'm not an actor," he growled.

"Well, you'd better learn a few tricks, because otherwise..."

"Yeah? You gonna fire me?"

"Don't make me go there. I want to think positive. You start thinking of the Junior Search and Rescue program if nothing else works. I know how you love those kids and the program. If nothing else matters to you but that...then know that the success of this project is resting on your ability to play nice."

Great. Thanks for setting me up for failure.

Time to practice that fake smile.

And with impeccable timing, just as Trace was exaggerating his "nice" face, Delainey walked in looking like a winter Barbie doll with her Ugg boots, skinny jeans, sweater and scarf wound around her neck, and Trace couldn't help but stare just a little because the woman knew how to turn heads. Too skinny. Too fake. Too Hollywood.

Remember that.

CHAPTER NINE

DELAINEY WALKED INTO the conference room, determined to keep her head held high, but when she saw Trace her nerves trembled and her resolve faltered. Why did he have to be so handsome? After all these years, couldn't time have stomped on his good looks a little? It would've been far easier to hold the memories at bay if she'd returned to Alaska and found Trace looking nothing like she remembered. But of course, that wasn't the case. If anything, the man had become even more handsome—which didn't seem fair—and even though there wasn't a hint of warmth in those eyes, a woman could still drown in their depths if she weren't careful.

"Gentlemen," she announced with a smile as she entered the room. "I appreciate you meeting with me this early to go over the production schedule. If, while we're going over the schedule, you see something that concerns you, please let me know and I'll make a note. We want this production to go as smoothly as possible for everyone, and I want you to feel your input is important."

"This is going to be a new experience for us all," Peter said cheerfully. "And to be honest, I've always been curious about the movie business. Seems like a whole different world. It's not often we get a glimpse of what happens behind the wall. Right, Trace?"

"Personally, a world full of fakes and liars doesn't interest me," Trace muttered, and before Delainey could say anything Peter shot Trace a warning look. Trace got the message but didn't take back his sarcastic comment, not that Delainey expected him to. Trace was as intractable as a brick wall. "Let's get this show on the road," Trace said brusquely. "I've got more on my plate than going over your production schedule. Some of us are less than thrilled over this sudden detour in the norm."

"Of course," Delainey said, forcing a smile at the difficult man. Trace and her father could write a book on how to alienate people. "If you'll turn to page one in the production schedule packet, you'll see a breakdown of the typical shooting day. Now, it will be very important that we all stay on track so that we can stay on budget. It is very easy to lose daylight hours and start spinning into overtime. Nobody wants that to happen. Least of all me. The sooner we get our shots, the sooner we'll be done for the day."

"Wait a minute…" Trace started, a frown building on his forehead. "This is a full eight-hour day. What the hell are we going to do for eight hours in front of a camera?"

"Actually, eight hours is fairly conservative. It's likely we will have several ten-hour days. Filming, particularly on location, has certain challenges. We can't always stick to the schedule as it is planned. However, I would like to try."

"And how am I supposed to actually do my job, if a camera is stuck in my face all day?"

Delainey smiled. "Don't worry about the cameras. Just go about your day like you normally would."

"That's a contradiction. Most days I don't even keep my cell phone on. And now I have to have a camera crew in my face? I don't know. This whole idea sounds stupid."

Peter cleared his throat and the two shared a look. After a tense moment, Trace finally backed down with a glower, saying, "I think this will be the most boring show ever aired, but it's your dime. As long as the check clears for the program, I guess that's all that matters."

"Great. Now back to the schedule. If you'll turn your attention to the second page, you'll see that we have a reenactment scheduled. Part of the reason that you attracted the attention of my boss is because you saved that little girl. So I think it would be great if we could start off the series with a reenactment of you finding her. Of course we will hire actors to play the governor and his daughter, but I think that would be a really great way to garner interest in the pilot."

"A reenactment?" Trace, clearly displeased, muttered, "This is getting better by the minute."

"I know it sounds weird, but I think it'll really translate into good footage. I've watched the news coverage and I've read the newspapers, but I'm really going to need to interview you to get a feel for how it actually happened, as I'll be writing a short script for the segment. And I would like to do that today. Do you think you could clear your schedule to talk with me about that incident?"

Peter answered for Trace. "No problem. I'm sure Trace would enjoy telling the story. It's nice to have a story with a happy ending. As you can imagine, we don't always get to save the day."

"Thank you, Peter. Now that that's settled, I need to ask where can I possibly find lodging for my crew. I can't have my crew staying with me at my dad's. There has to be at least one hotel that isn't booked solid. I thought maybe you could help me find one."

"Well, unfortunately, it's moose season so all the best hotels will be taken." Peter looked perplexed, scratching his chin in thought. "But, if you're not picky about your accommodations, there might be a hotel with some vacancies that I can look into for you. It won't be the Hyatt, but it'll be warm and dry with a clean bed."

"That's all we need," Delainey said, smiling with relief. If Peter managed to scrounge up a hotel for them, she'd happily kiss the man because it would mean she could get out of her father's house. "I'll need about five rooms, six if you can get it. How soon can you find out?"

"I can have an answer for you by the end of the afternoon."

"Excellent. In the meantime, Trace and I will conduct the interview and get that out of the way."

Peter rose. "You need me here for the interview?" She didn't know if Peter was asking for her benefit or Trace's, but when Trace gave a minute shake of his head, Delainey realized it had been for Trace's. "All right then, I'll leave you to do your interview while I try to find a hotel."

Sooner than she was prepared, she was sitting alone in the conference room with Trace. Her heart hammered hard against her chest and she tried to tell herself he was just like any actor she'd prepped for a role. Except, that was complete crap. "Do you mind if I record this?" she asked, pulling out her recorder. "I take notes, but I like the safety net of the recorder so I don't miss anything important."

"What did you come back here for?" he asked, throwing her off. He leaned forward and she actually found herself holding very still so as not to betray a single emotion. There was something about Trace that was primal and always had been. His energy buffeted her, and for a moment she rocked against the feeling that there were tangible sparks between them. It had always been this way between them, except before they'd had no reason to pull back. The sex between them had been explosive, and she'd yet to find a lover who could make her body sing like Trace had. More's the pity. She colored at the sizzling memories that jumped to mind, and she had to refocus on the here and now before she embarrassed herself.

"You know why I'm here," she answered, busying herself with straightening her pad and readying her pen. "Shall we begin?"

"What was the first thing that went through your mind when you heard *my* name in your little meeting? Did you think for a second that I was just going to fall into your arms and do whatever you say because at one time we had a history?"

Her hand trembled as she straightened her papers again, needing something to do. She couldn't stand the subtle sneer in his voice. It was such a contradiction from the Trace she remembered. Maybe she deserved his hatred, but it hurt just the same. Be that as it may, he needed to get a grip. "Trace, unlike you, I don't live in the past. I was just as surprised when your name came up in my meeting. It just so happens that I was the best person for the job. It really wasn't personal," she lied. If she were going to go to hell for lying her ass off, this would've been a prime example used to send her to the hot seat. "Can we get back to the interview, please?"

Trace chuckled and leaned back in his chair, regarding her intently. "You'd do anything to avoid talking about anything of substance, wouldn't you?"

"This is neither the time nor the place."

"Well, as I recall, you didn't give anyone a chance to talk about anything before you left. As far as I know, you haven't even talked to your old man or brother. It was like you just wanted to forget everyone and everything from your past."

She couldn't deny it, and having it pointed

out to her didn't make her feel any less like a self-centered jerk. "I talk to Thad now and then, but we're both busy people. As far as my father… You know he and I have never had a close relationship. I'm sure he was happy to be free of me."

"You're so delusional," Trace said, shocking her. "Whatever you need to tell yourself so you can sleep at night."

"What's that supposed to mean?"

"It means you turned your back on everything and everyone. Plain and simple. Yeah, you and your dad weren't close, but he was still your father and you abandoned him and your brother like day-old bread."

"What a hypocrite," she countered, unable to hold back. "Funny thing about small towns. Everyone seems to know everyone else's business and just loves to share. I happened to run into Molly Cavanaugh at the gas station, and you'll never guess what she had to say." Delainey didn't wait for Trace to jump in, gaining speed as her anger rose. "Word on the street is that you've become a hermit and your own family is falling apart. I left Alaska, and in doing so, left behind some people in my life. But you stayed right here and did something far worse— you just ignored everything around you because you didn't want to be bothered."

"You don't know what you're talking about," he said, glaring. "Neither you nor that busybody Molly Cavanaugh knows shit about my life or my family."

"No, but plenty in town know enough to gossip. Everyone likes to talk about the Sinclairs, and you all have given them plenty of topics to choose from."

It was a low blow—one that would've shamed her if she'd had any integrity left, but she'd long become conditioned to seeking out the vulnerable spots of her opponent, and she didn't hesitate. The kidnapping and murder of Simone Sinclair had been the town's most shocking tragedy, and as such it was still the favorite topic of gossip because Simone's killer had never been found. At Trace's stony silence, she said, "Doesn't feel good to be judged, does it?"

"No, it doesn't," he agreed in a hard voice.

"Then I suggest you stop throwing stones in your glass house and start focusing on the here and now."

"Do you really think we can work together?" he asked, and she realized he wasn't asking to be a jerk.

She had similar concerns. They had too much baggage between them to pretend that they didn't. But she didn't have a choice. Her career was on the line.

"I can start with good intentions, but the minute I see you…I'm angry all over again," he said.

"You signed a legally binding document, so I suggest that you try and figure out a way to be professional." She sighed. "Trace…it's a few weeks of your life. Surely, you can find a way to shelve your personal feelings about me for that long."

"Maybe." His answer was noncommittal, and she knew that was the best she was going to get from him at this point. If she were braver, she'd admit to him that she wished she'd handled things differently when she'd left, but that would mean admitting that she'd made some serious errors in judgment, and that would lead to admitting she may well have sacrificed everything she had for nothing. Tears threatened at the idea, and she sucked them back before they had a chance to betray her. She could not show any hint of weakness to Trace.

"Do you want me to apologize for leaving? Would that make everything better? Is that what you want from me?"

His stare became two chips of ice, and she knew she'd said the wrong thing. "Honey, I don't want *anything* from you except your absence. But since I can't have that and I'm stuck in this devil's deal, I guess I better make the best of it. Let's get back to the interview and leave the personal stuff out of it." *Oh, that was rich. He was advising her to keep things professional?*

"I don't need you to tell me to be professional. You're the one who is being a jerk." She stabbed the recorder on and fixed him with her most glacial stare. "Interview One with Trace Sinclair— the rescue of the governor's daughter. Please tell me in your own words how you came to rescue a lost little girl."

CHAPTER TEN

TRACE KNEW HE WAS being difficult. A part of him was appalled at how easily she'd gotten under his skin, but logic played no part in how he reacted when she was around. The adult side of his brain told him to cooperate, to get it over with so he could move on with his life and try to forget it ever happened. The more efficiently they were able to finish the project, the more quickly she could leave. The childish and immature part of his brain—quite possibly the area that was still holding on to the pain and the anger—wanted to make her job as difficult as possible.

"Why did you change your hair?" he asked. "You don't look right as a blonde."

"We're not talking about personal things, remember?" she reminded him coldly. "Besides, not that it's any of your business, but I happen to prefer my hair blond."

"You looked fine the way you were. Did somebody in L.A. tell you to change it?"

She looked exasperated. "No more than ten

seconds ago you were saying keep the personal stuff out of the conversation, and now here you are asking personal questions. Make up your mind. You want to know why I changed my hair? I'll tell you. Because I was tired of looking like the drab little mouse. Mice get eaten in Los Angeles. I wanted to fit in, and I knew I couldn't do that looking the way that I did."

"Did it ever occur to you that maybe you're not meant to fit into a place where you have to change who you are as a person?"

Her fingers curled around her pen, and he wondered if she might snap it in two. Knowing he'd gotten under her skin gave him a perverse pleasure. Maybe if he antagonized her enough she'd determine the project wasn't worth her time and leave. "I'm not going to discuss my personal life with you. Let's get back to the interview, please."

"So what's so great about Los Angeles? Is it everything you wanted it to be?"

"Everything and more."

Hell, he hadn't expected her answer to hurt. He supposed he wanted her to admit regret for leaving behind everything she'd ever known, but more important for leaving him behind. God, when did he become such a sap? He shifted in his chair, fighting with himself. Finally, he said, "Search and Rescue got the call from a hysterical father saying his daughter had been lost while camping. We didn't know at the time that it was from Governor Errington. It wasn't until we were suited up and hitting the trail that we got additional information that we were looking for the governor's daughter. Not that it would've mattered. When we found out the little girl, Clarissa, was lost in the woods, we would've put all resources toward finding her, no matter who her father was."

Momentarily startled but obviously relieved that he had returned to the interview, it took only a second for Delainey to catch up. "How long did it take you to find her?"

"Too long. She'd left the trail and tried to double back, but she got turned around and it was several hours before we were able to find her. Another hour and she would've died from hypothermia." Trace didn't like to think about how closely they'd come to losing the little girl. It reminded him too much of his sister Simone. He stretched his legs beneath the table and looked away. "We were lucky. The little girl was lucky."

"Forgive me for paying you a compliment, but I don't think luck had anything to do with it," Delainey said quietly. "There's a reason you're the best. If you couldn't find that little girl, no one could."

Her praise shouldn't have meant anything to

him, but her confidence in his abilities wormed their way into a private place, one that he kept guarded fiercely, and he found himself yearning for more. There'd been a time when Delainey's opinion had meant everything to him. At one time he believed Delainey was his other half. Of course she'd proved him to be a fool. "I was just doing my job. I'm uncomfortable with the accolades."

"Why?" she asked, perplexed. "There's nothing wrong with accepting well-earned praise."

"As quickly as someone will praise you for doing a good job, the same person will ride you into the ground for failing. I'm not always able to bring everyone back."

"Are you talking about Simone?" she asked tentatively.

"Among others," he admitted. "Two years ago, a Carolina man, Stuart Dillinger, went hiking up the ridge and didn't bring the proper gear. The snow disoriented Dillinger, and before he knew it he didn't have a clue where he was. No compass, not enough water and not nearly enough cold-weather gear. Fresh snow had erased his tracks, another storm was barreling down and we were running out of time. By the time we did find him, it was too late. He froze to death."

"No one expects you to be a superhero. Sorry

to say this, but you and I both know that anyone who doesn't have proper respect for the Alaskan wilderness will pay for it. It's like the people who die on Mount Everest because they didn't prepare properly. It's unfortunate but in a way they were asking for it."

"Try telling that to their families. Dillinger was a father, a brother and a husband. Now he's resting six feet under in a North Carolina graveyard."

"That doesn't have anything to do with you. You're the best tracker there is. Maybe it was just his time to go."

"You know I don't believe in that shit," he said sharply, uncomfortable with how easily the words came out of his mouth. He despised talking about his feelings, much less his failures, and yet somehow Delainey had managed to pull the words right out of his mouth. He stood abruptly. "I have to go. We can finish this at another time. I have another appointment," he lied, needing to get some air.

"Well, when do you want to finish, because I have to get the script ready. Can we finish tonight?"

He frowned. "What do you mean *tonight?*"

"I could bring the tape recorder and meet you at your place?"

"Hell, no. I don't want you in my house."

She drew back, stung. "That was rude and mean. Do you think I relish the idea of spending gobs of alone time with you? Get over yourself, Trace. This is a job that you agreed to do."

Could he handle her in his home? What had almost become *their* home? The idea made him instantly sick to his stomach and apprehensive and yet strangely curious. "Fine. We'll finish the interview at seven o'clock."

"Perfect." She clicked off the recorder. "Thank you for your cooperation, Trace."

He narrowed his eyes. "I'll give you a half an hour. If you don't get what you need by then, you're out of luck."

He didn't wait for her to negotiate, because he knew she would try. He couldn't get away fast enough; if he weren't careful, Delainey would find a way to make him dance to her tune no matter the cost.

DELAINEY KNEW SHE OUGHT to shelve any feelings Trace had awoken to the far reaches of her mind, but he'd always had a way of getting under her skin. He hated her hair color. She touched the strands and winced at the fairly brittle feel of her bleached tresses. It was a brutal process to strip out the natural light brown to create the platinum she sported now, and she was well overdue for a deep-conditioning treatment. But with her precarious finances she hadn't been able to see clear to pay the exorbitant amount that a treatment would require.

"Pooh on you, Trace Sinclair," she muttered as she gathered her documents, reminding herself that Trace's opinion didn't matter in the big scheme of things. In the land of fake smiles and plastic bodies, Delainey had stuck out like a country bumpkin before her makeover, and it had been painfully obvious that in order to make deals, you had to turn heads.

"Oh, honey, what is happening here?" Rafe Solange, the premier hairstylist in Beverly Hills, had exclaimed, lifting one limp mouse-brown lock in distaste. One look at her new zip code and she knew a trim was in order, so she'd gone straight to the top even though she couldn't actually afford it yet. He tsked as if surveying a hot mess and wondering where to start. "Oh, baby child, this has got to go. We're talking strip, color and style, and I'm talking *tout suite*."

"Is it that bad?" she'd asked with embarrassment. In Alaska no one had put much store in fancy hairstyles because half the time, your hair was tucked up into a knitted hat to stay warm. She cringed when he simply stared, placing one hand on his hip with flamboyant flair, and she had her answer. "Okay, do whatever you need to do."

"Thank you, baby Jesus! We're going to make you shine, girl. Los Angeles isn't going to know what hit it."

And Rafe had transformed her from a mouse to a lion, and the transformation had given her the shot of confidence she'd been lacking from the moment she'd stepped off the plane, scared and nervous about her big, life-changing decision to leave Alaska to pursue her dream.

And she was never going back to who she was—and that included her mouse-brown hair.

"So you can just suck it, Trace Sinclair," Delainey said, bracing herself against the chill as she hurried to her car. She may have left a mouse, but she'd returned a lion, and she wasn't going to take any crap from anyone. "Not even you, you big, judgmental jerk."

CHAPTER ELEVEN

DELAINEY FINISHED SELECTING her crew and checked her watch. Peter still hadn't gotten back to her about a hotel, and she was starting to sweat. There was no way she could expect her crew to sleep crammed into her father's tiny house. She could just hear the Teamsters union shrieking at the thought.

She rubbed at her forehead and then rummaged through her purse, looking for something to take the edge off the headache that was building but realized with a groan that she'd tossed back the last of her Tylenol on the plane. A trip to the store was in her future, and it was something she'd really like to avoid, as the local market was much like the town hall. She had a pretty good chance of running into someone she knew just by stepping through the front doors. She groaned and climbed into her car for the quick drive.

Intent on getting in and out, she went straight to the medicine aisle, grabbed the Tylenol and tried to beeline to the cash register, only to nearly run over one of the last people she wanted to see.

"Miranda!" Delainey exclaimed, forcing a bright smile, her gaze lighting on the small boy beside her, watching the two grown-ups with interest. "Oh my goodness, I'm so sorry, I didn't see you there."

Miranda, startled as well, offered an awkward smile as they both wondered how to treat one another. How does one greet a former best friend and sister of your former boyfriend?

"Hi," Miranda said, putting her arm around the boy, whom Delainey could only assume was her son. A sudden lump rose in her throat. At one time she would've been in this child's life as his aunt. *Egad, where'd that come from?* "Trace said you were in town."

"Yeah, and I'm sure he was really thrilled about it," Delainey retorted, unable to stop herself. She stopped and shook her head. "I'm sorry. I have a splitting headache and it's made me a little irritable."

"No need to apologize. And you're right, he's not happy about you being here, but can you blame him? I mean, not to be a stickler for fact, but you broke his heart and never looked back."

"Yes, I'm aware of how things went down between he and I," Delainey said coolly, not appreciating Miranda's quick reminder. "And he's been sure to remind me every second how he felt about my decision to follow my career."

"We should go to lunch," Miranda said, surprising Delainey with her sudden offer. Delainey regarded Miranda warily and Miranda laughed. "I won't bite and I promise I'll only give you a little bit of a hard time over the past. It'd be nice to catch up."

Delainey started to decline—the last thing she needed was to know more about everything she'd left behind—but she missed the simple pleasure of knowing that someone was being straight with her, whether she liked what they had to say or not. Back in L.A., she was constantly trying to decipher what people were truly saying because no one actually said anything without layering it with double-speak or a veneer of lies. Or at least that's how it appeared to her after eight years of constantly watching her back for the knife that was always poised to strike. "Promise me you'll be gentle?" she asked, half joking. "It's been a rough day already, and from what I remember about you, you never pull your punches."

"I'm a kinder, gentler version of me these days," Miranda said.

"Oh? How'd that happen?"

"Long story short, I found happiness and I

learned how to forgive myself. The long story you'll have to wait until lunch."

"Where are we going?"

"How about my place? I was just stopping by to pick up some peanut butter for Talen—my son is currently refusing to eat anything but peanut butter for lunch, and wouldn't you know it, I was completely out—and I think a little privacy would be good for our conversation."

Delainey smiled. "I'd like that." She could've hugged Miranda for her kindness, but she was still a little surprised at how easily Miranda was letting her off the hook. She'd half expected Miranda to lay into her as sharply as Trace. "You're not being super nice just to lure me to your house so you can stab me without witnesses, are you?"

"If I was really still angry about the past and your part in it, I would simply knock your lights out and be done with it. But I'm not mad. In fact, I understand why you left. I just wish you hadn't abandoned everyone when you split. It didn't have to be that way, you know?"

"I didn't mean to abandon anyone," she said, shifting against the pinch from her conscience. Hadn't she, though? She'd severed ties for a reason—she didn't want to ever give herself an out. If she failed, she had nothing or no one to fall back on. At least that'd been her thought when she'd been poised at the precipice of her big jump. It had all seemed so logical at the time. But she was beginning to feel as if she'd made a huge mistake, and it wasn't only because of Trace. "So where do you live?" she asked. "And should I bring anything?"

"I live at 213 Rochester Road, just around the corner from the Rusty Anchor."

"All right. I'll meet you there in a few minutes."

"Sounds good. In the meantime, I'm off to find peanut butter...."

Delainey watched as Miranda and her son walked away, chatting to one another as they searched for their peanut butter, and Delainey suffered that pang of loss again. She wasn't maternal and never had been, but watching Miranda with her son, plainly delighted at being a mother and all it entailed, made her wonder what life would've been like if she'd stayed. For one, she would've married Trace. And two, likely they would've had kids. Maybe she would've found a job in Anchorage and did the commute thing, or maybe she would've taught at the local university. A sudden shudder rippled through her. That's exactly what she hadn't wanted. Domestic bliss was not her dream, so why even wonder what would've been? Her life was amazing. She lived in a desirable neighborhood, she had a job most people dreamed about and she rubbed elbows with really important people.

Well, almost really important people. *Vertical Blind* had pretty much kicked her reputation to the curb, and now not even the D-list people were taking her calls.

But all that was going to change, she told herself. Soon she'd be the one turning down lunch meetings and triaging the scores of people looking to spend a little time with her. For once, she'd be the important one.

Ugh. But first… She cracked the seal on the Tylenol as she walked to the cashier. She needed to quiet the pain slicing open her brain. After that—anything was possible.

MIRANDA KNEW THE probability of running into Delainey at some point was probably high, but she hadn't expected to *literally* run into her.

Talk about shock to the system. At one time, they'd been thick as thieves, and Miranda had been just as stunned as Trace when Delainey had left town right when they'd all needed her the most. But Miranda had had some time to think since Trace had informed her that Delainey was in town, and she'd come to the conclusion that they couldn't continue to hold a grudge against the woman for following her dreams. It hadn't been Delainey's fault that

Simone had died, and it wasn't fair for them to assume that she should've put her life on hold because of the Sinclair tragedy. Time and distance had eased that wound for Miranda, but Trace was a different story. Miranda didn't think Trace would ever forgive Delainey, but Miranda could do her part and extend the olive branch.

About fifteen minutes later, the sound of a car pulling into the driveway signaled that Delainey had arrived, and after cleaning up the peanut butter mess her son had left behind from inhaling his sandwich, she put on his favorite movie and started making sandwiches for Delainey and her.

Delainey walked in tentatively, gesturing toward the door. "I figured it was okay to walk in because you invited me to lunch…."

"Laney, at one time you and I were practically sisters. You don't have to knock to come into my house," Miranda said, and for a split second she thought she saw Delainey's eyes well up. Miranda wondered what was really going on with Delainey after all these years. Something told her that her former best friend was putting up a good front, but the question was why? "I hope you don't mind egg salad," she said as she dished two plates.

"I haven't had egg salad in years. Sounds perfect."

Miranda slid the plate over to Delainey, and they both sat at the counter like old friends, even though there was plenty that needed to be said between them. "How weird is it to be home after all this time?" she asked, trying to break the ice slowly. "It must be like going back in time. Not much has changed since you left."

"*Weird* isn't the word," Delainey admitted. "The worst part was having to stay at my father's place. He hasn't changed, either."

Miranda nodded. Harlan and his daughter had never gotten along, and Harlan, like many Alaskan men who made their living by the harsh conditions of the sea, could be difficult at best. "How'd that go?"

"Not well. He didn't like me before I left, and the only thing that's changed is that now he hates my hair, too." Miranda took in Delainey's appearance and noted all the differences. Delainey touched her hair and shrugged. "He said I was a stranger to him."

"I think it's safe to say that he never really knew you in the first place, so how can you be anything but a stranger now?" Miranda pointed out, and Delainey laughed at the logic. God, she'd missed Miranda. She'd forgotten how easily Miranda had always gotten straight to the point of an argument. "But you know, maybe it's time you introduce yourself. He might find that he likes the real you."

"I doubt that. I don't value anything he does and vice versa. It's a colossal joke that I was born his daughter. I hate fish, I'm a dreamer, I hate the snow… Shall I go on? We're so different sometimes I wonder if I was switched at birth. I wouldn't be surprised if somewhere out there is a woman who can spit like a man, would feel right at home hauling rigging and slipping around on the deck of a boat, and can shoot a moose between the eyes at several hundred yards. That's the daughter who should've been born to Harlan Clarke. Not me."

Miranda laughed. "I am that woman, if you recall, and I can assure you, I'm not Harlan's daughter. You're stubborn like him, and you're not afraid to take risks. I'd say those are pretty cool characteristics to have."

Delainey stared at Miranda in somewhat disbelief. "What's happening here? You should be angry with me. We shouldn't be gabbing like old girlfriends and playing catch-up. I don't understand why you're being so nice."

"Laney…there was a time when I would've been exactly as you think I would act because I was eaten up with anger and working myself into becoming a full-blown alcoholic, but I've recently come to realize that being angry about things I can't change isn't doing me any favors. So, I guess, it's your lucky day. Do you want me to yell at you? Would that make you feel better about how things went down?"

"No." *Maybe.* "I just don't know how to feel about this. I guess I feel guilty for how I handled leaving."

"You had to do what was right for you. I don't begrudge you your happiness. I wish I could say the same for Trace. He's still pretty hurt. He covers it up with anger, but he's really never gotten over you. And he'd *kill* me if he heard me say that because he'd go to his grave denying it. But I know my brother, and he's never been the same since you left."

"Why didn't he meet someone else and move on?" Delainey asked, a pained expression on her face. "I would've expected someone to snatch him up the minute I left."

"I don't know. I got him to go on a few dates, but beyond the superficial dinner and a movie… nothing really materialized. But it's not all your fault, Laney, and I want you to know that. Simone's murder did a number on us all. There's no saying that if you'd stayed he would've been different. Being the one to find Simone…it did something to his head."

Delainey's eyes glazed and Miranda knew she

was reliving that moment as only Trace's girlfriend could. But because Miranda didn't want to wallow in a painful past, she made an effort to redirect the conversation to less depressing ground. "Okay, enough about sad things. Tell me about your glamorous career in Los Angeles as a movie producer."

Delainey emitted a short laugh and her gaze skewed away as she answered with a bit of a flush, "I'm not a movie producer—yet—but I've produced a few television shows here and there. It's a difficult business and the players are constantly changing. One minute you're on top and the next the bottom, but one thing is for sure—you're never bored."

"Oh, wow…sounds…" Miranda searched for the right words so as not to offend Delainey. "Well, it sounds like an adventure. If you're happy, then that's all that matters, right?"

Delainey's smile was blindingly bright—too bright—as she bobbed a nod. "Yep. And I am so happy. Deliriously so, actually. I mean, I live a life most would dream about. I live the Hollywood lifestyle. Rubbing elbows with the important people. Making dreams come true. Yep. It's everything Alaska isn't…and that's what I love about it."

CHAPTER TWELVE

TRACE TRIED NOT to check the time, but his nerves betrayed him as his gaze continually strayed to the small wall clock above his fireplace. Each minute ticked closer to the time he'd agreed to finish the interview with Delainey. He didn't know why he'd agreed to talk with her after hours when his instinct was to flatly turn her down.

And now, it was too late to rescind his reluctant agreement.

It seemed a lifetime ago that Trace and Delainey had been planning to start a life together. When he thought of how stupid she'd made him look, leaving him crying as she'd bolted, he wanted to throw something. She'd done a number on his pride, for sure. So why'd he allow her to manipulate him into this late-night interview? He was baffled by his own behavior, and he didn't like the obvious reason staring him in the face.

He hated himself for it, but seeing her again had awakened something he'd much rather ignore. Something inside him was thrashing around, banging into the furniture and roaring to be free, and whatever it was scared the living hell out of him.

The fact was, he was still insanely attracted to Delainey, even after all this time and in spite of what she'd done to him. And that shamed him to his core. He forced himself to remember what a terrible person she was deep down in the marrow of her bones, because if he didn't, he was afraid of what he'd allow himself to do.

He remembered with crystal clarity how it felt to touch her skin or hear her soft, little moans of pleasure as he'd plunged his tongue deep into her most private flesh. He remembered everything. Time hadn't dulled his memory or lessened the ache of his loss.

He rubbed at the heat gathering in his cheeks, recalling how he'd succumbed to using an erotic memory of Delainey from his mental cache to pleasure himself recently when he hadn't relied on those memories in years. Delainey had gotten under his skin in rapid time, and he was a fool to allow her into his private space.

That's it, he thought resolutely, as soon as Delainey arrived, he would tell her he'd changed his mind. Besides, how professional was an interview conducted in a person's home?

Right on time, a soft knock at his front door

told Trace Delainey had arrived, and he jumped from his chair, nearly stumbling on the end table in his haste to send her away. But as he opened the door, all good intentions fled and he couldn't help but stare. Maybe he was losing it, because her platinum blond was starting to look pretty to him. The exotic, unnatural color turned his crank in an unexpected way, and he itched to touch it. Hell no, a voice screeched in his head, causing him to take a step away as if she were contagious with something life-threatening. "Let's get this over with. I don't know how much more you're going to get. I told you everything back at the office," he said gruffly.

"Well, I need more than a few details if I'm going to re-create the scenario correctly," Delainey explained as she walked into the living room, taking in details as she went. "Everything looks the same." She looked to him questioningly. "What did you do with the stuff I bought for the house?"

"Some of the stuff I gave away, other I threw out. I didn't understand why you'd bought the stuff anyway since you never planned to stay. And I didn't want any reminder of you." He hadn't wanted anything from Delainey after she'd left. It hurt too much to see stuff she'd purchased when he'd been under the assumption that they were going to build their life together in that house. Frankly, there'd been a moment when he'd considered selling the house, too.

"I really did some damage, didn't I?" she asked quietly, and he was stunned by her question. The open regret in her tone stilled the immediately caustic retort that came to mind. Instead, he remained silent. His silence was answer enough. "I didn't mean to hurt you. I don't know if that matters or not. Things were moving so quickly and I panicked. I saw my life flash before my eyes, and I couldn't handle what I saw. I'm not sure that I realized that there was no way you would leave Alaska, and then when it became apparent that you weren't going to budge, I reacted."

"The idea of life with me caused you to panic?" he asked, blinking against what felt like an insult.

"No, it wasn't a life with you that scared me— it was life here with you in Alaska. I didn't want to be a housewife. I wanted a career, not just a job. Too many people allowed their dreams to die because circumstances changed in their personal life, and I didn't want that to happen to me."

Trace didn't want to remember how Delainey had always been open about her dreams and goals; he certainly didn't want to remember how he'd given them very little weight. Too much retrospection and he'd start apologizing for God only knew what. "I don't need an explanation of why you did what you did," he said. "It's done and over with."

"If that were true, you wouldn't still be holding a grudge," she pointed out, and he hated to admit she was right. "Can't we talk about it and get everything out in the open?"

"I doubt it."

"Why not?"

"Because I don't want to talk about it, and it takes two people agreeing to hash things out in order for that to happen. Let's just stick to the professional aspect of our relationship and leave the past where it belongs."

"Trace, why won't you let me explain? Maybe if I could get you to understand why, you could move on with your life."

"Move on? What are you talking about? I did move on with my life."

"That's not what Miranda has said."

Damn his sister for opening her big mouth about his personal business. "Miranda doesn't know what she's talking about. And when did you see Miranda?"

"I saw her earlier today. We had lunch together."

Great. Now his sister and Delainey were best

buds again? Wasn't there any justice in the world? "I don't know what gave Miranda the idea that it was okay to talk about my personal business with you, but I wish she'd just kept her mouth shut. The fact is, I've moved on just fine."

"Trace—"

"No. I'm done with this conversation," he said firmly. How could Miranda betray his confidence like that? To Delainey of all people? "If we're not going to talk about the project then I'd rather just put an end to this visit, if you don't mind." Delainey looked dejected at his curt response, and he didn't for the life of him know why he allowed her feelings to affect him. She'd made her bed and she could lie in it. But as soon as her eyes welled with sudden tears, he knew he was sunk. "That's not fair and you know it," he said, hating how easily her tears moved him. "What do you want from me, Delainey?"

"I want you to stop hating me," she whispered, wiping at her eyes. "It hurts more than I ever realized it would to see you look at me with such hatred. I never meant to hurt you. I was just trying to save myself. Is that so bad?"

DELAINEY SHOULD'VE STUCK to the plan of simply conducting the interview and leaving, but the information Miranda had shared had been stuck in her head on a loop that just wouldn't quit.

Somehow she'd thought if perhaps she began a dialogue with Trace the floodgates would open and they'd spend the evening healing old wounds with open communication. Now in the face of his rejection, she felt like a complete fool. Now she really wanted his forgiveness and she wasn't likely to get it.

"You don't get to break someone's heart and then act wounded because they don't want you around," Trace said. "We're never going to be friends, Delainey."

"I know that," she said, wiping at her eyes. "But I'd hoped that maybe we could look at one another without being assaulted by our past. I made mistakes, more than I'm comfortable admitting, but I'd like to think that I've changed and grown a bit since making them."

Trace pulled a beer from the fridge and cracked it. "I'd offer you one, but seeing as you're going to hit the road soon…"

She frowned, her fists clenching with the urge to pummel some sense into the man. "You don't have to be such an ass all the time. That's all I'm saying."

"Maybe I'm not a nice person." He shrugged.

"You used to be."

"Yeah, well, I used to be a lot of things."

"Ugh. You're impossible."

"I've heard that, too." He swigged his beer.

"Tell me, how did you envision all of this going down between us?" he asked. "I mean, truthfully, did you think that I was going to be so overwhelmed with nostalgia that I'd completely blank out everything that had happened when you professed regret at how you destroyed our relationship?"

"No, of course not," she shot back, embarrassed to admit she'd dared to hope such a thing could happen. "But I never thought you'd delight in treating me so badly just to assuage some messed-up sense of revenge. If you were so heartbroken over my leaving, why'd you let me leave without a fight? You never even tried to change my mind, or better yet, you never entertained the thought of leaving with me."

"My home was here. Why would I leave?"

"And I made it no secret that I never wanted to stay!" The moment stretched between them as they held each other's angry stare. The tension in the room was palpable, but neither was willing to back down. Delainey couldn't believe how cold Trace had become. At one time, he'd been sweet and kind, generous and loving. And he was blaming her for the change? What a cop-out. "Playing the blame game is fun when you know you're cheating to win. Admit it, Trace. You were content to let me eat my dreams so your world remained the same. You didn't care that I wanted so much more than this place could give me, because you never considered my career choice a real one. In your mind, I was never leaving Alaska. Did you imagine me popping out a few kids and then dutifully putting my hopes and dreams on indefinite hold while you pursued your dreams?" The charged silence was enough of an answer for her. "You selfish bastard," she muttered. "Well, screw you. If you want to vilify me for chasing my dreams, so be it. I'm not looking for your approval. Not anymore." She grabbed her purse and stormed past him, but his arm snaked out and grabbed her, pulling her roughly to him. She squeaked in alarm but he wasn't actually hurting her. Her heart beat like a wild thing and her breath seemed in short supply, but she held his stare, determined to seem unaffected by his close proximity. "What now, Trace?" she taunted him, the tip of her tongue wetting her lips. "You slap me around or something?"

"You know I would never hit a woman," he said, his eyes burning but his voice changed to a silky timber that sent shivers of awareness tripping down her spine. "Not even you."

"So what do you want to do with me?" she asked, painfully aware of how Trace's touch sent her logical brain scurrying for shelter. She ought to wrench her arm free and leave, but she didn't want to go. The honest truth was that she craved Trace's touch even if she would die before admitting it. Leaving him had been the hardest thing she'd ever done, and it wasn't only because she'd loved him. She'd known that Trace was the only man who would ever make her heart and body resonate. And she'd been right. No one had managed to make her feel as Trace had. He'd known her body instinctually, as if they'd been cut from the same cloth, and he'd known exactly where to pleasure her until she was hoarse from crying out, her body completely wrung out and limp. And, God help her, she missed that! Was she a terrible human being for hoping beyond hope that he would simply throw her down on the bed and make love to her as he used to?

She was afraid to breathe, afraid to say another word. Time ticked by with the slowest of increments until Trace lowered his mouth to hers. And then she was fairly certain time definitely stopped, and she was glad because she wanted to savor this illicit moment until its sweet, inevitable end.

CHAPTER THIRTEEN

TRACE DIDN'T WANT to think about what he was doing or the possible ramifications. He just wanted to feel. He gently twisted Delainey's arm behind her back and pulled her close as his mouth sought hers. Her lips opened with very little coaxing and her tongue touched his in a tentative motion that set his blood on fire. His tongue slid along hers, exploring hungrily as she rose on her tiptoes to press herself against him more securely. No words were said or needed, as if both knew one single utterance might destroy the fragile moment.

Need flowed between them as if time evaporated, and suddenly they were two young lovers desperate to feel each other's body, mindless of what tomorrow might bring. Within seconds Delainey's sweater was ripped from her body, and she tilted her head back with a groan as Trace pressed a trail of urgent kisses down the column of her neck. She smelled of citrus and a cool mountain breeze, two scents that should've been discordant but created a harmony of sensual awareness throughout his body.

She clung to him as he lifted her into his arms and carried her to his bedroom—the room that had once been *their* bedroom—and laid her on the bed. He snapped the bedside lamp on and the room filled with soft, hazy light. He quickly unlaced her boots and she kicked them free so he could help her wiggle out of her jeans. Within moments, she was in nothing but her matching set of bra and panties, looking like an exotic pinup girl whom most men only dreamed about but never had the privilege of touching.

She smiled shyly under his perusal and he jerked his shirt over his head, tossing it to the floor. She couldn't hide the way her eyes warmed with blatant hunger as her gaze traversed the muscles of his chest and dipped to the softly furred trail disappearing behind his zipper. Her pupils dilated with arousal, and he could barely contain his own.

She started to unhook her bra, but he stopped her with a gruff "Let me" and proceeded to release her beautiful breasts from the dainty cups. So much was different about her—her hair, her nose—but her breasts were exactly as he remembered. He cupped the pert, rosy-tipped globes of soft womanly flesh and nearly lost control as he slipped a tight nipple into his mouth. She'd always thrilled at his rough hands touching her tender skin, saying she enjoyed the feel of a real man. Time hadn't dulled that appreciation, as evidenced by the way her mouth fell open on a gasp and her fingers threaded through his hair and gripped almost painfully. But the sensation spurred him on, and he suckled harder, squeezing the other breast with his free hand.

"Trace," she cried softly, rocking against him, her feminine core rubbing against his erection almost frantically, but the thin scrap of silk of her panties blocked his way. Her breathy moans were like gasoline to his fire, and his hands trembled as he framed her face and claimed her mouth again, slanting his tongue deeply inside, desperate to taste her again. She clutched at his back as he moved over her, pressing her into the bed with his body. He ground his erection against the sensitive spot between her thighs and she groaned into his mouth, her nails digging into his back. "Tell me you want this," he said against her lips, needing to hear her say the words.

"I want this," she whispered, almost desperately. "I want this more than anything."

"What do you want me to do to you?"

"Everything."

He reached between them and pressed the

heel of his hand against her, causing her to squirm. The damp heat of her arousal smelled of heaven, and he couldn't wait a moment longer. He rose to his hands and knees and then bent down to pull her panties free from her hips with his teeth. Her stomach trembled and she put her hand over her eyes, as if she were embarrassed to watch what he was about to do. He chuckled at the memory of her doing that very thing each time he had plunged his tongue deep inside her. He'd always found her bashfulness so sexy because it was part of who she was. And seeing that that part of her hadn't changed made him all the more intent on touching her so intimately.

He settled between her legs and buried his face against her sensitive skin, grazing the swollen nub with his teeth and causing her to jerk, her breath coming in short pants. He teased her with slow, deliberate motions until she was writhing beneath him, begging him not to stop. Her soft cries were better than the sweetest music, and before long she shuddered beneath his tongue, thrashing against her climax as it claimed her. He smiled as the sweet, responsive nub pulsed with pleasure, and he pushed up to climb her body as she gulped in air, trying to recover. Before she could speak, he kissed her deeply, and she melted beneath him, her body limp and sated.

He ignored his straining erection to focus on her, loving how soft and feminine she looked with her eyes at half-mast and her mouth slightly open as she swallowed, trying to catch her breath. "I just need a minute," she said, but he shocked her when he rolled her to her stomach and pulled her to her knees. Her round behind had lost some of its cushion, but it was still the loveliest one he'd ever seen. "You have the best ass," he couldn't help but murmur, intent on impaling her on his length. But before he could bury himself inside her, she looked back at him with a panicked expression, saying, "Condom!" and he realized belatedly that he'd used the last one several months ago.

At his chagrined expression, Delainey realized he didn't have one and she dropped her head in disappointment to the bed. "Crap," she muttered, which didn't even come close to the expletive that he wanted to say. "I'm sorry… not without a condom. I can't take the risk," she said and rolled away from him. She worried her bottom lip when she saw his erection and he knew she felt bad for refusing him, but she surprised him with a suddenly coy look, saying, "But there is more than one way to get the job done," before pushing him down on his back. His eyes rolled back into his head as the warm, wet heat of her mouth enveloped him and he discovered that she'd remembered his particular likes and dislikes just as easily as he'd remembered hers. Seconds before he lost his mind, he wondered how he'd ever let this woman get away from him.

She was damn near perfect.

DELAINEY AND TRACE lay sated and quietly reflective, neither saying a word. After their heart rates had settled into a normal rhythm, Trace broke the silence first.

"Have you had many lovers since moving to Los Angeles?" he asked.

"That's probably not a question you should ask," Delainey warned. "You might not like the answer." Trace knew she was right but for some reason he needed to know. When he remained silent, waiting, Delainey sighed and answered, "A few. Nothing serious. It's hard to start a relationship in the field I'm in. Well, I should say, it's easy to start a relationship but hard to maintain it."

"Why?"

"Well, for one, it seems everyone is always looking for the bigger, better deal, and sometimes you're on the losing end of that arrangement. Plus, when you're on location, away from your loved ones and whatever your particular reality is, you turn to the people you spend so much time with, and that creates a false attachment. There are a lot of affairs that happen," she explained with a shrug. "And I'm not one for an open relationship. I'm old-fashioned that way."

"Is there a lot of that going on? Open relationships?" He couldn't fathom being okay with someone else touching his woman. Even though they'd been apart for eight years, he hated the idea of someone else occupying space that had previously belonged to him.

"Yeah," she admitted. "It's an incestuous little circle. Everyone is doing someone that someone else knows. I hate that part. Feels dirty. I tried to date outside of the business, but it's complicated and they often don't understand the long days and, worse, the politics. In the end, it's just easier to date within the circle." She turned to regard him with open curiosity. "How many women have you dated?"

"Not a lot. My job makes it difficult to make too many attachments." Plus, he wasn't about to let another woman get her claws into him. He'd learned his lesson, but he didn't see the sense in ruining the tentative truce between them. "Besides, I'm not the boyfriend kind."

She stilled and he knew she was thinking of

their time together. "Because of me," she surmised quietly, and he didn't deny it. She held his gaze and he felt his heart lurch. She was so beautiful in this light, almost ethereal, and he wished this time together were real and not an illusion. "I hurt you pretty bad."

He shrugged. "Things happen. I'm not hurting now."

"I don't believe you. If you weren't still hurting, you would've settled down with someone else. I know you, Trace. You're meant to be a husband and a father. You have a kind and generous heart that was meant to share a life with someone else."

Good feeling fading, Trace moved to the edge of the bed and started to collect his discarded clothing. "Let's just leave it alone," he suggested as he pulled his shirt on and reached down to grab her bra. He tossed it to her and stood to slide into his jeans. "I'm sorry about...*this*—" he gestured between them "—I never planned to..."

"Yeah, I know. Me, neither," she said, quickly dressing, and he could feel the awkwardness growing like mold on bread. "Well, for what it's worth, I enjoyed myself, but we probably shouldn't do it again. It's not very professional."

He tried not to take offense but he bristled all

the same. "Sorry. I'm new to this Hollywood game. My apologies for breaking the rules."

"Don't be like that, Trace. I'm just saying, that even though it was great, I can't afford to lose my objectivity. This project means everything. It's imperative that it succeed."

"Nothing stops you from succeeding, does it?" he said with a subtle sneer in his voice, and even though he was ashamed of how it made him sound, he was helpless to stop it. "Delainey Clarke, ambition personified. Homer still has the boot print on its back from the last time you marched on by in your quest for success."

"Oh, this again?" she said sharply, her eyes flashing. "I thought we were past this petty crap."

"Why? Just because we fooled around a little? Honey, in your business, I thought this was just part of a normal day's work."

She gasped at his insult and slapped him hard. "How dare you! I can't believe you went there. I thought we were sharing some private information and you just used mine against me. Real classy, Trace. Real classy." She scrambled from the bed and quickly gathered her clothes and jerked them on. "If my job weren't depending on this stupid assignment, I'd tell you to go screw yourself and find someone else to play your part. I didn't want to believe it, but you're right, you have changed and not for the better! Forget the damn interview. I'll get what I need from the news footage. The sooner I'm done with Alaska—and you—the better."

"That goes for the two of us, sweetheart!" he called as she slammed out the front door. *Damn it!* Trace wanted to yell to the rafters and do collateral damage to anything in his path, but he reined in his rage and frustration by the thinnest margin. What was wrong with him? Why couldn't he just keep his mouth shut and play along? Because he wasn't that kind of person, he answered himself. He wasn't the kind of guy who shared his woman, or laughed when he wanted to scowl, or handed out false compliments to someone who was plainly an idiot and *he never would be.* And as such, he couldn't pretend that everything was all right between him and Delainey just because their bodies still craved one another even when their brains said *bad idea.* He could make love to Delainey all day, worshipping her body until they were both soaked with sweat, and it wouldn't change a damn thing between them. He didn't trust her and he never would, and she was never going to stop chasing that elusive dream, no matter the cost. Nothing had changed—except now they had brand-new baggage between them.

Well, hell.

So much for using sex to mend fences. By the feel of things, they'd just started a whole new war.

CHAPTER FOURTEEN

THE FOLLOWING DAY Trace found Miranda during her lunch break and pulled her aside. "What the hell are you doing telling Delainey anything about me?" he asked, still angry. "She came to me saying that you'd shared personal details with her about my life, and I didn't appreciate that at all."

"First of all, calm down," Miranda said, unruffled by his ire and calmly continuing to enjoy her sandwich. "Yes, I talked to her, and yes, I told her some things. But I think they were things that needed to be shared for everyone's sake. You know, our family is pretty screwed up, and until I got my head on straight I was pissed off most days and blaming everyone but myself for the circumstances in my life. Don't you think it's time to let the past go?"

"You're one to talk. You've only just recently started being the kinder, gentler Miranda, so don't start preaching to me just because you've suddenly had an epiphany."

"Well, I will preach to you because you're my

brother and you're likely going to keep screwing up your life if I don't. You have unfinished business with Delainey, and until you get it figured out, your life is going to suck."

"Who are you to judge my life? Maybe I like my life just the way that it is and I don't need my nosy little sister poking around where it's unwanted. And I definitely don't need Delainey pitying me either because she thinks she broke me when she left. I was doing just fine until she started coming around again."

"That's a matter of opinion," Miranda quipped under her breath, and he returned with a glare.

"Yeah, it is—mine, and I say I was doing just fine."

"So is that what this visit is all about? You yelling at me for caring about you?" Miranda crumpled her trash, her stare just as hard. "Like it or not, we're family, and if I see an opportunity for you to get over the past, I'm going to take it."

"How does pushing Delainey at me help the past?"

"Because when she left, you changed, and frankly I need the old you back."

"What does that mean?"

"You promised me you'd help me with Mom and Dad, and yet you've avoided the situation since you returned from your last trip," Miranda said, pulling no punches. "I need your help. There was a time when you would've done whatever you could to help and it wouldn't have taken strong-arming you into doing it."

He stared, hating that she was right. "I've been busy. In case you haven't noticed, my life has been hijacked by the very person you've been trying to shove down my throat."

"Yes, I heard. Even though Fish and Game is a separate department from Search and Rescue, it seems everyone is twittering about how lucky you are and how lucky the Search and Rescue program is to have a little unexpected cash flow. Not to mention, you're getting a nice little payday from this gig, right?" At his reluctant nod, she said, "And you're getting to hold on to your Junior Search and Rescue program, right?" Again he nodded. "Well, then I say suck it up, put a happy face on and stop being such a sourpuss about it all. So you have to deal with Delainey—something that's well overdue if you ask me—big whoop. Put your big-boy pants on and just deal with it."

Had his little sister just schooled him? And worse, had he deserved it? Maybe. But he still wasn't happy about Miranda spilling his secrets. They were secret for a reason. "Next time you want to share life stories, keep to your own, okay?" he bit out, but his argument was losing steam. Hell, he was losing his grip on everything since Delainey came back to town. He rubbed at his forehead. "I'll stop by Mom and Dad's after work today. That work for you?"

"Fine by me, but you're on your own this time. Mom doesn't want anything to do with me right now. She's refusing to let me into the house, saying the last time I came over I picked a fight with her. It's not true but that's how she remembers it."

"How do you remember it?" he asked, knowing Miranda and their mom had always butted heads over one thing or another.

"Talen and I came over to help her clean up. It was so bad I couldn't stay. It smelled like something had died in there, and I didn't know if it was safe for Talen—or any human being—to be in there for too long."

"What does Dad say about it?"

"Nothing. He never goes in the house any longer. He pretty much lives in his garage."

"Typical," Trace muttered. "The old man is content to ignore everything around him while he does whatever the hell he wants. And before you say I've been guilty of the same thing, it's different. My life and schedule is far more hectic than Dad's."

"I have this instinct to defend him but I can't. That's about the long and short of it right now,"

Miranda agreed sadly. "Have you talked to Wade lately? Maybe if Wade came home they'd snap out of their funk."

Trace shook his head. He hadn't talked to his older brother in a really long time. Terribly long, actually. "It's hard to coordinate our schedules," he said. "And we're both busy."

"Yeah, I know. But I think we really need to get him home. He needs to see what's happening, too. Besides, maybe if Wade came home…"

"We'll see," he said, not sure having Wade return would make things better or worse. Of the conversations he'd had with his older brother, Trace knew Wade had no respect for their father since he'd started growing and selling marijuana, and the two clashed as readily as Miranda and their mother did. "Let me take a look at the situation first and then I'll give you my honest assessment."

"Do you think you'll have time between being a movie star?"

Trace realized Miranda was teasing him, and he offered a small grin. "I guess I'll have to make time. Do you want my autograph?"

"Only if I can turn around and sell it for big money on the internet," Miranda quipped. "I have a wedding to pay for."

He suppressed a shudder and turned to leave. "Better you than me."

"Maybe someday that'll change," Miranda called after him, and he answered with a wave as he left her to enjoy the rest of her lunch break.

DELAINEY SPENT THE morning securing her crew and getting their flights scheduled while jotting notes for the reenactment script. She still needed to hire a few actors and find a hotel because Peter had come up empty.

"I'm so sorry," Peter said, looking wretched at having failed her, but she didn't have time to coddle anyone as panic threatened to rob her of her senses. "I tried to find a hotel with enough vacancies, but we're having a banner moose season and wouldn't you know it, all the hotels are booked solid."

"Thank you for trying," Delainey said, forcing a smile as she added "Find Hotel ASAP" to her to-do list. "I have twenty-four hours to find a place to house a crew of eight. At least it's not a full crew," she said, trying to find the silver lining.

"I feel terrible," Peter said. "I thought for sure that I could find a place. Maybe not the best of places, but a place to hole up while you're here."

"It's okay," she assured him, but her heart was racing. "I'll figure it out. That's what I do—I problem-solve."

He smiled with relief and she almost wanted

to slap him silly, but that was only because she was still out of sorts after her interlude with Trace and definitely confused about why she'd let it happen in the first place.

Trace was like a flu virus—she'd just have to wait out the symptoms. She stomped on any memory that dared to pop its head from her mental cache before she found herself aching for a rematch. Why did Trace know her body so well? Even after all this time, his touch still had the power to make her quake. She thought of the men she circulated around in Los Angeles and she wanted to laugh. There was a marked difference between the men who work out religiously to hone their physique and a man hewn from hard work. Delainey couldn't stand a man with soft hands. She'd discovered that fact about herself in a rather unfortunate episode that had ended with a not-so-great bridge burning.

It'd been her first big producer gig, and she'd been heady with the thrill of being in charge. She'd naively found herself flirting with a big-name actor who was known for his playboy ways. Before she knew it, they were in bed together. But the minute those soft, girlie hands had touched her skin, she'd found her desire deflating like a punctured balloon. Of course, he'd noticed that she'd gone cold and unresponsive, and he'd taken offense. Suffice to say, they would never work together again.

Delainey shook off the horrid memory and chuckled to herself. The actor had paid fanatical attention to his supplements and calorie intake so as to maintain his killer physique, but the man had never worked a hard day's labor in his entire life. Trace ate like a red-blooded American man should—if he could catch it, he could eat it. Trace could trap, fish or track anything. A warmth suffused her body and a private smile followed. Trace, for all his faults, was the sexiest man she'd ever known. And that fact had not changed.

Her cell phone interrupted her musing, and she saw Miranda was calling. They'd exchanged cell numbers after lunch, and it seemed Miranda was keeping up with her promise to keep in touch, though Delainey didn't expect a phone call so soon.

"Hey, Miranda, what's up?" Delainey answered, her mind returning to the problem at hand.

"I heard through the grapevine that you need a place for your crew to hole up for a week or two during your production. I may have what you need," she said, and Delainey immediately perked up.

"Yeah? How so?"

"Do you remember Otter?" Miranda asked.

"Yeah, sort of. Why?"

"Well, he's been getting into real estate over the years and he just so happens to have a good-size house that just came up for rent. I'm sure if you make him an offer, he'll take it. Otter loves making a deal. I know you were looking for a hotel, but this might do in a pinch."

"Actually, at this point, any roof over their heads is good for me. Thanks!"

"No problem." Miranda paused before adding, "Hey, one more thing… Trace came by and he was pretty mad at me for sharing some details about his private life. My guess is that you and him talked?"

Talked? Ha. Perhaps if they'd stuck to talking, there wouldn't be this awkwardness now. But then again, maybe not. "Yeah, we talked. I hope he wasn't too mad with you."

"Oh, he was but don't worry about that. I can handle my brother. Besides, I didn't say anything that didn't need saying. I really hope you two can work out the kinks from the past. Even if you're not meant to be together, maybe we can work toward being friends again."

Hearing Miranda say she and Trace weren't meant to be together pinched, even if she'd been saying it for years. It was one thing to think something privately but quite another to have another agree with you. Somehow, it made her want to prove Miranda wrong.

She rubbed her forehead, wondering if she was ever going to feel normal about relationships. She'd run away from the one solid, stable romantic attachment in her life and then found every relationship since lacking. "We'll see," Delainey said. "Trace and I have some pretty big boulders in our way."

"Don't we all. But it can happen. You know, I carried a pretty big chip on my shoulder for a long time, but now that it's gone…it makes me wonder why I didn't chuck that thing a long time ago."

"Well, I don't carry a chip. I don't carry anything with me that doesn't serve the moment," Delainey said.

"That's how it may seem but we all have baggage, even if we don't realize we're still packing it around."

"Geesh, the years have turned you into a philosopher," Delainey teased, half joking. "What happened to my favorite ballbuster, tomboy kind of girl?"

"She grew up," Miranda answered with a small chuckle. "But I can still shoot better than most men."

"I believe that," Delainey said. "I haven't shot

a gun in years. I'd probably shoot my damn foot off."

Miranda laughed. "You and Trace ought to go target shooting back behind my parents' property. Remember when we all used to do that?"

Yeah, Delainey remembered. Those were such good, innocent times. Seemed a lifetime ago. She drew a deep breath and decided to put an end to the conversation. "Listen, I have to go. I appreciate your help with the accommodations. Text me Otter's number and I'll hit him up."

"No problem. That's what friends are for, right?"

Even friends who didn't qualify as friends anymore. Delainey thanked Miranda again and clicked off.

Thank God for old connections. For a long moment, her gaze traveled to the scenery outside the conference window and she wondered why she'd severed ties with everyone. She'd been so stupid, so naive. And so selfish. She missed her friends, even if their lives had turned out so wildly different. Miranda had been her best friend in the entire world. And Delainey had walked away without looking back. Yet, Miranda was actively working to forgive her. Why? She couldn't fathom a reason, but she was inordinately grateful.

Was it too much to hope for Trace's forgiveness? She knew the answer, and it hurt. Trace would never forgive her. She'd taken something beautiful between them and smashed it into the ground—deliberately.

The bigger question was how could she forgive herself?

CHAPTER FIFTEEN

Trace pulled up to his parents' place and took a moment to put himself in the right frame of mind. The happy memories of the past had been eclipsed by the reality of a family broken by tragedy, and he could no longer deny that he'd been avoiding facing the situation as it was today.

His father's garage/shed had once been his workstation where he'd created beautiful carvings for the tourist trade, but his dad had stopped the pretense of carving many years ago. Now, his father made his living selling and growing marijuana in an elaborate greenhouse operation, and it made Trace sick to his stomach to see how far his father had fallen from the morals and values he'd once had. But he wasn't here to see his dad. He needed to see if there was any validity to Miranda's claim that their mother was living in a dangerous situation.

As he walked to the house, he desperately hoped Miranda was exaggerating. But as soon as he came within a few feet of the door, his hope died under the stench that was escaping from the interior. He covered his nose. If he could smell something outside, what did it smell like on the inside?

He knocked but when no one answered, he tried opening the front door but found himself barred by something. He pushed hard and the sound of something toppling to the floor followed, but at least the door could swing open. "Mom?"

He navigated the narrow walkway that was clogged with various boxes of who-knew-what, and he immediately covered his nose as the smell nearly bowled him over. Holy hell, what was that stench? A horrid thought occurred to him. What if that smell was his dead mother buried under a wall of garbage? This was unreal. He never in a million years could've imagined that his mother had let things get to this stage, and he immediately felt guilty for ignoring Miranda's pleas for help. Clearly, their mother was a hoarder of the worst kind.

The door leading to the bedroom that had once been Simone's opened and his mother peered out, her eyes widening in distress when she saw it was Trace. "What are you doing here? You should've called. We could've met in town for lunch or something," she said, quickly closing the door and making her way toward him.

It'd been only a few months since he'd seen his mother, but in that time it seemed she'd aged tremendously. Whereas gray had peppered his mother's dark hair, now it blanketed it, and deep lines were etched into her face. Dark circles ringed her eyes and her skin tone looked sallow.

"Mom, come outside with me for a minute," he said, concerned. "It's not sanitary in here and it's unsafe."

At that her expression crinkled into a disapproving scowl and she crossed her arms and refused to budge. "You've obviously been talking to your sister. She's somehow gotten you to sing the same tune as her. I'm perfectly fine right where I'm at."

"No, you're not," he said firmly. "And you're not staying another minute in this house. What's happened here? I don't even know where to begin," he admitted with a flush of panic. Everywhere he looked, he saw filth and clutter. His mother had always been a bit of a collector, but she'd never been dirty. He couldn't even make a path to the kitchen, which was where the smell seemed to be originating. His eyes smarted and began to burn. "Mom, outside now. If not for yourself but for me. I can't breathe in here."

Jennelle softened and relented. "Fine. But only because it's a beautiful day and I need to water my plants," she said. Trace didn't care what excuse got her to step outside as long as they were no longer in that toxic place. "I really wish you would've called," she said, going to the hose and unraveling it to start watering her marigolds. "We could've eaten at that new place on Bluegill Street. I've heard it has great fish and chips."

"Mom, I'm sorry it's been a while since I've visited and now that I'm here I have to be the jerk, but Miranda is right. That house isn't safe. What happened? It looks like a war zone. And what does Dad say about it?"

"Your dad is busy with his projects," she answered with an evasive shrug, but Trace saw the hidden hurt hiding behind the motion. "We live separate lives."

"Why? And since when?" Had he really been that absent in his family's life to have missed this total and complete breakdown? Simone's death had done a number on them, but he hadn't realized that the very fabric of who they were as a family was disintegrating to dust. "Mom...talk to me. You have to know that you're in trouble. That house is...not safe in any way."

"It's just a little cluttered is all," she said. "I have so many projects going at the same time. All I need is to prioritize a little."

"You need a wrecking ball at this point. How do you get into your kitchen to cook your food?"

"Oh, I don't cook that much anymore. No sense in making a full meal just for me. Your father prefers his microwave meals and I enjoy a can of soup, which I can make on my hot plate. It's much better this way, actually."

Trace couldn't wrap his head around the situation and felt a little sick to his stomach. "Mom, I can't let you stay here. Now that I've seen it… God, I don't even know where to start. I can't believe things have gotten this bad. This is borderline ridiculous. You're not blind. You have to know that you're living in a bad situation. Your health is at risk! Hell, I was in there for five minutes and thought my chest was going to cave in."

"It's not that bad," she scowled. "And I don't appreciate your judgment. You can't come around and tell me how to live when you haven't seen fit to visit or call. You all were cut from the same cloth. Except Simone, of course," she added with a sniff, and Trace felt slapped.

He tried not to bristle as he said, "If Simone were here she'd say the same thing we are. In fact, she'd probably never step foot in this place again if she saw it."

His mother lifted her chin. "My Simone would never abandon me," she said resolutely. "I know that in my heart."

This was a dead-end conversation, Trace realized too late. Bringing up Simone was always a land mine of heartache no matter how innocent. "Okay, Mom, I don't want to strong-arm you, but you're going to force my hand. This place needs to get cleaned up. Plain and simple. Me and Miranda will come help you. Pick the day."

"Don't tell me what do to or how to do it, Trace Sinclair." His mother's strident tone reminded him of when he was a boy and he'd royally screwed up. "I will live my life as I see fit, and no one is going to tell me otherwise. Next time, call before coming over." And then she turned on her heel and returned to the wretched dump that had once been his childhood home and slammed the door. He was tempted to follow so he could pull her forcibly from the house, but he knew that was a bad idea and likely to make things worse. His gaze turned to the shed, and he strode resolutely in that direction to take things up with his father. It was time for Zed to take control of the situation before the house collapsed and buried the man's wife.

Trace didn't bother knocking and went inside. The sharp scent of marijuana permeated the hazy room, but the smell wasn't nearly half as bad as what Trace had just endured in the main house. He found his father tending to his garden, examining a leaf for some sort of imperfection. When Trace walked in, Zed looked up and for a moment stared as if he wasn't sure what to say, but when he saw Trace's expression he went back to his project with a barely audible grunt of a greeting.

"Dad, we have a situation, and I know you have to know about it," he said, going straight to the point.

"And what might that be?" his father asked, slipping a pair of specialized goggles over his face to examine his plants more closely.

Trace tried to ignore the fact that his father was tending an illegal garden—that was a fight for another day—and focused on the immediate threat. "Mom is going to die in that house. She's trying to bury herself in crap. Have you seen the inside of your house lately?"

"That's your mother's house and I tend to leave her to her business. I suggest you do the same."

"No, that's not going to happen," Trace said firmly, trying to keep his anger in check. "You need to help us get Mom out of that house so we can get a crew in there to clean it up. We have to get moving before the winter sets in and we have to wait until spring."

"And what do you propose to do with her while you're cleaning?" he asked, still absorbed in the plants.

"I don't know. Maybe she can move in here

with you. I see you've turned the garage into a serviceable apartment. I'm sure if she doesn't mind the smell of garbage, she surely won't mind the nose-burning smell of marijuana. Besides, in case you've forgotten, she's still your wife and you're obligated to care for her."

At that Zed turned a jaundiced eye toward Trace and said, "I don't need a pup like you telling me how to tend to my business."

"I disagree," Trace countered boldly. He'd been taught to respect his elders, but Miranda was right—things were out of hand and neither of their parents was taking care of business, which left it up to the kids to see it done. "I don't want to do this, Dad. I'm worried. Mom's living in an unsafe environment. Please tell me you care."

"Of course I care. She's my wife," he answered gruffly. "But your mom's a stubborn woman. I can't make her do anything she doesn't want to do, and for whatever reasons she's happy to live like she does. Hell, do you think I moved out here because I wanted to? It just sort of happened."

"Then, make it *unhappen,* Dad," Trace urged, seeing a glimmer of hope in his father's admission. "Maybe she just needs to know that you still care enough to put your damn foot down."

"What she needs I can't give her," Zed said,

looking away. "Besides, she'll come to her senses on her own time. We just need to give her some space to figure things out."

Trace's hope died as quickly as it had flared. "Dad, you're giving me no choice. I'm going to call Social Services to come out here and evaluate her living situation. You know if they come out here they're going to insist she get it cleaned up."

"Your mother isn't going to care about a piece of paper telling her what she needs to do and what not to do. Besides, we don't need a bunch of government types traipsing in on our land. It's private property for a reason."

Understanding dawned on Trace, and he shook his head in disgust. "The real reason you don't want anyone coming around is because of this—" he gestured to the plants "—isn't it?"

When his father refused to answer, Trace bit back an expletive. "Unbelievable. Dad...you've turned into a selfish bastard, you know that? Your wife needs you. Hell, your family needs you, and you're content to bury yourself in here. You aren't the man who raised me. The man who raised me taught me to be a man—and you aren't that person. I never thought I'd say this, but I'm ashamed of you."

"If you've said your piece, you can go," Zed said, but his lip trembled and Trace knew he'd hit a nerve. Good. His old man needed to hear it. Trace left before he said something he really couldn't take back, although he couldn't be sure that he hadn't already.

CHAPTER SIXTEEN

TRACE FOUND HIMSELF at the Rusty Anchor needing a drink. The place was filled as it usually
was, and the minute Russ saw him belly up to
the bar, he poured a shot of whiskey. "How'd
you know?" Trace asked, lifting the shot in gratitude before he downed it in a single practiced
move.

"You had a look that said beer ain't gonna do
it," Russ answered with a knowing grin, and
Trace nodded. Either the man was a freaking
psychic or Trace had his day written all over his
face. "Troubles of the rich and famous?" Russ
teased gruffly, and Trace wished that were his
problem. Somehow that seemed easier to navigate than the situation with his parents.

"It's my folks."

"Say no more. We've all got 'em and some
are worse than others. Yours, though, have
been through a lot. Losing Simone... Hell, that
would've tore up the most stoic."

"Simone died eight years ago. Isn't it time we
all stop using her death as a crutch for every sin-

gle bad thing we do in our lives?" Trace asked, tapping the bar for another shot. "I don't know… it just seems her ghost lingers a helluva lot."

By his third shot, he was feeling good and he'd finally lost the tension cording his shoulders. The music was toe-tapping good and he was enjoying himself, shooting the shit with fellow bar patrons and laughing at raunchy jokes told by the deckhands.

That was until he heard a particular laugh filter through the noise. He swiveled on his barstool and searched the dim light for the source. He zeroed in on Delainey sitting in one of the corner booths, a single glass candle lighting the cubicle, with Otter Stout. Delainey was laughing at something and Otter was beaming at having been so witty. Something primal and possessive washed over him and after three shots of whiskey, his good sense had completely left the building. He signaled for a beer, and after Russ had put one in his hand, he sauntered over to where Delainey and Otter were having their little tea party for two.

"Hey, Trace," Otter exclaimed with a smile. "How you doin'? I haven't seen you in a while. Miranda said you've been out busy with Search and Rescue lately. Any good stories?"

"Just the ones the news sees fit to blab about," Trace said, his stare going straight to Delainey.

Why was she so pretty? She was like a delicate piece of chocolate, sweet and decadent. And he was suffering from a sweet tooth something bad. "You guys catching up on old times or something?" he asked, trying to sound nonchalant, but he really didn't like the way Delainey's eyes had lit up. He knew he didn't have the right to care but he did, and the three shots of whiskey were telling him he had *every* right.

"Did you want to join us?" Otter asked, preparing to move over, but Delainey cut him off before he could answer.

"I'm sure Trace has his own friends to visit with. He doesn't need to horn in on our time. Besides, I want to hear all about your decision to go into real estate. I've always dreamed of having a few investment properties."

Trace snorted and she glared at him for the rude noise. Otter seemed to catch the odd current flowing between them and his brow furrowed. "Hey, you guys should catch up or something. We can chat later, Laney. I'll have those short-term rental papers to you first thing in the morning." Delainey started to protest but Otter had scooted out and made his way through the throng of people to the front of the bar, where he then disappeared.

"Are you happy?" Delainey asked, glaring. "That was incredibly rude."

"I know," Trace admitted, but he smiled nonetheless. "You look really pretty tonight."

His unexpected compliment seemed to rattle her, and he liked the effect. "How much have you been drinking?" she asked, standing and grabbing her purse and jacket.

"Probably too much," he allowed with a shrug. "Are you going to be my designated driver tonight? I probably shouldn't drive."

"I'll call you a cab," Delainey said, moving past him, but he caught her hand and brought it to his lips, startling her. "What are you doing?" she asked, her gaze darting to see who was watching. "I can't be seen canoodling with the talent."

"You haven't even begun to witness my true talent," he murmured with a wicked grin. He ought to stop, but the whiskey was running the show now. He swigged his beer, but before he could finish she took it from his hand.

"That's enough of that," she said, putting the half-finished beer on an empty table. "Let's get you a cab."

"First, let's dance," he suggested, pulling her into his arms and moving sensually against her to the beat of the music. She gasped and if the lighting wasn't so dim, he could've sworn she'd blushed. "C'mon, one dance, sweetheart. For old times' sake," he said softly against the shell of her ear, and she relented with a shake of her head even as she looped her arms around his neck. "There...see? That wasn't so hard was it?"

"You're drunk, and if you weren't you wouldn't be wanting to hold me like this," she reminded him with a sad smile.

"True and not true."

"What do you mean?"

"It's true I'm drunk. Not true that I wouldn't want to hold you. Delainey, I always want to touch you. The difference being, when I'm sober I remember why I shouldn't."

Delainey accepted his answer with a nod and instead of coming back with a sharp quip, she settled against his chest and they danced, a slow sensual movement in tandem with each other, as if the entire bar had disappeared and it was just them and the music. "Maybe I should get you drunk every night," she said lightly.

"And why is that?" he asked.

"Because you're not as angry. This is how I remember you," she said. Trace let that comment sit between them and finally the song ended and she drew away. "So, are you going to let me call you a cab?" she asked.

"No, but I'm going to let you drive my truck."

"And how am I supposed to get home?"

He pulled her back into his arms. "You and

I both know you're not going anywhere until the morning."

She bit her lip. "We really shouldn't…"

"Honey, you're preaching to the choir, but I don't feel like being a good boy…. How about you? Do you feel like being a bad girl?"

Her gaze widened and she swallowed as she slowly shook her head. "Yes," she whispered.

His grin widened. "Then let's get out of here before we both come to our senses."

"Lord have mercy…"

You got that right.

Trace knew he was making a big mistake, but at the moment he didn't care. The morning would come soon enough. Until then…he was going to show Delainey all that she'd been missing the past eight years.

DELAINEY WAS LOSING her mind. But the idea of feeling Trace's body against hers one last time was too big of a temptation for her to ignore. Screw good sense. They managed to make the front door and slam it behind them before they were both tearing each other's clothes off. Trace, smelling of whiskey and male, drove her insane with need as he ripped her shirt off, popping buttons as he went. She laughed and pushed his shirt from his shoulders and then giggled as they tumbled to the leather sofa, the room encased in darkness. Fingers, tongues, hands, even feet, went crazy as they explored each other in a frenzy that took her breath away. He never stopped, moving from one pleasure spot to the next, seeking out her erogenous zones like a bloodhound intent on finding the next target. She lost her mind several times, babbling and crying out as Trace wrung an orgasm out of her within seconds. And then just as she was coming to her senses, she heard a rapper tear and she mouthed "Thank God" because she wasn't going to be content with intense foreplay this time around.

She wrapped her legs around his torso and lifted her hips, and he drove himself home, burying his length deep inside. She cried out with pure, unadulterated pleasure as Trace rocked her body. The darkness and the taboo nature of their union pushed her to greater heights, and she was soon sobbing as another, more powerful orgasm clenched every muscle and stole her ability to think like a normal, rational human being. At that moment, she would've given Trace anything he wanted—even it meant leaving her career and popping out his babies. It was that good.

Had she ever been so consumed by another person? No. Not even close. She considered herself a sexual being, but this was ridiculous.

Were those stars? Delirium, that's what this was. Orgasmic lunacy. And she wanted more. God help her…she wanted more.

Delainey recovered lying on top of Trace, their sweat drying in the cold room. After a long moment, she reached up and grabbed an afghan draped on the edge of the sofa and covered their bodies with it.

"Good thinking," he murmured sleepily, his arms curling around her and holding her tight. "This is nice," he added, and she wondered if it was the alcohol speaking. Probably, but she closed her eyes and savored it just the same. This felt right. She'd spent the past eight years bouncing from one bad relationship to the next, blaming circumstances for their failures instead of examining the real reason. She didn't want them to succeed. None of them had that essential quality—none of them was Trace. This man was like a drug in her system, and she'd been unaware just how much she'd needed a fix until this moment.

"I can hear you thinking," Trace said, interrupting her thoughts.

"Sorry," she said, feeling guilty for allowing anything to ruin the moment. "Are you cold?"

"I'm perfect. How about you?"

"I'm fine."

"Want me to build a fire?"

"No. I don't want you to move."

She felt him chuckle and she smiled. "Good, because I don't want to move yet, either," he admitted, tightening his hold on her.

"Why were you drinking at the bar tonight?" she asked, hoping it wasn't her that had sent him straight to the bottle. She'd hate to think she was fodder for the chorus of a melancholy country song.

He exhaled a heavy sigh. "My parents."

"What's wrong with your parents?"

"I didn't want to believe it but…my mom's a hoarder. Pretty bad actually. I don't know what to do other than calling Social Services."

"What does Miranda or Wade have to say about it?"

"Miranda was the one who told me about it in the first place and Wade doesn't know. I haven't told him yet."

"Maybe Wade should come home to help you deal with it."

"Yeah, that's what Miranda said, too."

"You're worried about your mom, aren't you?"

He nodded. "She looked old. I've never seen her age so quickly. And after I saw her living conditions, I knew why. It made me sick to my stomach."

"What about your dad?"

Trace made a sound of disgust. "He's no help.

He's just watching her bury herself as long as it doesn't interfere with his pot planting. That man's not the man I grew up with, that's for sure."

Sadness for Trace and his family filled her chest. At one time, the Sinclair family had been like her own—more so, seeing as her family had been so dysfunctional. She didn't feel it was her place to offer advice nor did she think Trace would welcome it, so she remained silent and instead pressed a quick kiss to his bare chest. "I'm sorry, Trace," she said quietly.

"Yeah…me, too," Trace said, his voice heavy with more than drink and sexual satisfaction. "Let's go to the bed," he suggested.

"Oh, are you ready for sleep?" she asked, surprised. Maybe the alcohol had sapped his stamina. She tried not to be disappointed, but then Trace surprised her by scooping her into his arms.

"I never said I wanted to sleep," he said, thrilling her with the sensual suggestion in his tone. "I just thought you might like the bed more than the sofa when I bend you over."

"Oh!" She gasped and buried her burning face against his chest, yet she was secretly delighted. She loved his dirty mouth. But she loved what he did with that dirty mouth even better…

As far as that little voice at the back of her

brain whispering that she was making a huge mistake? She answered with, "Go big, or go home."

And then she told that little voice to shut the hell up.

CHAPTER SEVENTEEN

AWKWARD BE THY NAME was the morning after a hookup that never should've happened. Trace remembered everything—three shots and half a beer wasn't enough to obliterate his memory— although as he stared at the ceiling, wondering what the hell was wrong with him, he wished it were.

Delainey stirred beside him and he tried not to think about her naked body beneath the blankets and how they'd blown through an entire minipack of condoms. At least he was proud to say he'd left a good impression if this was the last time they ever knocked boots again. *Yeah, that's what's important right now.*

He scrubbed his face with his hands and climbed from the bed. The sunrise hadn't touched the horizon yet, which was a surprise given how little sleep they'd gotten. He pulled on jeans and an Alaskan Aces sweatshirt before padding silently from the bedroom to start a pot of coffee. A few moments later, Delainey appeared, looking delectably tousled, wearing his old bathrobe, with a blearily grateful expression the moment he placed a hot mug into her hand. He remembered how Delainey was a zombie before her morning coffee. Did it bother him that he remembered so many tiny details about her when he ought to have discarded them as useless information? A little. But then, he was also glad to have remembered certain things in the bedroom.

He waited until they'd both enjoyed a few bracing sips of coffee before launching into the most obvious question in the room. "What are we doing?" he asked.

She closed her eyes and shook her head. "I don't want to talk about that right now. I'm exhausted and I have a full day on the schedule. Can we table this conversation until later?" she asked.

"Later when?" Another eight years from now? "Seems to me we've stirred a hornet's nest. I never imagined we'd ever be naked in the same zip code again, if you know what I mean, and frankly I'm not even sure how it happened. I could blame it on the whiskey, which is the easy answer, but I'm man enough to admit that I know there's more to it. So, I have to ask, what are we doing and are we going to keep doing it?"

She opened her eyes, irritated and frustrated. "I don't know," she answered. "All I know is that

I have a crew of eight coming in today and I still have auditions to hold for the reenactment. There are a million different details to handle before we can start shooting, and I don't have time to hash out the emotional aspect of our hookups. Maybe it's just rebound sex or reunion sex, or whatever they call it when exes hook up. It was fun—I enjoyed it immensely—but I really don't want to sit here and dissect the why and how. Okay?"

"You're such a grouch in the morning," he muttered, fighting the absurd urge to laugh. Talk about déjà vu. He should've known better to come at her with a serious question before she'd morphed into a human through the power of intense caffeine. "I have to shower. Are you going to join me?" he asked, moving toward the bedroom.

"Yes," Delainey answered grumpily. "Just stop talking."

He laughed. "You are the only person on this planet who would ever accuse me of talking too much. Hurry up and drink your coffee. We have just enough time for a quickie before heading to the office." Coffee and sex…he didn't know a better way to start the day. He supposed the questions—and their answers—could wait.

DELAINEY GASPED AGAINST the shower wall, still trying to catch her breath. If Trace's arms weren't wrapped around her torso, she might slide to the ground. He flipped her around and buried his tongue in her mouth as deeply as his length had impaled her only moments earlier, and she melted against him. After a long, deep kiss, they broke apart and she said with a breathy moan, "Good God, I'll never be the same," as she slowly recovered. Trace's powerfully built body glistened in the steam and moisture as he slowly let her go once she could stand on her own. "Why are you so amazing? You big jerk," she added weakly, hating that he could turn her to Jell-O with a single touch. "You know it's not fair to do those things to me."

"A man's got to have his advantages when it comes to women," he said, smoothing a hank of wet hair from her face, his expression inscrutable.

"Yeah? And why is that?"

"Because women are much smarter than men. We have to level the playing field somehow."

She grinned. "Well, that's true," she said, grabbing the soap and beginning to lather it along the hard planes of his body. Her fingers glided across every muscled valley and corded length of skin, openly delighting at the feel beneath her palm. "I find it fascinating how much you've changed and yet stayed the same. Your body is as I remember it, only harder and more mature, and your face somehow became even more handsome, which isn't fair, of course, but your eyes are different."

"Different how?" he asked, plainly enjoying her touch on his skin. She smiled a tiny smile at how his penis had begun to plump again. She thrilled that her touch had that effect on him, and she rewarded him by gripping the shaft with her soap-slicked hands. He sucked in a tight breath and his voice was strained as he warned, "Be careful or we'll never make it out of the house today."

For a moment she contemplated how lovely it would be to spend the entire day holed up naked with Trace Sinclair, but then she remembered her many obligations and reluctantly let go of him to return to less sensual cleaning tasks. "Your eyes used to be soft and warm. Now your gaze is hard and filled with scrutiny, except when you're aroused.... Then they're fathomless."

"Fathomless? How so?" he asked, regarding her with interest.

"I used to be able to read your thoughts because whatever you were thinking was reflected in your eyes. It's not like that anymore," she answered softly, running her soapy hands gently over his chest. "You hide your thoughts behind a wall because you don't trust me anymore. Do you trust anyone?"

"No," he admitted. "But that's not your fault entirely. A lot has changed. It's only natural that I would change, as well."

She didn't have to say Simone's name to know she was the root. Poor Simone. A brilliant life cut short by circumstance. "I could see if my network might be interested in Simone's story... maybe get some more eyes on the case. Maybe her killer could finally be brought to justice."

"Don't go there," Trace warned, his voice hardening until he added with a softer, "Please" to lessen the sting. He drew a deep breath and she murmured an apology.

"I was just thinking out loud...thought maybe it might help. I'm sorry."

"I know. No more talk of Simone, okay?" he asked, forcing a small smile. "It's a tough subject."

She nodded and felt wretched for being so thoughtless. But Trace seemed intent on erasing all remnants of bad feelings as he removed the soap from her hand to return the favor, starting with her breasts.

"I think they're clean," she teased after it seemed he'd spent an inordinate amount of time in that one area. She smiled when he pulled her close and their soaped bodies slid against one another, rubbing in all the right places. She glanced up at him with a coy expression.

"Now, if we're not careful, we'll get dirty all over again."

"Yeah, I was thinking the very same thing," he said in a low tone that sent shivers ricocheting down her back. "The difference between you and me is that I don't mind getting dirty. In fact…it's one of my favorite things to do."

And then he claimed her mouth again, and she knew they weren't leaving that shower anytime soon. In fact, they might run out of hot water before that happened.

"Only one more time," she gasped as he lowered to his knees to press his hot mouth to her feminine core. "Only… Oh!"

And then she forgot what she was talking about.

ZED SETTLED INTO his favorite chair and tossed the wad of cash from his last "friend" who had come by for a "visit" and pulled a ready-rolled joint from his personal stash. Normally, he rewarded himself after a good visit from loyal friends with some private time with his cache of pot, but this time as he lit up he wasn't celebrating. He was trying to escape the memory of his son's disappointment. At one time, he and Trace had been so close. He'd taught Trace everything he knew about tracking that he'd learned from the natives, and he'd been proud to pass it on to his children. Of his kids, Trace and Miranda had exhibited the most talent for the lost art; Simone and Wade had found the teaching tedious and a waste of time. It seemed a lifetime ago that he'd been of use to teach them anything.

One summer day, when the sky had been the bluest and the grass had smelled sweeter than honey, Zed and his kids had tromped into their back forty, armed with supplies in their packs and an adventure on their minds. Trace and Miranda had eagerly walked beside him, chattering about their discoveries, each clamoring for his approval, while Wade and Simone had hung back, both taking their sweet time and complaining about the miles they were going to log before they reached their campsite.

"Dad, this is dumb," Simone had exclaimed with a pout. Her cute face puckered into a sour expression. "Sara invited me to a sleepover tonight and I really wanted to go. Now, instead, I'm looking for bear poop and staring at broken leaves."

Miranda and Trace had scowled at their little sister's complaints and Miranda had said, "You just wanted to go to Sara's so you could flirt with her older brother, who is way too old for you anyway."

"Shut up," Simone had shot back, but Zed could tell by the way her mouth had tightened

that Miranda had hit the nail on the head. Good
Lord, he was going to have a time with that girl,
he'd thought. Too pretty for her own good was
what he'd thought. And he'd been right.

They'd spent the weekend tracking a bear for
a few miles until they'd finally spotted him in a
clearing. They'd stayed downwind so as not to
spook him, but he wanted his kids to know how
to navigate the forest and to know what lurked
in the shadows simply by the clues they left behind. He hadn't thought to teach them about the
threats that walked on two legs.

They'd ended the weekend hunting down a
deer for Jennelle to cook up, and even though
Simone had hated it, she did her share in skin-
ning the animal and cutting up the meat to bring
home. He'd been proud of his princess for rolling up her sleeves and getting the work done
when he'd been sure she was going to shriek
and protest. Sometimes Simone had shown that
she was more than just a pretty face.

Had her killer been drawn to her beautiful
face? Had that been her downfall? Too many
times he'd wondered if there was anything he
could've done differently in her childhood that
might've saved her from dying at the hands of
a murderer. Maybe he should've been more insistent that she pay attention to the tracking
tools he was trying to teach. Maybe if she'd

known how to navigate the forest by her wits, she wouldn't have frozen to death in the very woods she'd hiked as a child.

Eight years was an eternity when navigating through the bleak landscape of regret. He drew on his joint, the faint crackle of burning paper the only sound in the room, and held the smoke in his chest until it burned his lungs. He exhaled slowly and closed his eyes, absently spitting a stem from his mouth as he waited for the sweet oblivion to take him to a better place.

But his mind was stronger than the smoke, it seemed, because he couldn't escape the condemnation in his son's eyes nor the memory of Simone's smile. Worse, he knew his son was right and he'd never see his pretty baby again.

How could he tell his son he was aware of what was happening but was helpless to stop it?

Jennelle was killing herself in that house. And he didn't have the balls to do a thing about it. In his imagination, he saw himself marching in there and pulling her bodily from that prison and telling her that things were going to be different from now on. He was going to quit selling pot and go back to carving, just as Jennelle and his kids wanted him to. But as he mustered up the energy to make it happen, he remembered that it didn't matter if he stopped selling pot. His daughter was still dead; his kids never visited;

and his wife was slowly losing her mind from unchecked grief.

The reality of his life wasn't a Hallmark card. There were no happy endings and nothing would change, even if he wanted desperately to try to fix what had been irrevocably broken.

And suddenly, faced with that knowledge, the will to change evaporated like the smoke that he'd come to cherish so much.

In the end, there was simply no point—so why bother?

CHAPTER EIGHTEEN

DELAINEY SCRIBBLED LIKE MAD, jotting down the script for the reenactment while her crew got settled in the two-bedroom house Otter had provided. Thankfully, the house was already fully furnished, which was one less headache for Delainey to worry about, though she could already hear the squabbling over who was going to get the beds and who was getting the floor and sofa.

"Listen, the accommodations aren't deluxe, but it's better than the alternative, which was sleeping outside," she reminded them when the complaints came to her.

"This is what happens when you're not in the union," grumbled Trevor Gann, the camera operator. "This would never fly. I'm not sleeping on the floor," he announced, returning to the master bedroom to stake his claim. Trevor was a good cameraman but a bit of a pain. However, it was a short shoot so she wasn't too worried about handling his little outbursts of petulance. At least that was her hope.

It was an all-male crew, which alleviated her

other worry about housing men and women in the same place without proper privacy. Now, they could all bunk together and pretend they were at camp.

"How are we supposed to start shooting if you haven't completed the script yet?" Trevor asked, returning to the kitchen, where Delainey was seated. She didn't look up as she answered.

"It's an easy script. A reenactment isn't too complicated. Besides, let me worry about the shooting schedule, okay? Your job is to worry about capturing the footage." She smiled and he got the point, but she could hear him grumbling under his breath. She sighed and returned to her scribbling, all the while checking her phone for an update on the auditions from her production assistant. She trusted Brett could handle the auditions, and frankly it was the least of her worries. The members of the crew, accustomed to sunny California and only rare location shoots, were not properly outfitted for an Alaskan outing. In short, they were going to freeze their L.A.–acclimated asses off.

Her phone went off and a text message came through from Brett with two photo attachments of little girls. Brett wanted her opinion on which looked the part. She gave the girls a quick once-over and then texted back, "Doesn't matter what she looks like—make sure she can act!" She wondered if she'd overestimated Brett's abilities. Well, there wasn't anything she could do about it now. She read over her script notes and nodded to herself. She'd give her notes to Brett when he returned so he could transcribe the scribbled mess into a script form and then run off copies. In the meantime, she and Trace had to scout the location. More alone time with Trace. She hated that she looked forward to that most of all because it was a bad sign. She couldn't afford to get attached, not again. It'd been hard enough to leave in the first place. She didn't think she could handle doing it again. Plus, if she played with Trace's heart a second time, well, she didn't like to think what Trace would do.

She scooped her papers and headed for the door with instructions to the crew. "I will be out and about all day. I suggest each and every one of you visit the store for some more appropriate cold-weather gear. A light windbreaker isn't going to cut it here, and if I have to have any of you airlifted to a hospital for treatment of hypothermia, I will not be happy. Got it?"

There were head nods and grumbles but no outward dissent, which was a miracle given that Trevor was already in one of his querulous moods. Why'd she hired him? She second-guessed herself as she hurried to her rental car.

She was meeting Trace at the Search and Rescue parking lot and they were taking his truck from there.

Her body ached in private places from all the action it'd seen after a long hiatus, and she couldn't help the happy smile that followed. Trace was a god between the sheets. Time had definitely honed his natural skill. Good gravy, what was she doing ruminating on activities she shouldn't have done in the first place? She was sinking in quicksand and she didn't know how to stop from going under. Thoughts of Trace still managed to take her breath away, and now that she had fresh memories—heaven help her, she couldn't stop thinking about him.

Was she a terrible person that she caught herself daydreaming about spending the evening curled up next to Trace, worshipping each other's bodies? Her cheeks flared with heat and she touched them, glancing around furtively to see if anyone else had noticed her flushing red in the face. Delainey trained her thoughts to more appropriate subjects, such as keeping the production on schedule, but before she reached the Search and Rescue, her cell phone went off and she saw that it was Thad. She hesitated, nearly sending his call to voice mail, but guilt for being a largely absent sister made her answer.

"What's up, Thad?" she asked via her Bluetooth as she navigated the roads.

"Laney…it's Dad," he said, worry in his voice. "He's in the hospital."

"What?" Delainey hoped she'd heard her brother incorrectly. "Did you just say that Dad is in the hospital? What happened?"

"Yeah.…" He hesitated and then said, "I would've told you sooner but he made me promise not to say anything. The thing is…he's real sick and the doc is throwing around words that scare me."

"Such as?" she asked, her lips suddenly numb. "What's he sick with?"

"It's something with his pancreas," Thad said, his voice clogged with tears. "I don't think he's going to last much longer."

Delainey knew Thad expected her to drop everything and go to the hospital to see Harlan. That's what would happen with a normal family. But the Clarke clan was anything but normal. Sweat dotted her brow as she considered what to do. "I'm sorry about Dad, but I have an appointment that I can't miss," she started, not sure she wanted to see her father in the hospital. It was selfish and cowardly, but she wasn't ready to say her goodbyes. She and her father had too many conversations that needed to be said to let it all go. It wasn't fair. Irrational anger flooded her chest. "I can't. I'll check in on him later. I'm sure the hospital staff are doing everything they possibly can for him."

"Laney—" Thad's voice was incredulous and tinged with disappointment. "He needs you now. There might not be a later."

"I can't... I'm sorry, Thad. I...have work to do." She clicked off and pulled her Bluetooth from her ear to toss it to the passenger seat, tears blurring her vision. She had a production to shoot and her career to save. She didn't have time to star in her own Movie of the Week with a dying father. He'd been a miserable father anyway. Maybe it was a mercy that she wasn't standing at his bedside. Besides, wouldn't that be hypocritical of her to profess some sort of daughterly concern when he'd been a mean SOB her entire life? If she were writing that script, she'd immediately find that character development inconsistent. She nearly barked a hysterical laugh. He didn't get to die and get off the hook so easily. Not fair. Just not fair. And why was Thad so damn loyal to the man? Just because he took him out fishing? Hell, if that'd been the magical key to her father's heart, maybe she ought to have learned.

By the time she pulled into the Search and Rescue parking lot, she was nearing a full mental breakdown and was holding on to her sanity by the tiniest threads. Trace's expression changed when he saw her and immediately sensed that something was wrong. It took everything in her not to fall into his arms and cling to him as if the world was ending. "Something the matter?" he asked.

"My dad…he's, I don't know, sick or something. Thad called me and said he's in the hospital." She pushed away the hair in her eyes and shouldered her purse, determined to get her job done, no matter what stood in her way. Why was her life always so damn complicated? "How far is the location from here?" she asked, her voice shaking as she glanced at her watch. "I want to let my production assistant know how long I'll be so we can set the production meeting."

"Delainey, what are you talking about? If your dad is in the hospital, you need to go see him. I doubt Thad would exaggerate the situation."

"I don't have time to sit around a hospital bed and pretend that I had a rosy relationship with my father. I have a job to do and people are depending on me to get it done."

"Your dad was a gruff man, but he did the best he could by you and Thad."

"Trace, please stick to things you know, such as tracking and hunting. You don't know the first thing about my relationship with my father, so butt out."

His mouth tightened as anger flashed in his eyes, but she didn't care. She didn't need anyone telling her how she should act or feel when it concerned her father, because they hadn't lived her life. "You're making a mistake," Trace said. "You're putting your career in front of the people who matter, not that I'm surprised—just disappointed. I'd hoped you'd changed in the eight years since you'd split, but I guess I was wrong."

"Yes, well, apparently. Because I am the job and the job is me. Anything else is just window dressing. My father made his bed, he can lie in it. He has Thad and Brenda.... He doesn't need me."

Trace held her stare but she didn't back down. Couldn't he just leave it be? It wasn't his business anyway. She needed to work. Otherwise, she might crumble and cave. Harlan Clarke didn't deserve her sympathy and he didn't deserve her tears. He was a bitter, angry, short-tempered brute with a tiny fuse and absolutely no interest in his daughter, and she wasn't about to forgive that because suddenly he was sick. How could Thad so easily forgive the man after their wretched, bleak childhood? Because Thad was good and sweet and had a heart big enough to make up for their father's shortfalls, a voice answered.

Well, it's poetic justice that her heart was fashioned after her father's because it felt cold and barren right about now.

She walked away from Trace and went to his truck, turning to ask sharply, "Are we going? We're wasting precious daylight."

Trace's mouth firmed as if he were holding back what he really wanted to say and he followed. "You're the boss," he muttered and climbed into the driver's seat.

Yes, that's right. She was the boss.

And the boss did not have time for family drama. No matter how dire.

CHAPTER NINETEEN

TRACE CLIMBED INTO the truck and Delainey followed. He knew Delainey needed to go see her father, but he didn't know how to convince her to do so. She was digging in her heels pretty hard and he couldn't say he didn't understand, even if she didn't think he did. The truth was, everything that Delainey had said was true. Harlan had been a terrible father to his children, but Trace also knew that Harlan had done the best that he could have, given the circumstances.

And now Harlan was sick? Trace knew a thing or two about abrupt goodbyes. There was never enough time when it came to losing a loved one. And he knew that if Delainey didn't say her piece to her father, she would live with the regret forever. However, it wasn't his place to tell her how to live her life, even if she was screwing it up. All he could do was offer his advice, and if she didn't want to listen he had to let it go.

"How far will we have to hike from the main

road to get to the location?" she asked, seemingly back to business as she scribbled notes in her notepad, her father forgotten. "I have a small crew, but they're definitely not used to hiking. We might have to take some liberty with the location if it turns out to be prohibitive for the crew. I'm not too worried though. We can fake it. The terrain is similar enough that no one is going to point a finger and say, 'Hey, that's not where that happened!'"

"It might've been better to hire a crew from Anchorage. At least they'd have a better idea of what the terrain is like," Trace said. Was she going to ignore the fact that her father was in the hospital as if it was no big deal? Trace slanted his gaze at her, troubled. "The city boys you flew in aren't cut out for the Alaskan wilderness. Those yahoos are more accustomed to midmorning lattes and lunchtime pedicures than tromping through rough brush and rocky terrain. We'll end up having to save them from breaking their fool necks."

"Don't worry about my crew. I've got it handled. I'm more concerned about the weather holding. I can't afford to be losing shooting days because of snow or rain."

"Can't control Mother Nature. Last time I checked she ran by her schedule and no one else's."

"More's the pity. Location shooting is such a nightmare. It's almost as bad as shooting with kids or animals. Anything that can and will go wrong usually does. At least that's been my experience."

"I know this isn't your first gig, but how many have you done before this one?" he asked.

"This is my fifth production. Well, fifth production where I'm completely in charge. I've been an associate producer on a number of other shows. You might have heard of a few.... Did you catch *Vertical Blind?* I think you would've enjoyed that one. It was about rock climbers. It was a challenge to shoot but I was so proud of it." She paused, a subtle, pained frown following. "Ultimately it didn't test as well as I'd hoped. I think if the network had given it a little more time we could have had a hit on our hands. Some shows aren't quick flares of success, but rather a slow burn. Unfortunately, the network disagreed and yanked it after only four episodes aired."

"What happens when a show fails?"

"Depends. In my case, it was one failure too many. Unfortunately, Hollywood is an unforgiving town and the people who hold the money even more so. It's been rough. I had a bunch of other ideas but no one wanted to hear them. It wasn't until your name popped up that anyone even remembered who I was."

He frowned. "And you *like* this place? Sounds like a hellhole."

"Yes, I like it," she said, bristling a little, then she clarified. "Well, I don't like the backstabbing and the double-talk and the politics, but I enjoy creating something from start to finish and seeing it succeed. I can't draw, I can't sing, but I'm a good producer. If it's true that everyone has one talent where they can really shine... this one is mine."

Trace heard the desperate pride in her voice, as if she were clinging to that one single thing about her that was worth talking about, and sadness followed. If she based her value solely on the successes that other people deemed good or bad, by his estimation that seemed a recipe for a lifetime of misery. It wasn't that he felt the way he lived his life was better, but at least he didn't live and die by the expectations or the opinions of others. "Why did *Vertical Blind* fail?"

She shrugged. "Who knows? Bad time slot, wrong demographic, plain bad luck...take your pick. In the end excuses don't matter—all that matters is results. And *Vertical Blind* didn't measure up. But this show we're shooting here, it's going to be amazing. I just know it. I have a feeling that this is going to make you a star."

"I don't want to be a star," Trace reminded her quietly. "I want to live my life the way I always have. I don't think being a star would allow me to do that." He valued his privacy, and from what he knew about celebrities, they didn't have any. The thought of having his private business splashed on the television for all to see was akin to standing in front of the high school marching band in nothing but his underwear. He didn't understand why Delainey would want anything close to that. "Let's not get ahead of ourselves. The reasons I'm doing this job haven't changed. After the pilot's shot and finished, I'm not interested in seeing it go on to make a full series."

"Your feelings might change when you see it all cut together," she said with confidence. "I think once you see what a good job I can do, you'll change your mind."

He hated to burst her bubble but he had to set her straight. "I won't. It's not a reflection of how well you do your job. It's that I have no interest in pursuing that lifestyle."

"You could be a household name," she protested with open consternation. "A job like this could make you a very wealthy man. You'd never have to worry about money again."

"I don't worry about money now because I don't have expenses I can't afford. And I don't want to be a household name. People have been talking about the Sinclairs for long enough. I don't need to give them more to gossip about."

Delainey's expression dimmed and she fell quiet. After a moment she said, "I know. I'm sorry. I know this isn't what you want. And it's not something you would ever seek out. But I need this. Without it, I might as well stay here in Alaska because I'm through in L.A. No one will take my calls, no one wants to hear my pitches and I'm dangerously close to losing my condo. The fact is, Trace, I'm on the verge of losing everything, and that's why this pilot has to be successful. I know I'm asking a lot, but I don't have a choice."

"Everyone has choices. It's your perspective that needs changing."

She looked at him sharply. "If you're suggesting that I give up on my career, it's not going to happen. And frankly, I'm tired of you giving me the same advice—quit your career. What if I told you to quit yours? How would you feel about that? I always supported you in your endeavors, but you couldn't support me when I needed you. So I think you owe me this one."

A hot retort danced on his tongue, but he held it back. Was she right? He hadn't always been supportive and there had been times when he had plainly patronized her goals, and that didn't make him feel very good. Certainly didn't paint him in a very nice light. Maybe if he'd been less rigid in his perception of how their life should be she wouldn't have left. But then again, maybe it wouldn't have made a difference. Delainey was consumed with ambition, and that part about her personality hadn't changed.

"You know what the worst part about failure is?" she asked, surprising him with her question. "It's that when you fail you are defined by that failure. People look at you differently, and then they don't listen when you talk. Suddenly you have no value because you failed. My shows have not been successful, not because I didn't do a good job in producing them but because of circumstance or things that were out of my control. However, there are no excuses that will change anyone's perception, which is the reason no one will take a meeting with me and they laugh behind my back when I walk by."

Trace hated the idea of Delainey being mocked, and an old sense of protectiveness rose up inside him before he could stop it. "Why do you put up with that crap?" he asked. "In the past you were never one to put up with bullying. Why do you do it now?"

"Because in the real world, schoolyard bullies grow up to be CEOs, and they're the ones who make or break careers. So I have to swallow my pride and pretend not to hear the whispers and turn a blind eye to the snickering and tolerate the blatant disregard if I want to stay in this game. I *will* have a hit and I *will* succeed. I just have to bide my time and be patient. I knew the right project would come along. And it did, because here I am. This project is going to be successful."

The conviction in her tone nearly had him agreeing with her, but that scared him. He didn't want it to be a success. He wanted this whole mess to fade and go away so he didn't have to go through this ever again. He wanted to go back to his life the way it was, quiet and secluded. He wanted to be able to go hunting when he felt like it and not have to constantly look over his shoulder for the paparazzi. Were there paparazzi in Alaska? He didn't know but he had a feeling they were everywhere, kind of like cockroaches. But if by hoping the project failed that meant that Delainey would fail as well, he had a problem with that. He shouldn't care—it was her business and her life—but they'd opened Pandora's box by sharing time together again and sharing intimacies that they shouldn't have. The box was open and the old need to protect and shelter her was too strong to ignore. Privately he bit back some swearwords. If Delainey needed this project to succeed, how could he not help her?

He exhaled long and deep as he pulled the truck off the side of the road and put it into Park. He took a moment to simply enjoy the sounds of the forest. He knew by taking this next step his life was never going to be the same, but Delainey needed him and he felt he couldn't deny her. But first, he had something to say. "I'll stop fighting you on this project and I'll do what I can to make it successful. But you have to do one thing for me." Her eyes lit up. She was prepared to give him anything until he said, "You need to settle this with your dad. We've all got problems and issues with our family, but they're the only family we've got and when they're gone, they're gone. We don't get do-overs and we don't get a say when our time is up. If your dad is dying, you owe it to yourself and him to say your piece."

"You're one to talk," Delainey said, scowling. "Don't you think that's a bit hypocritical? I don't see you busting down your parents' doors to work out your problems."

"Totally different and don't change the subject."

"It's not different," she maintained stubbornly. "You just don't want to talk about it."

Trace bit back the immediate hot retort and choked it down, knowing it would only make things worse between them. "Let's just say you're right and I am avoiding a few situations with my parents, but you and I both know that my relationship with my parents is entirely different from what you had with your dad."

Delainey couldn't deny that and jerked a miserable nod, her argument deflating, revealing the pain beneath. "What am I supposed to say to him? That he was a miserable father and he doesn't deserve the comfort of his children standing by his side as he dies? Don't you think that's kind of harsh?" Her eyes darkened, and when she looked away her whole body was vibrating with emotion. "I know I look like the bad guy in this. I know I sound like a selfish bitch for not wanting to go to his side. But there are just some things that I can't forgive or forget. Those are just the facts, and I can't change them."

"What did he do that was so bad that you can't forgive?" he asked, realizing for the first time that maybe he didn't know the whole story between Delainey and her father. "Did he…hurt you in a sexual way?" He hated to ask but he needed to know. If Harlan Clarke had touched his daughter inappropriately, there was no way he was going to insist that she make peace with him.

"No, he never touched me in that way," she answered with a slow shake of her head. "But he hurt me in plenty of other ways. Nothing was ever good enough, no matter how I tried. Everything I did was wrong. He never had a kind word and he never encouraged me. He made me feel like I was worthless, and it took me a long time to realize that he was wrong. I *am* worth something. *He* was the one who was worthless."

Finished with the conversation, Delainey exited the truck and stalked away. Trace thought of his own father and how much he'd changed. Zed had gone from being a loving, caring father to a man who didn't give a shit about anything or anyone as long as he had his marijuana. Whereas Harlan had realized too late that he'd wasted every opportunity to grow close to his children. Both fathers had wounded their children, and likely neither had the strength nor the knowledge to fix what he had broken.

Deep down, for all of her outward sophistication, Delainey was still that young girl searching for her father's approval that she would likely never get. Even worse, she was only perpetuating the cycle by chasing after a dream populated with people who couldn't care less about her. His heart hurt at the painful realization, but what could he do?

The bigger question was, should he even try?

CHAPTER TWENTY

DELAINEY WIPED ANGRY TEARS from her cheeks and stomped away from the truck, hurt and betrayed that Trace would force her hand like this. He knew she'd do anything to make this project succeed, and to have Trace make her a devil's bargain was reprehensible.

"Delainey, wait," Trace called out, chasing after her. She ignored him and kept walking, but he caught up to her fairly quickly. She couldn't outrun him, so instead she cast him a dirty look. "Listen, I know you don't like what I have to say, but someone has to tell you things straight. Your dad might very well be a bastard and a terrible father, but if he goes to his grave without you being able to say what you need to say, you're the one who's going to suffer."

"How do you know? Maybe I'll be just fine," she shot back. "Last time I checked you weren't a psychologist."

"No, you're right. Maybe I'm not qualified to give anyone advice, but I've seen plenty of situations where pent-up emotions have caused a lot of damage to the person left behind. I don't want to see that happen to you."

Delainey's heart leaped at his admission, and she berated herself for the involuntary reaction. "Why do you care?" she asked in a low voice, almost afraid of his answer.

He pushed his hand through his hair and then shrugged as if he didn't know the answer. "I'm not ready to look that deep. All I know is how I feel."

What had she expected—a declaration of undying love? And if she'd gotten that, how would she have handled the responsibility? It was better this way. She accepted his answer and nodded. "Okay, so even if you're right and I should hash things out with my dad, don't you think that's selfish on my part? I mean, if the man is dying, why should I make things worse by burdening his last days with my childhood scars?"

"I'm not saying you should march into his hospital room and start detailing all the ways he was a terrible person," he clarified. "I'm saying you need to find your peace. The truth is, he can't change the past, no matter how remorseful he may be."

She cut him a sharp glance. "What makes you think he's remorseful?"

"What makes you think he's not?"

Delainey snorted. "My father is remorseful

for nothing. To feel remorse, one has to admit guilt, and my father doesn't apologize for anything."

"Dying has a way of softening a person. Maybe you ought to give him a little slack and see what he does with it."

She closed her eyes and slowly realized maybe there were signs if only she'd been open to seeing them. She worried her bottom lip as she considered everything Trace had said. Finally, she looked to him and said, "Okay, I'll go. But if he turns out to be the same bastard I grew up with, he can die and go to hell for all I care. Got it?"

"Sounds fair to me."

She prodded him. "And in return?"

"In return I'll stop fighting this production and do what I can to see it succeed."

Delainey smiled in relief and jumped into his arms, mindless that it was inappropriate and confusing, grateful for his presence—however brief—in her life. "Thank you," she murmured, loving the feel of his embrace. "You don't know what this means to me."

He sighed and tightened his hold on her. "I think I have an idea."

TRACE WAITED IN the truck while Delainey went into the hospital, her heart pounding and her stomach a little sick. What if she couldn't handle the reality of her father being gravely ill? Trace was right about her needing to do this, but she was scared out of her mind and she wished she'd taken Trace's offer for him to accompany her. Right about now, she could use a little shot in the courage department.

She checked in at the nurse's station and was directed to the ICU. She found the room and was temporarily taken aback by the stark truth of the sterile environment, with its multitude of equipment beeping and monitoring, and the smell of antiseptic assaulting her nostrils. Brenda, who was sitting by her husband's side, rose when she saw Delainey, a tremulous smile on her face. "Oh, girl, I'm so glad you came. I had my doubts, but I knew deep in your heart there's love for your daddy," she said, gripping Delainey in a fierce hug that shocked her. "Thad just left, the poor thing. He's taking things pretty hard."

Delainey nodded as if she understood, but in fact she was a little knocked left of center and she felt like a terrible sister for not realizing how things had changed between her father and her brother. But how could she have known if she never kept in contact? Yet another notch in the "bad sibling/daughter" category. "Thad didn't tell me exactly what's going on..." Delainey said, letting her sentence trail, knowing Brenda would elaborate.

"Oh, honey, I wanted your daddy to tell you what was happening with his health, but he didn't want to burden you with his problems. Your daddy was diagnosed with pancreatic cancer a year ago, and it's been a miracle he's lasted this long. But he's a fighter." Brenda smiled lovingly at her sleeping husband, tears sparkling in her eyes. "He's a strong man but the body can only take so much."

What? Delainey stared, unable to believe what she was hearing. "He's…dying?" She could barely get the words out. It was one thing to hear the news and another to face it. Her knees wobbled and she leaned against the wall, her vision swimming. Her father was a mean old crusty fisherman. She always figured the sea would take him when it was his time to go. There'd been times when she'd wished he would drown out there, but those were the heated, heartbroken cries of a child who'd never been properly loved by the man who was supposed to be her protector. And now that he was truly facing imminent death? She felt squeezed by the lack of time between them. Could they have fixed things? She didn't know and she never would.

Before she realized it was happening, she was sliding down the wall and tears were tracking down her cheeks. Brenda fluttered around her, clucking like a mother hen, and although it was a foreign feeling to have an older female in her life, Delainey didn't fight it when Brenda joined her on the floor and held her as if she was a baby, crooning to her and patting her head.

"There, there, let it out, honey," Brenda said, rocking her. "I know it hurts. God, I know. And your daddy has told me how much he wished things were different between you, but he'd plain run out of time."

"Why didn't he call?" she asked, sniffing back tears. "Why didn't he pick up the damn phone and tell me what was happening? He didn't even give me a chance. I might've come home earlier."

"Would you?" Brenda asked softly, knowing.

Delainey couldn't lie, and the knowledge made her cry harder. "No, probably not," she admitted shamefully. The only reason she'd come tonight was because of Trace. She squeezed her eyes shut and cried until her eyes felt wrung out. She didn't know how long they sat on the floor, but Delainey's rear end was numb and her head ached. Brenda let go and they struggled to their feet, Brenda rubbing her behind ruefully with a watery chuckle, saying, "I'm no spring chicken no more. Sitting on the floor is hard on these old bones, no matter the extra padding."

Delainey sniffed and allowed a tiny smile. Her gaze strayed to her father, oblivious to her meltdown and barely clinging to life. How messed up was this? Her life was slowly crumbling to dust right before her eyes, brick by brick. She had a crew of eight waiting to go to production at first light, and her career was resting on the pointy end of a blade with everything depending on this shoot going well. And now her father was dying? She rubbed her forehead, fighting against another impending meltdown. She swallowed and drew a deep, halting breath, needing to focus. One thing at a time, she told herself. One thing…

"How much longer does he have?" she asked, cringing at the question.

"Hard to say. Days, hours? Only God knows. But the doctors have assured me that he's not suffering any longer. He's so high on morphine he doesn't even know where he is or likely who he is any longer."

Delainey nodded, pulling herself together thread by thread. "I know this will sound terrible, but I have a production ready to start first thing tomorrow and—"

"And you don't have time to sit at your father's bedside waiting for him to draw his last breath," Brenda finished for her. For a minute Delainey wasn't sure if Brenda was chastising her, but Brenda smiled and patted her hand. "You come when you can. Your daddy wouldn't want you putting your life on hold for him. He was proud of you for making your own way. He'll understand."

Delainey stared. Her father was proud of her? She couldn't believe it. "I…" she didn't have words.

"Go." Brenda nudged her gently. "Do your thing. I'll let you know if anything changes."

Delainey nodded, her vision blurring as she escaped that room. Her nausea returned and she forced it down as she made her way back to Trace's truck, where he was waiting. She jerked open the door, climbed inside and said, "Go! I need to leave this place." She had to get far away before she completely dissolved into a weeping, hysterical mess that put her first meltdown to shame.

TRACE KEPT HIS EYES on the road, helpless as Delainey wept into her hands, unable to stop. He didn't know if Harlan was dead or what the situation was, and he was afraid to ask. He'd never seen Delainey break down like this before, and it freaked him out a little. He didn't ask but drove straight to his place.

When they pulled up in the driveway, Delainey jumped out, gulping great big swallows of air as she tried to compose herself. She paced in the cold night air, her breath pluming. "I waited my entire life for one ounce of affection or kindness from my father, and now that he's dying he dares to say he's proud of me?" she asked, angry. "What is this crap? Is he trying to get into heaven? Does he think by throwing around desperate apologies I'm going to forgive a miserable childhood at his hands? I can't believe how messed up this is. I have a full production slated to start first thing tomorrow, and now my father chooses to die. Perfect timing." She threw her hands up as she raged. "You know, the thing that kills me is that he could've picked up the phone and given me a heads-up of what was going on. But he didn't. And now I've been blindsided by this news and I don't have time to deal with a dying family member."

Trace knew she was only venting and that deep in her heart what she was saying wasn't how she actually felt but she didn't know how to deal with her feelings. "Let's go inside and you can tell me what's going on," he suggested. She stopped pacing but stared at him with such bleak heartache that he wanted to pull her roughly to him and promise everything was going to work out.

"I probably shouldn't stay here, but I can't go back to my father's place now that I know he's sick. And although Brenda means well, I'm not ready for her to be a mother figure to me. I don't know if I'll ever be ready, and I know that's terrible of me because she seems like a really nice person. I don't know how my father even met a woman like her. I keep waiting for some hidden darkness to reveal itself, but so far Brenda is as sweet as a stereotypical Southern woman who's all about family, good food and the Lord's Prayer. And I can't deal with it. Trace, I'm a terrible person because I just can't deal with it."

"You're not a terrible person," he assured her, shepherding her firmly into the house. "What you are is hurting and dealing with a lot in a short amount of time. Now, tell me what's going on with your dad."

Delainey removed her jacket and hung it on the hook beside the door, rubbing her arms for warmth. "Can we build the fire first? I'm frozen."

Trace quickly built up a fire in the woodstove, and within minutes the house started to warm. Trace took his place beside Delainey on the sofa. "So how bad is it?" he asked, ready for the worst.

"Pretty bad," Delainey answered, staring at her fingers. "Brenda said he's been diagnosed with pancreatic cancer and apparently he's had it for a while. I guess it's a miracle he's lasted this long."

"Well, Alaskan fishermen are made from tough stock."

"Apparently," she agreed with a mild smile. "Pancreatic cancer is brutal. Brenda said that he could have days or hours left. I don't know what to do. Do I cancel the shoot? I know I should be by his side so that I'm there when he dies, but the thought of sitting in that room just waiting for him to take his last breath just makes me want to run away." She stopped and her voice wobbled as she admitted to him, "I'm not ready for my dad to die."

"I don't think anyone is ever prepared for death, but what would you say to him if you could?" he asked.

"I don't know. I'd probably say something really mean because I'm so angry with him, but Brenda told me some things that I don't how to process. She told me that he was proud of me for chasing my dreams, for not letting anything get in my way. She said that he understood why I stayed away and he never blamed me. She also said that he knew he'd been a terrible father but he'd run out of time to fix things. What am I supposed to do with that information? I feel like a jerk for being angry with him. I mean, isn't it bad form to beat up on a terminally ill person?"

"Is there an option to delay the shoot?"

She shook her head. "No. Even if we don't start shooting I still have to pay the crew, and I can't afford five days with nothing to show for it. This budget is already tight enough it squeaks. I just can't stop, no matter what's going on in my life. The shoot has to go on as scheduled."

"Then that's what happens. From the sounds of it, your father doesn't want you to make special allowances for him. It's probably why he didn't call you in the first place. He'll understand."

"How can you say that? He's dying. If I don't go to him during his last hours, everyone's going to say I'm the worst daughter on the planet."

"Who cares what anyone thinks? It's not their life. I have some experience with people talking about business that isn't theirs, and you just have to ignore it. Go with your gut. If Brenda says that your father was proud of you…chances are it's the truth. What does Thad say?"

At the mention of her brother, Delainey winced. "He tried to tell me that Dad had changed, but I didn't want to listen. I can't even fathom my father being different from what I remember. How can one man change the entire fabric of his personality? It's impossible. So, I didn't listen to what he had to say, and I think I hurt his feelings."

"You can smooth things over with your brother. You two have always been close, and he'll understand."

"How can you be sure? The one thing I seem to be really good at is pushing people away."

Trace suppressed a chuckle at the truth of that statement but said, "Because your little brother always looked up to you. And that hasn't changed. He always had something nice to say about you even when you were gone. He was so proud of his big sister making her mark out in the big world. He didn't begrudge you your success or your need to leave."

New tears welled in her eyes. "Really?" Her expression filled with shame. "I've been a terrible sister. I don't deserve his love or admiration. I never gave my brother a second thought. I mean, I called him now and then just to let him know I was still alive, but they were really perfunctory calls without any real meaning to them. But I love my brother. I really do."

"I know you do. He's going to need you when your dad dies. Are you going to be there for him?" Trace asked, wondering.

"I will try to be."

Under different circumstances Trace might've called her on her noncommittal answer, but he didn't feel it was necessary to pound her over the head with more guilt. She definitely had bigger fish to fry at the moment, and he knew she was barely holding it together. Fate had a funny way of jerking the rug out from beneath your feet when you least expected it.

Of all the troubles he had with his own family, he knew if either of his parents were to die, their absence would leave a hole in his heart. When Simone had died, the pain had been surreal. To never hear her laugh, never tell her funny jokes or make fun of her incessant chatter were things he could barely manage to accept. In the early days, he'd dreamed of her every night. Sometimes it'd hurt to close his eyes, knowing Simone would be waiting for him in the landscape of his dreams. But he had soldiered on, and that's what Delainey would have to do when her father died. "Are you hungry?" he asked.

"No," she answered, rubbing at her eyes. "I think I need a hot shower and then to go to bed. I'm exhausted and I don't want to think anymore. Is that okay?" She looked to him for permission. When he nodded, she smiled with gratitude, saying, "I know I don't deserve having you with me right now, but it means so much. I don't want to think about what we're doing or what's going to happen later. All I want to do is feel you next to me and know that for a short time everything is going to be all right. Can we do that?"

He answered by brushing her lips with a soft kiss. He had questions, misgivings and concerns about what he and Delainey were doing, but he knew he couldn't walk away from her, not right now when she needed him the most. He wasn't hardwired that way. He'd probably end up paying for it later, but for now he was looking forward to crawling into his bed beside her and forgetting the world.

CHAPTER TWENTY-ONE

DELAINEY'S EYES OPENED before the sun came up, and for a long moment she wondered if she ought to call the shoot off. It was one thing to say that the show must go on but another to march on when faced with something truly catastrophic. She'd slept like a baby wrapped in Trace's arms, and for a heartbeat she'd been able to forget what was awaiting her. But with the breaking dawn, she knew it was time to make a decision.

She really couldn't fathom sitting in a hospital room, watching the clock as her father's life slowly ran out. It was too horrific for words. She also knew that if she managed to force herself to sit in that room with him, her mind would return to the production and all that was being lost. If she let this project go, it would mean saying goodbye to everything that she had worked her entire career for. And she wasn't ready to do that. Not by a long shot. She hadn't sacrificed and endured every indignity foisted upon her in the past eight years to back down now.

Perhaps that was a testament to how her father had made her strong. It was a backhanded compliment for sure, but she couldn't deny that being raised by Harlan Clarke had definitely strengthened her backbone.

Trace stirred beside her and she regarded him silently. He always looked so innocent, so sweet when he was asleep. She used to love to watch him in the quiet moments before the dawn, before their life had taken a disastrous turn. She remembered the phone call as if it were yesterday.

Young, pretty Simone. Gone. The news had been too awful to comprehend. Everyone had loved Simone. She'd had that effervescent quality you couldn't fake—either you were born with it or you weren't. Some called it charisma, others called it an angel's grace, but whatever it was hadn't kept Simone alive.

If Simone hadn't died, maybe Delainey would've stayed. Not because she didn't have dreams and aspirations—no, quite the opposite. It was that Delainey might have swallowed her dreams and goals in an effort to hold on to the one person she loved more than anything. But when word came down that Simone had died, the shock of it had created a sonic wave of awareness that had made Delainey desperate to get out of Alaska. Simone's life had been cut short. Her death had been the wake-up call to Delainey's slumbering psyche, and she'd kicked to life with a vengeance. Tomorrow wasn't promised to anyone, and by God she was going to take her tomorrow by the throat.

"If you're going to lie there and stare at me, the least you could do is make coffee," Trace said, his sleep-roughened voice teasing. Without opening his eyes, he reached over and pulled her to him. "You still talk in your sleep," he said. "You'd make a terrible spy. No state secrets would be safe with you."

She smiled. "And what exactly did I say?"

"Something about walking the dog and feeding the parakeet. Do you have pets?"

Delainey with a pet? She could barely keep a plant alive. "No. My condo doesn't allow pets. It was one of the top selling points for me."

He chuckled and nuzzled her neck, still sleepy. "About that coffee..."

"I'm a guest. Isn't that your job to see to my needs?"

"I don't normally allow my guests to sleep in my bed, but then again I don't have guests, either."

His admission made her feel warmly possessive. It was wrong and selfish, but she was so grateful that he hadn't married or found anyone to replace her. A sudden, wild thought came to her. "You know, you could come visit me in Los Angeles sometime." She let the offer dangle, almost holding her breath as she awaited his reaction.

"And why would I want to go to L.A.?" he asked.

"One of the best things about California is the weather," she answered. "And you don't have to wear a lot of clothing. In fact, there are days I walk around my condo in nothing but my G-string. It's hard to do that here."

Just as she anticipated, she felt his erection nudging her leg, and she laughed. "That was easy," she teased.

"What can I say? Men are simple creatures," he quipped, seconds before climbing on top of her. Fully awake now and raring to go, Trace stared down at her with open desire in his eyes. "If you're not going to make the coffee, then we might as well make good use of the time we have before we have to leave. If your production schedule is to be believed, call time is at 8:00 a.m. That gives us just enough time for a little of this—" he bent down and suckled her neck "—and this—" he claimed her mouth in a searing kiss "—and definitely this—" he pressed his stiffening length against her pubic mound, teasing her with his hard shaft.

She gasped and squirmed beneath him, delighted with his version of a wake-up call. "We can always pick up coffee on the way in," she managed to suggest, groaning as he began to remind her of all the reasons why he was hard to forget.

Her last thought before she could think of nothing at all was that a girl could get used to this.

And that wasn't necessarily a good thing.

An hour later Trace and Delainey were heading into town to round up the crew. The afterglow of their morning interlude was already fading and nerves were setting in. He was walking into a foreign environment, completely out of his element. It'd been a long time since he had to do anything that he wasn't prepared to handle.

"It's going to be great," Delainey assured him, noting his sudden quiet. "I know you're nervous. But it's going to be fine. I'll help guide you through this process. But you're going to have to trust me."

"I'm no actor," he warned her. "I don't want to end up looking like an idiot, either."

"You think that I would let you look stupid? This is my career on the line, not only your reputation. People want to know about how you do what you do. The fact that you saved a high-profile person is the icing on the cake. Your rescue of Clarissa Errington was heroic. I know you hate that word, but it doesn't change the fact that it was. Please trust that I know what I'm doing."

He wanted to trust her, but Trace was short in the trust department, particularly with Delainey. He didn't know what they were doing and he didn't know where it was headed, and the fact that he already wanted her to stay when she was likely planning to go only served to put him on edge. However, he'd made a promise and he planned to stick to it.

He pulled up the driveway of the rental house where Delainey's crew was staying. He followed Delainey into the house and tried to remember not to be antisocial. He hated meeting new people. He hadn't always been this way, but having a younger sister die the way Simone did had caused him to be wary of strangers. Seemed as if no one wanted to talk about anything but his sister's death and how it'd affected him and his family. Eight years of that crap was bound to change a person.

They walked into the small living room and nearly tripped over camera equipment. "Trevor," Delainey called out, clearly irritated as she moved the camera equipment herself. "I've told you not to leave the cameras lying around like this. If you have a couple hundred thousand dollars lying around to buy a new camera, then so be it. But somehow I doubt that's the case. Take care of the equipment, please."

A tall, lanky man in his late twenties or early thirties with spiky hair emerged from the bathroom wearing an artfully shaved face that told Trace the man spent more time in front of the mirror than Trace had his entire life. "Watch out, the boss lady is here. She's already busting skulls."

"Yeah, that's right. Keep it up and I won't hire you again," Delainey muttered before heading out of the room to find the rest of the crew.

Trevor sauntered over to Trace with a cocky smile on his face. "You must be the golden boy. The man of the hour. Pleasure to meet you. I'll be the man making you look good. The name's Trevor Gann." He held his hand out for Trace to shake, which Trace did reluctantly, already finding the man irritating as hell. "So, you're a tracker? Are you like an Indian or something?" he asked, pulling a North Face sweatshirt on and bouncing up and down to settle the garment. "That's wicked, man. I have totes respect for you and what you do."

"Thanks," Trace said, looking for Delainey. "So…you're a camera guy."

"One of the best," Trevor bragged, earning a

snort of derision from another of the crew rolling up his sleeping bag and tucking it away.

"Yeah, Trevor is the best at whatever he does, just ask him," the man said, moving to his equipment bag, which looked filled with sound equipment.

"Don't mind Neal," Trevor said with a crooked, arrogant smile. "He's just jealous because he doesn't have what it takes to do my job. All he can do is hold a boom mic, which I'm pretty sure a monkey can do."

"Boys," Delainey warned, returning to the room. "Try to be professional. Trevor, start loading the gear since you're already set to go."

"No problem, boss," Trevor said, hefting the large camera box. "I'm on it."

Once Trevor had left the room, Neal introduced himself, and already Trace liked the quiet, unassuming young man. "Pleasure to meet you. I remember watching the news footage of the rescue and all I could think was, that man is one badass. I mean, without GPS most people would drop off a cliff. No sense of direction at all. What you can do is…pretty damn awesome."

"Thank you, but anyone can do it. Just takes time to learn."

"Maybe you could teach me a few tricks," Neal said, and Trace shrugged.

"Sure. It's not that hard. If you're an observant person, you can pick it up."

"Well, I think I have the patience of Job to put up with Trevor for months at a stretch. He's the most annoying man on the planet."

"My thoughts exactly." He turned to Delainey and gestured to Neal. "More of this guy, less of that other. Sound good?"

She laughed. "Trevor is a character but he's good at what he does, just like Neal is good at what he does. My crew is handpicked for this project. Nothing but the best for you, Trace. Remember how I said to trust me? This is part of that request." He grunted a nod and let it go. Guess there was no turning back now. Delainey smiled and gestured for him to follow her into the bathroom. He furrowed his brow and she explained. "We'll do your makeup here. It'll be easier than trying to apply it on the location."

"Makeup?" He took a step back. "I'm a man. I don't wear makeup."

"You do when you're on camera. Not a lot, just so your face doesn't look washed out. Everyone does it."

"Well, not me. I don't care if my face looks washed out. It's my face. If your audience wants the real thing, they're going to have to accept all of me. Washed-out face and all."

"Trace," Delainey protested, her brow scrunching in irritation. "Just get over here so I can put some powder on your face so you don't shine."

"Just powder?"

She sighed. "Just powder. I promise." But once she'd gotten him into the bathroom, she added under her breath, "And maybe a little foundation…"

He reached around and pinched her sweet little behind. He smothered a grin as she glared at him and grabbed a wand of something, saying, "Just for that…mascara."

"You get near me with that mascara and I'll ruin your reputation."

"And how would you do that?"

"Easy. I'd push you up against that wall and remind you how quickly I can make you weak in the knees. It'd probably be quite a show for your crew."

She flushed and dropped the mascara tube back into the makeup container with a hasty, "Powder is all we need," and he smothered a laugh. Maybe this celebrity gig wouldn't be so bad after all. He kinda liked working with Delainey.

But he liked undressing her more.

Too bad there wasn't a way to do both more often.

CHAPTER TWENTY-TWO

ONCE THE CAMERAS started rolling and the focus shifted from her problems to the immediate needs of the production, a heavy weight slid from her shoulders. She was in her element and loving every minute of it, even though she felt a lot like the chief cook and bottle washer of the small production as she wore many hats to accommodate the tight budget. Trace, on the other hand, was not having as much fun.

She could tell he was trying to be accommodating, but each time Trevor got too close, he'd look straight into the camera with an irritated expression, breaking the fourth wall, which was a sin unless the script called for it. And the script they were working from did not.

"You have to stop looking at Trevor," she told Trace when they'd taken a lunch break. "I know it's unnatural for you to have someone at your shoulder filming your every move, but I need you to pretend that Trevor isn't there."

"I'm not sure I can. Part of what I do, I do in silence, and having a crew tromp along beside me is weird and distracting. Plus, I feel like an idiot pretending to follow tracks that aren't there."

"*You* know the tracks aren't there but the *audience* doesn't. In postproduction we'll add the voice-over track, and it will be very convincing."

"I don't like it. Feels like a bunch of crap."

"C'mon, you're doing great," she assured him. "We need a few shots of you looking pensively into the distance, though. Just try to remember how it felt when you were searching for Clarissa." He graced her with an expression of open annoyance, and she smiled. "Go grab something to eat. I think we have sandwiches."

Trace muttered something under his breath that she probably didn't want to hear and stalked off to get something to eat. Maybe after he'd eaten he'd be in a better mood, but she wasn't holding her breath. Whether he liked it or not, the camera loved Trace. She had butterflies in her stomach watching him do his thing, and she knew America was going to fall in love with him—which, of course, Trace would hate and find intrusive. She withheld a sigh, fighting against what she needed for her career and what was best for Trace. Why couldn't they mesh for once?

"Make sure you get plenty of close-ups," she

reminded Trevor as she scribbled notes to remember later. "Oh, and if you can, give Trace some space. He gets unnerved by the cameras, and I'd like to be as organic as possible in his process."

"What process? He stares at dirt and leaves, and then pokes at them a bit. Are you sure this is a good idea?" Trevor complained, biting into his sandwich. "I mean, I'd hate to think we're wasting all our energy on another *Vertical Blind*."

She bristled. "Not that it matters, but this pilot was ordered by the head of the network, so whether we get hours of footage of Trace picking his nose because that's how he makes his magic work, that's what we're going to deliver. Got it? What is your problem, Trevor? You're always an insufferable ass, but since landing here in Alaska you've been an aggravating jerk at the same time."

"Sorry...I just think this shoot is boring. There's nothing to look at but trees and more trees. Whoever said we're facing deforestation has obviously never come here."

"Well, a better attitude, please. I have a lot riding on this and I need you at your best. Okay?"

"Yeah, sure. One spiffy new attitude coming right up."

Ugh. The man was incorrigible. "Great," she

said drily as she walked away to check with Scott, her second camera operator. "Tomorrow, I want you shooting plenty of B-roll footage, okay? Crowd shots, small-town life, et cera. But today, I need you to get some different angles of Trace." She probably had enough but seeing as she was wearing the director hat as well, she wanted to be sure.

"No problem," Scott said readily, and Delainey smiled, wishing Trevor were as amenable as Scott. If only she could switch jobs between her two camera operators. Unfortunately, Trevor had seniority and would screech like an angry blue jay if she assigned him the B-roll footage. Besides, Trevor was connected to people in high places, which was why everyone put up with his crap. But just once, she'd love to tell Trevor to stuff his attitude up his ass and get the hell off her set. Delainey smiled at that cheery thought and went off to double-check with Neal that the audio was coming off without any problems.

"Everything good?" she asked Neal just as he was finishing his sandwich.

"We're just catching ambient sound, but so far, so good. Trace doesn't seem like much of a talker, not that there's anyone to talk to, I guess."

"I tried to get him to talk out loud about what he was doing, but he refused, saying it felt stupid to talk to no one. So, we'll record it later in a voice-over track. Speaking of, do you think you can rig a soundproof room? Something tells me there's no way in hell I'm going to get Trace to L.A. to do that."

"Sure. I can rig the closet with decent enough soundproofing to suit our needs. I mean, it won't be perfect but we can clean up any noise in post-production."

"You're a godsend," she said, smiling. "Go ahead and buy what you need from the hardware store, but try to keep it modest. I don't want to go into the red over a soundproofed closet."

"I got your back," Scott assured her and went off to do his thing before they started again. She watched her crew going about their business, enjoying their break before resuming again, and she relished the warm-and-fuzzy feeling her job created when things were going smoothly. She had to take the good moments where she found them because they weren't always so easy to find. Location shoots were a mixed bag. At least her crew was small and relatively manageable. Aside from Trevor, the rest were very cooperative and easygoing. A few were excited to see Alaska and the others, if they weren't happy about the cold locale, kept their feelings to themselves.

She exhaled and her breath plumed before

her. The sun was slowly sinking and they were losing light. Time to cut the break short before they lost the opportunity to get any shots at all.

BY THE END of the day Trace was grumpy, feeling out of sorts and wondering what the hell he'd signed on for. Filming was everything he'd thought it was going to be—which wasn't much. After the crew had struck the location, they all headed back to their respective places and Trace and Delainey detoured to the Rusty Anchor. Delainey had been against it, but he needed a beer in the worst way.

"Why don't we just have a beer at your place?" she suggested, plainly uncomfortable. "My crew is here and I don't want them seeing me hang out with you in a bar."

"Then stay behind. I need a beer and I need a change of scenery." He tried not to snap, but his nerves were on edge. He was trying to be accommodating, trying to be the good guy, but he was rapidly losing that battle. He did not know how people did this every single day. He wasn't cut out to be a reality star—thank God. He cast her an irritated glance. "Besides, you're not their mother. What? You're not allowed to have a drink now and then? Last I checked you were a grown-up."

"It's not that," she said, following him. "It's

that I'm trying to set a good example. I don't need my crew drinking in bars, either. Particularly here. You know the locals are not all that friendly to people who aren't from here. The last thing I need is a bar fight."

"Well, if they mind their manners, you won't have to worry about that."

"You and I both know that sometimes the locals can provoke a fight even if it's unwarranted."

He shrugged. "Again, you're not their mother or their jailer. Let them take responsibility for their own actions. Listen, bottom line, stay or go—either way I'm getting a beer, end of story."

"Fine," she muttered, then tried to add a stipulation that grated on his already frayed nerves. "One beer, okay?"

"I'm not making deals. The last deal I made with you put me in this position."

She scowled and groused. "Well, aren't you a bowl of sunshine."

"Honey, you ain't seen nothing yet, but you will if I don't get that beer," he promised darkly.

They walked into the Rusty Anchor, and the familiar noise was a comfort to Trace as he selected a booth in the corner, away from everyone but with a good vantage point. Delainey slid in beside him and muttered, "This place never changes. I don't know if that's a good thing or not."

Trace rubbed his eyes and rolled his shoulders to release the tension, and Delainey caught the motion. "You were great today," she said, trying to butter him up with flattery, which she should've known wouldn't work with him. "A natural."

He slanted a dubious look her way. "I highly doubt that. Listen, you don't have to patronize me. I probably look like a fool."

"I would never allow you to look like a fool," she said quietly. "Please have a little faith in me."

"I got a question for you… If you're the producer, why are you directing, too?"

She smiled at being able to answer a question with authority. "Ordinarily, I would hire a director, but because of the rushed nature of this shoot, and the limited budget, I figured I could do it on my own. If the shoot were more complicated, I would definitely hire out, but I didn't think it was necessary. Why? Do you think I'm not good enough to wear so many hats at once?"

"I have no opinion on that, I was just curious. Hell, I don't know shit about this business or how it works. This isn't my element—I don't know what I'm doing and I feel stupid."

"I think you're doing a great job," she offered, but he shrugged off her earnest praise.

"I'm not like one of those Hollywood men you're so used to, saying things they don't mean, making promises they'll never deliver and who care more about their wardrobe than how they treat people, and I never will be."

She blinked at him, stung. "I know that and I wouldn't want you to be. Why would you say that? Where is this coming from?"

An angry and raw place, he nearly growled but didn't. Instead, he shrugged. "Right about now I'm wishing I hadn't signed on for this gig. It's not me and I'm not cut out for it, but I'm doing it for you."

"Don't act like a martyr. You're not doing this for me. You're doing it to save your program, remember? Don't make it sound as if you're sacrificing yourself selflessly, so please spare me the *poor me* act."

He knew she was right but he wasn't in the frame of mind to admit it. "Don't pick a fight with me, Delainey," he warned.

"I'm not picking a fight. I'm setting you straight. I don't need you thinking that you're doing me some kind of favor when you're coming out of this deal with something for yourself, as well. Listen, I know this isn't your idea of a good time, but I hate to be the one to remind you that you signed a legally binding contract. And I'm going to make you stick to it."

He narrowed his stare at her. "I never said I was going to quit. But I don't have to like it, and I never will like it. I was just letting you know."

"Don't worry. I never would have made the mistake of thinking that you're enjoying yourself." She stood, shouldering her purse and staring down at him with a cool look. "You know what? I've changed my mind about that beer. I'm going to stay at my dad's place tonight. Call time is 8:00 a.m. tomorrow. I'll see you there."

"Delainey, wait—" he called out after her, but she was already gone. He probably should've run after her to smooth things over, but he didn't have it in him. He was too out of sorts and too deep in the wrong frame of mind to do anything but more damage. So he let her go, and he enjoyed his beer just as he'd planned to do in the first place.

What did he care anyway where she stayed? He and Delainey were messing with each other's heads by playing house. As soon as the production was over, she would hightail it out of there, leaving him behind as surely as she'd left him behind the first time. And he knew what that felt like. He ought to put some distance between them and save himself some pain later.

Yeah, he knew that was the smart thing to

do. But as he finished his beer, finally loosening up, he also knew with a certainty that he wasn't going to stop whatever they were doing. He couldn't. Delainey was like a drug in his system, doing its damage yet coaxing him to want more. He craved her touch, needed her in his bed, and even if it ended up killing him, he'd do what he could to make this dumb production a success.

That was plain masochistic right there, he told himself with a dark smirk.

Yep.

And since he was determined to stay the course, he also knew he was going to drive to her dad's house and pick her sweet little ass up, because the only place she was sleeping was in his bed.

End of story.

CHAPTER TWENTY-THREE

DELAINEY WALKED INTO her father's home and found Thad trying to repair a fishing line. Country music played faintly from the old radio and the house was otherwise empty. She figured Brenda was at the hospital with Harlan, and although she probably should've stopped by, after her spat with Trace she didn't have the emotional strength to tack on a visit to her father's deathbed, too.

Thad looked up briefly when she walked in, and the first thing she noticed was his cast was gone. She frowned and took a seat at the table opposite her brother. "What happened to your cast?"

"Took it off. Can't do no work with it on."

"But you need another week or so, don't you?"

He stopped and flexed his arm, wincing only a little as he shrugged. "Feels fine to me. Besides, with Pops in the hospital, I figure I need to pick up the slack for the business."

Delainey remained quiet for a moment and then moved her chair closer to Thad and started helping. She and Thad had been repairing fishing line since they were little, and although it'd been close to ten years since she'd picked up a line, her fingers remembered what to do.

"Why didn't you call me and tell me that Dad was sick?" she asked.

"He didn't want no one to know. His pride and all. I wanted to tell you, but you were so far away and it didn't seem as if you were in an all-fire hurry to visit anytime soon. So why put worries on your shoulders that weren't going to change nothing? Plus, I know how you and Pops never got along. Figured, well, you might not care."

Shame crawled over her. Thad was right. She didn't know if she would've cared. Her life in L.A. was all-consuming and she didn't know if she would've made time for the drama of family life back in Alaska. But she should've. "Why are you so forgiving?" she asked. "You remember how our childhood was. When he wasn't beating the hell out of us, he was ignoring that we existed. That's hard to forget."

Thad stopped and said, "He can't change the past. He knows he was a terrible father, and maybe he changed because he wants to make amends or because he's afraid of what's waiting for him at the end of his life. But who am I to say that I shouldn't give him that chance to be a better dad? He's trying, Laney. Don't that count for something?"

"If he had changed so much, he would've called. He never called me. Not once."

"Neither did you."

Delainey dropped her fishing line and glared at her brother. "What do you want me to say? I'm not capable of being the bigger person? Fine. I'm not. I'm selfish and self-centered and shallow. All I care about is myself, and if that's who I am, then he helped to make me that way."

She rose and moved away from the table, needing to get some space. She was in a lose-lose situation, and she hated those kinds of battles. She shook out her hands when she realized she was clenching them. "How is it that I'm the bad guy in this situation? I don't understand. Trace blames me for leaving to focus on my dreams, and my father blames me for remembering that he was a terrible dad. Blame the victim, I guess."

Thad snorted and she whirled to face him. "What's that for?" she demanded.

"You. Being the victim. Laney, you've never allowed anyone to make you a victim. Ever. Yeah, maybe you're selfish and self-centered, but you're also ambitious and determined. I don't fault you for it and never have. Hell, I wish I had an ounce of your drive. Maybe I'd have my own fishing outfit instead of fishing on someone's else's boat. But don't ever say you're a victim, because you're not. Whatever you're going through, you created for yourself. And that includes Trace."

She bit her lip, her eyes smarting from the tears that were building. When had her younger brother become so insightful? Seemed somewhere along the way, he'd grown up and she'd totally missed it happening. He wasn't a kid anymore and he saw way more than most young adults his age. He saw more than she ever had. She wiped at her eyes. "So, what am I supposed to do?" she asked, her words choked by the sudden squeezing of her throat. "I don't know how to be different even if I wanted to."

"I don't know. Maybe you're not supposed to change," he offered with a shrug. "The world will keep spinning. I guess it's up to you to find your place in it and then make peace with yourself wherever you end up."

Make peace with herself? She wasn't even sure if that was possible. Part of her was so locked up with anger and resentment and fear that she wasn't sure if that would ever change. She hated that about herself, and she knew that she used the excuse of work to cover up the dark places that she didn't want anyone to see. The fact that she hadn't done a very good job of covering up those ugly spots was a painful revelation. "I want to forgive him. I want to be able to walk into that hospital room without any hang-ups and simply hold his hand as a daughter with a dying father should. But each time I try, my feet won't move and my fists ball and I'm pissed off all over again."

"Why?"

"Because he was the only parent we had and I needed him to be better."

"But he wasn't. He was who he was and it's up to you to decide what you're going to do with that. In the eight years that you've been gone, he's changed. But he'll never be that guy who gives out hugs and tells funny jokes and who is that warm-and-cuddly person who everyone loves to be around. That's just not who he is. I came to that realization a long time ago, and when I did it made accepting who he truly is a lot easier."

"And who is that? Who is he?"

"Pops is the kind of man who is loyal, hard-working, quiet, but he's not afraid of saying what needs to be said. He doesn't care if he's the unpopular opinion, and he's taught me a thing or two about integrity. He doesn't make excuses. He just gets the job done. Doesn't matter if it's raining, it doesn't matter if he's sick—if he says something's going to get done, you can take it to the bank that it'll get done. In this day and age, I think that's pretty rare."

Delainey stared at her brother. How had she missed so much?

"There were times when Pops went over the line. But it wasn't all bad. I think you've blocked out the times that were good."

"What are you talking about?" she asked, stiffening. "Are you implying that my memory is faulty? Because I remember quite clearly the bruises and the fear."

"No," Thad said, shaking his head. "But there were good times."

"Maybe before Mom died but not after."

"If that's how you remember it, nothing I can say is going to change how you feel. All I can say is I disagree. So if you're going to be mad at our dad for a past he can't change, at least be sure that you're remembering it right."

"I can't believe you would even suggest that I'm not," she said, fighting back the urge to cry. "I spent half my childhood trying to protect you from his temper. I took the brunt of his anger so that you wouldn't go to bed with bruises. It hurts that you would turn this around on me. I don't regret protecting you, because it was the right thing to do, but to have you sit there and judge me for the aftermath of that protection really stings."

"I know you protected me. That's what big sisters do. But I'm not a baby anymore and I'm not a child. I've grown up a lot in the last eight years, and I see things a little more clearly than you do right now. I have no doubt that you'll come to it on your own, but right now your vision is all messed up. Pops used to take us fishing. I remember the both of us taking turns unlacing his boots when he came home after a long stretch on the water. I remember him playing the harmonica for us and dancing. Can you tell me that you don't remember any of that?"

Delainey opened her mouth to deny it, but snippets of memory surfaced and the echo of childish laughter followed. She remembered unlacing her father's boots and pulling them off his sodden feet. She remembered how white his toes were after being stuffed inside the boots for more than nineteen hours at a stretch, and she recalled how her father used to smile at her enthusiasm when she tried to rub the wrinkles from his saturated skin. "I remember those things," she admitted. "But those times did not outnumber the bad."

"Well, I choose to remember the good stuff. The man is dying. He ain't gonna get a second chance to make things right. The way you decide to handle your goodbyes is your business."

Delainey felt chastised, even though her brother

hadn't said anything that wasn't true. She wiped the tears tracking down her cheeks. "I don't know what to say," she admitted. "Maybe there isn't anything to say."

Thad nodded and returned to the fishing line. She supposed everything had been said that needed to be said. Her soul felt shredded. She was forcing Trace to do something that went against his nature, and she was looking like the bad guy in her family's personal drama. Nothing about this trip seemed right. Nothing about her life seemed right. "Do you hate me?" she asked.

"I could never hate you, Laney. You're my big sister and I love you, but I think your priorities are really screwed up."

She winced. Yeah, she was beginning to realize that. "If I agreed with you, how do you think I should go about changing that?"

Thad grinned and he looked every bit her younger brother with his boyishly handsome face and his beautiful eyes. "I guess I'd just start changing what you don't like. But then I'm a simple guy."

She laughed and wiped the remaining moisture from her eyes. "That's some pretty good advice. I guess life doesn't always have to be so complicated."

"Nope. I always say if your socks are wet,

don't spend time complaining. Just change them and go on with your day."

Delainey's smile widened. That's what she'd been doing. Spending too much time complaining about wet socks. "Since you're so full of good advice, tell me what I should do about Trace."

"Can't help you there. Besides, I think you already know what you need to do about Trace. You don't need me to tell you."

"How is it that you're still single?" she asked, cocking her head at him. "The girls here have got to be dumb not to snatch you up, Thad Clarke. You're a good guy."

"Can I put that on my online-dating profile?" he teased, and she rolled her eyes. He chuckled as he returned to the fishing line, checking hooks and reknotting frayed line. "Are you going to help me finish this line, or are you going to take off?" he asked.

But before she could answer, someone else answered for her.

"Sorry, kid, but she's going home with me."

Delainey startled, her heart jumping into her throat as Trace appeared from the darkened hallway. "Good God, you scared me." She hadn't heard him come in, and she didn't know how much of the conversation he'd heard, either. But just seeing him standing there, his eyes blazing and brooking no argument, the possession in his voice obvious, she shivered and a smile trembled on her lips. She still hadn't answered, but when he grabbed her hand and began leading her out of the house, she didn't fight him.

"Bye, Thad!" she called out and followed Trace out the door.

CHAPTER TWENTY-FOUR

TRACE HAD EXPECTED Delainey to give him an earful as soon as they climbed into the truck, but surprisingly she remained silent. He didn't know whether to be grateful or worried. But as they drove the distance to his house, his truck eating up the miles in the dark, he didn't care what the outcome—he wasn't sorry. "You probably ought to just keep your stuff here," he said gruffly. "Because you and I both know this is where you're gonna be while you're here in Alaska."

"What about my crew? What am I supposed to say to them?" she asked absently, as if the question was simply a formality because she really didn't care about the answer. "I thought you said you're tired of people talking about you and your business. Openly sleeping with me will only make that worse."

"When it comes to you, I don't care. I don't understand a lot of what is happening between you and me, and I'm not even going to pretend to try. All I know is that if you're here, you're sleeping with me."

Delainey didn't argue. The fact that she didn't put up much of a fuss gave him pause. Frankly, he'd expected a bigger argument from his staunchly independent woman. "Are you feeling okay?" he had to ask. "Because you're not acting like yourself."

Her small smile confirmed that something was up. There was a wistful sadness clinging to her, and he had a feeling it had nothing to do with the little spat at the Rusty Anchor. His demeanor changed. He was no longer consumed with getting her to see things his way. He just wanted to be there for her. "What's going on? Did Thad say something to upset you?"

"No. Well, yes." She seemed to struggle with the words until they finally tumbled out and she was helpless to stop them. "I've come to the realization that I'm a terrible person," she said.

"What? No, you're not," he quickly disagreed, not liking where she was going. "Who told you that?"

"No one needed to tell me. I came to the realization myself, and I can't hide from that fact anymore. Thad says I need to get my priorities straight, and he's right. I value all the wrong things. My father is dying in a hospital room, and I can't bring myself to sit there next to him.

I can't hold his hand and pretend or forget what a terrible bastard he was when we were growing up. I *want* to be the bigger person and forgive, but I can't. Thad can, but I can't."

"It doesn't make you a terrible person. It makes you an honest person."

She shook her head in denial. "No, Trace. Don't you see? I have put so much value on all of the wrong things that I don't remember what it feels like to value the things that are true. I have an emptiness inside of me that I've been trying to fill with all the wrong things. But here's the worst part—even knowing this I know I can't change. I'm driven to succeed because everyone expected me to fail. I have sacrificed so much for that ambition, and what has it yielded me? Not a lot," she answered before he could try. She barked a short, miserable laugh. "Trace, I would've made a terrible wife. You probably would've ended up hating me if I'd stayed, and I definitely would've hated myself."

"You don't know that. You're taking a guess from the past about a future that never happened." He drew a deep breath. He needed to get her off this track because the journey wasn't going to be a smooth ride if they kept traveling that way. "Let's table the heavy stuff for the night. We have an early call in the morning."

KIMBERLY VAN METER 255

"You're so sweet. I should've seen that a long time ago. I'm sorry."

"Stop apologizing. We both made choices that in hindsight might not have been the best. Let's leave it at that."

Delainey followed him into the house, seemingly complacent with his suggestion, but after she brushed her hair and readied for bed, she pulled away from him to roll onto her side.

"What's wrong?" he asked, perplexed that she would insist on the distance between them.

"I need some space."

"That's the last thing you need," he disagreed on a low growl. "You're punishing yourself as some kind of needless penance."

"Trace, you've always been good at everything," she started. "You don't know what it's like to struggle to be good at something so that other people will recognize your skill. I've been struggling my whole life for someone to notice me, and sometimes I just feel like giving up. But I won't. Even if I should."

In spite of the fact that she wasn't facing him, Trace wrapped his arm around her belly and pulled her close. He nuzzled the back of her neck and kissed her softly. He hated the raw pain he heard in her voice. She was fighting demons he couldn't even imagine. "Tell me what you enjoy about your job. Help me to understand."

"Do you really want to know?"

"I wouldn't ask if I didn't."

She paused to reflect and then said, "I like being in charge of so many people at once and watching something materialize out of nothing. I like being able to turn on the television and see something I created for the enjoyment of others. *Vertical Blind* was the last major production that I produced. I liked that it wasn't a typical reality show but a drama about rock climbers. It was unique and different and exciting. I really thought it was going to shine. But it was expensive to shoot, and in the end the ratings didn't support the expense. We were axed after only four episodes. It was humiliating. But even though the show didn't make it, I was proud of the work. It was a good show."

"Sounds like something I would enjoy, if I watched television," he said. "So you had one failed show. It doesn't mean that you're no good at what you do. It just means that luck wasn't on your side."

"Logically, I know that, but deep down it just reinforced that belief inside of me that I'm not good enough. That I'm a fraud pretending to be someone when in truth I'm really nobody."

He wanted to shake her and make her see that she was somebody to him, but he didn't because he knew her insecurities had nothing to do with him and never had.

"Forgive me for playing into the stereotypes, but I would think that a place like Hollywood would reinforce those insecurities no matter how confident a person started off."

"You're right. The town is filled with people looking to tear someone down just so they could stand on top of the fallen on their climb up. I guess I thought I would fit in better because I never really fit in here."

Her admission was a shock to him. How could she have felt as if she didn't belong in her own hometown? "What do you mean?" he asked.

She shrugged. "I always felt like an outsider here. I could go through the motions, but I didn't feel as if I had anything in common with the people here. I don't like fish and I don't want anything to do with fish. The fact that my father is a fisherman makes me feel as if I'm betraying my roots in some way by admitting that. People who live and die by the sea cannot understand somebody who has no affinity for that lifestyle. I wanted to go somewhere warm, where I could wear my flip-flops year-round, and where when I put my feet in the ocean my toes don't freeze off. I wanted everything that Alaska wasn't."

"So you found happiness." He had a hard time

saying the words because it hurt to know that there was no way she would ever find happiness with him in Alaska. "Don't apologize for what brings you joy."

"I love that it was eighty degrees on Thanksgiving, and I love that I have more summer clothing in my closet than I ever did in my entire life in Alaska. But I don't like that I constantly look over my shoulder watching for the knife going into my back, and I hate that the men I meet are soft, posturing fools who have no idea what hard work truly is. Seriously, I stopped dating because if one more man touched me with those soft, manicured hands, I would throw up. Disgusting. I need a man with hands that are tough and roughed up from real work, not from tapping on a computer all day or texting."

He shifted and tried not to growl as he said, "I get the point. Can we not talk about the men you've been dating? I know I can't expect you to be celibate, but I'd like to pretend that you are. Otherwise, I will have to start sharing some of my dating experiences, too."

"Point taken," she murmured with a mild shudder.

"You were saying…" he prompted her, and she rediscovered her original point.

"I guess all I'm trying to say is, there is a lot

about the city that I don't like, but mostly what I hate is that you're not there with me."

Trace spooned her in stunned silence, his mind stuttering on her statement. Had she just admitted that she missed and needed him? She turned in his arms and he felt her gaze in the darkness. "If I asked you to go to Los Angeles with me, would you?" she asked, the vulnerability in her tone slicing at him.

He desperately wanted to give her anything she wanted, but he wouldn't lie to her, not even to spare her feelings. "Los Angeles is no place for me. I would be lost in a place like that," he said quietly. "My home is here and always has been. This is where I find my joy."

And he realized it was true. Alaska, with its savage beauty, was stamped on his soul, and that would never change. "I would give you anything you ask, anything that was in my power to give, but I can't give you that."

"How do you know if you've never been there?" she asked, almost desperately. "Wouldn't you be willing to give it a try for me?"

He felt like a jerk for denying her, but he could see the writing on the wall. "I need wide-open spaces, and the concrete jungle like Los Angeles would kill me. Or I'd end up killing someone else. We would end up tearing each other apart because I would be so desperate to leave and you would be desperate for me to stay."

She didn't deny his reasoning. Perhaps she knew he was right. But her grip tightened on him and she buried her face against his chest. "So basically we're back to square one. I won't stay. You won't go."

He held her close and closed his eyes. Yeah, back to square one. And square one sucked. "At least we have now. Let's not waste a single moment." She nodded and he felt something wet drop on his chest. Her tears burned his heart and he wished he could have been the one to give her everything she needed and wanted. God, he'd never truly stopped loving Delainey, and he realized he probably never would.

CHAPTER TWENTY-FIVE

TRACE HAD JUST finished his second day of shooting when Miranda showed up on the location in her Range Rover. Delainey and Miranda shared a smile as Miranda trudged past the crew toward him, and Trace was happy to see the two former best friends had begun to build a bridge to one another again. But he was curious as to why his sister would show up on location. "What's up, sis?" he asked, concerned. "Is everything okay?"

"No. I wish that it were. I know you said that you were going to do it, but I think we're running out of time and so I did it for you," she answered gravely, and he knew immediately what she was talking about before she even explained. "I called Social Services and told them about Mom and Dad's situation. I hope you're not mad that I jumped the gun, but I'm afraid that if we wait any longer she's going to die in that house."

Trace frowned, not because he was mad at his sister but because she was right. The production had eclipsed his life in more ways than one, and the situation with his parents had slipped his mind. He rubbed at his brows, sighing. "I'm sorry. I should've remembered to call. What did you say to them?"

"The truth. I told them I wanted to file a report of hoarding and illegal marijuana cultivation."

Trace stared. "You told them about the pot? Why did you do that? You know Dad can go to jail for this."

"I know but they're going to find out anyway and something has to give. We've been trying to get him to quit for years and he refuses. You said yourself that he's just being selfish. And I feel that we have to do what is right for Mom, seeing as he can't or won't."

Trace pushed his hand through his hair, frustrated. "I understand that, but I really wish you wouldn't have mentioned the marijuana. The investigation is going to go from Social Services to police services. There's a big difference between the two, and I don't think you realize what that will entail for this family."

"Trace, you agreed with me that this had to stop. You were supposed to make the call." She glanced around, her gaze settling on the film crew before continuing. "Listen, I know that you're busy with this shoot, but our parents' lives are at stake."

"I'm not disagreeing with you. I just wish you would've left the marijuana out of it. We could have let Dad know that they were coming and he could've—"

"Hidden his stash?" Miranda finished for him, growing angry. "Hiding the problem isn't going to fix it. If he needs to suffer the consequence of growing an illegal garden, then that's what needs to happen. He has to take some of his own advice. Remember when he used to tell us to face the music when we'd screwed up? Well, it's time for him to do exactly that."

What could he say? Miranda was right, but having the police involved was going to complicate things far more than she realized. "Well, it's done now," he said. "Don't be surprised when we get a call from jail because our father's been arrested on felony cultivation charges."

"Maybe they'll just give him a warning," she said hopefully. "I mean technically he's a first-time offender. I doubt they throw the book at people who have no prior criminal record."

"Are you willing to leverage our father's future on that hope?"

"I guess I'll have to. Anyway, I just wanted to give you a heads-up. Also, I think it's time for you to call Wade. Frankly, I don't think he'll listen to me. He thinks I'm being overly dramatic."

"To be fair, so did I." Trace had had no inkling that things were as bad as they were. It'd been hard to fathom, but now that he'd seen the truth of things, he wasn't about to let it slide and he knew his older brother would want to know. "But you're right. If it comes from me he'll probably take it more seriously."

"I'll try not to be offended as long as you can get him here. I know the next step is going to be a doozy. Having all hands on deck is going to be necessary to make it through."

"Wade has his own issues about coming home," Trace reminded Miranda. Wade had dealt with Simone's death and their father's marijuana dealing by leaving the state and never returning. But Trace was confident that his older brother would come back if they really needed him. However, he also knew it wouldn't be easy. "It'll be a struggle to get him on the plane, but I'll do my best."

Miranda smiled with relief and he realized he'd been putting too much on her shoulders these past two years. If Wade was guilty of running away from his problems, Trace had been equally at fault. "Listen, I'm sorry I overreacted to the news. You're right. Dad has to own up to what he's been doing. We've been tiptoeing around the situation for too long. I guess it's time for a Sinclair intervention."

"Oh, goody. Can't wait. Should I bring popcorn?" Miranda asked wryly. "Hey, on a separate note, how are things going with you and Delainey?"

He did not want to answer that. He couldn't rightly say, *Well, we really enjoyed each other's company in the bedroom, but we really haven't worked out anything otherwise.* "It's complicated," he finally said. Miranda laughed and he cast her a sharp look. "What? It's true. There are no easy answers and neither one of us has figured out anything, so I guess it's status quo."

"I'd hardly say it's status quo," Miranda said with a mischievous sparkle in her eye. "Before she came back no one could even mention her name without you snapping like a wounded bear. And now you're practically dating again. Oh, don't give me that look. You know word spreads really fast in this town. You can't hang out at the Rusty Anchor dancing and acting all snuggly without people watching and catching on. No judgment on my part, I think it's great, but I'm just saying people have noticed."

"When will people stop being interested in our business?" he growled. "Yeah, well, it's still complicated."

Miranda laughed. "Jeremiah and I had a complicated relationship, too. And now look at us. Happy as two bugs in a rug."

"Don't start buying towel sets for us yet. She's going back to L.A. and I'm staying here. Essentially nothing is going to change," he said, his mood rapidly souring. He hated being faced with the reality of his situation with Delainey because he hated how he knew it was going to end. He didn't want to talk about Delainey anymore and steered the conversation back to their parents. "So when do we expect all hell to break loose?"

"Well, I made the report today and they probably won't send anyone out there until the end of the week, so probably Friday or Monday at the latest." She gestured meaningfully to his cell phone hanging from his hip. "Take the ringer off Silent. I'll definitely need backup when it happens."

"All right," he agreed. Delainey started walking toward them and Miranda took that as a cue to leave.

Delainey frowned as Miranda drove away. "Where'd she go? I was about to invite her to dinner. I was thinking of taking the crew over to Harpies for burgers and fries. I thought maybe she could join us. I haven't had a chance to meet her new guy, Jeremiah. Her son, Talen, is adorable though. It must be fun having a nephew."

"He's a great kid. I don't get to see him that much though because of my schedule. I always try to take him out for a little man-to-man time when I'm home, but like I said, my schedule wasn't very accommodating until now. In fact, this is the longest stint I've been home in years. Usually, I'm gone for months at a stretch on assignment or training."

"That's too bad. I'll bet he loves playing with his Uncle Trace. You're probably the coolest uncle a kid could ever ask for," she said, giving him a little wink. He didn't want to let on how much her praise affected him, but his cheeks may have pinked because suddenly she smoothed her fingers over them and grinned. "Can you get any cuter? I love it."

He watched as she returned to her crew as they packed up the location, and he withheld a sigh. Things were about to get ugly in the Sinclair world just as Delainey's life was about to fall apart.

If he thought things were complicated before…he had a feeling they were about to get screwed in the near future.

TRACE DIDN'T SAY ANYTHING but Delainey could tell that he was preoccupied. After burgers and fries at Harpies, the crew dispersed for the night, leaving Delainey and Trace behind. She no longer cared if people saw them hanging out. Somehow it didn't seem to matter anymore. It was no one's business how she and Trace spent their time, and that was that.

Trace had barely touched his fries and had only eaten half of his burger, which told Delainey that something was really bothering him because Trace loved his food. "Are you going to tell me what's wrong or do I have to guess?" she asked. Trace looked up and smiled, caught. "Out with it, Sinclair. I know when something's on your mind."

"It's my parents. Miranda called Social Services and she also alerted the police to my father's *garden*." He sighed and dropped the French fry he'd been pushing around his plate. "It's not going to end well."

"Do you think they're going to arrest your dad?" she asked, worried. Her first thought went to the production. Reporters would find something like this and delight in splashing the news all over the media. The old adage "There is no such thing as bad publicity" wasn't always true. And she wasn't willing to take any chances. "What did she tell them? Do you know anyone over at the police department who could pull some strings?"

He looked at her sharply. "For what purpose? My father is breaking the law. There's nothing any of my connections can do about that. Besides, I'm more concerned about my mom. And if it takes my dad getting busted for his marijuana, then so be it."

Delainey knew she needed to tread carefully and so phrased her next comment with caution. "Absolutely," she agreed. "Your dad needs to stop doing what he's doing, and, of course, your mom's safety is paramount. But it's not a good idea to have a police investigation going on when we're trying to put together this pilot. We really can't take any bad publicity hits. It could damage the production. If there's anything you can do to lessen the impact, then I think you should do that."

He stared hard, and she tried not to fidget. He was mad but she had to do what she could to protect the production. "Delainey," he warned, "do not tell me that you are more concerned about the production than the safety of my mother."

"Of course not," she rushed to say. "I want your mom to be safe, and I agree she is in a bad situation. But maybe we could work together to help your mom instead of bringing in the police. That's all I'm saying."

"And what do you propose to do? She won't listen to her own children. What makes you think she's going to listen to you?"

"I don't know that she'll listen to me either, but I have resources that you might not have. Maybe I could have a professional organizer come in and help her—"

"Miranda already tried that and my mom kicked her off the property. Next idea?"

"We could have a professional cleaning crew come in—" Trace shook his head at her suggestion, and she bit her lip with true consternation. She didn't have the answers but she had to avoid bad publicity at all costs. Panic colored her voice as she said, "I'm sorry. I'm just trying to think of a solution that will help us both. I know it's coming off as if I only care about the production, but that's not the case. I do have to think of it, though."

"Damn it, Delainey," he said, anger rippling from his tone. "This is a new low. Don't try to sell me that you're trying to protect my parents when in fact your only concern is the production. Remember when you said that you value the wrong things and that your priorities were screwed up—well, this is a great example. The production should take a backseat to what is happening in my parents' personal life, what is happening in my personal life and for that matter what is actually happening in your own personal life. The fact that you're sitting here eating a burger, chatting with friends and joking with your crew when your dad is dying is further proof that you don't have your shit straight." He stood abruptly and his chair toppled to the ground. He jerked it upright, pulled a few bucks from his wallet and tossed the money to the table before muttering, "I need some air," and leaving.

"Trace—" She tried calling after him, but she knew better and stopped. She'd screwed up. She shouldn't have brought the production into the conversation and should've found a way around it herself. Why was she always caught between two impossible situations? She just wanted everything to work for once in her life.

She dropped her head into her hands and fought the tears. She felt sick inside. Seeing the judgment in Trace's eyes hurt, and she hated that he was right. Once again, she'd shown in vivid color that her priorities were screwed up. How was she supposed to fix that, without sacrificing everything that she'd ever worked for? It didn't seem fair. Why was she the one always asked to sacrifice? Well, one thing was for sure—the answers weren't going to be found here at Harpies.

She covered the rest of the bill and let herself out, but when she didn't see Trace anywhere, she didn't know what to do. They both came in his truck and she couldn't very well leave him without transportation. She stomped her foot in frustration. "Damn you, Trace." She fished her cell phone from her purse and dialed Miranda. "Can you come pick me up?" she asked, embarrassed. "I'm at Harpies. I'm fine, but I don't know where Trace is. We had a fight and he took off, but I don't want to take his truck and leave him without a ride."

"No problem. I'll be there in a minute." Miranda clicked off and Delainey had no choice but to wait. Within five minutes Miranda was there to pick her up. Delaine took one final look around the area, not having a clue where Trace had gone, and reluctantly climbed into the car. As they drove back to Miranda's place, Miranda asked, "What happened? Trace just up and left you there? Did you try calling him?"

"He doesn't want to talk to me right now," Delainey answered sullenly. "He probably walked over to the Rusty Anchor to cool off, and I figured I ought to give him the space."

"Sounds serious. Was it about my parents?" Miranda guessed. Delainey nodded and Miranda sighed. "I'm sorry. It's bad timing with your production, isn't it? I couldn't hold off any longer. Delainey, if you could see how my mom is living, you would agree with me. She's sleeping in the bathtub, for crying out loud—that's how bad it is. She's going to die in that house and my dad, well, all I can say is, he's not doing anything to help her."

"It's okay, I understand."

"I didn't mean to cause problems for you and Trace, especially when things seemed to be going so well."

"What do you mean?" she asked.

"Well, just that you two seemed to have been catching up on lost time."

"It's not like that," Delainey hedged, uncomfortable with what Miranda was implying. It was one thing not to care what strangers thought of her and Trace hanging out with each other, but she didn't want Miranda to get hurt by hoping something was building when it wasn't. "We're not dating again and I don't want to give off that impression. I mean, not to be crass, but we're just enjoying a sexual convenience."

"Oh." Miranda drew back in surprise. "Does… Trace know this?" she asked.

"Of course. We both know this is temporary." But the fact that Miranda seemed unsure made Delainey extremely worried. What if Trace wanted more? What if he thought they were going to work things out and she was going to become his little woman, just as he'd wanted eight years ago? The truth was, she didn't find the idea of being Trace's woman distasteful— not in the least—but he'd already shot down her invitation to return with her to Los Angeles, and she sure as hell wasn't going to stay in Alaska. So a future together…just wasn't in the cards.

Just as it wasn't in the cards eight years ago.

But a secret part of her had hoped, *that maybe,* this time would be different.

CHAPTER TWENTY-SIX

TRACE RECEIVED A TEXT from his sister saying Delainey was at her place, and he realized he couldn't avoid the conversation with Delainey for much longer. He'd stormed out of Harpies like a petulant child and he was ashamed of his knee-jerk reaction, but he'd be a liar if he didn't admit that he was still a bit angry.

She could dress up the facts as much as she'd like, but the glaring truth was that her first priority had been the production and nothing else. That hurt. He supposed he'd been hoping that she'd changed and maybe they had a future together, but it was plain naive of him to hold on to that hope now.

He texted his sister, "On my way," and climbed into his truck.

Trace arrived at Miranda's and, after a short knock, walked into her house. Immediately, Talen ran to him and tackled him. The boy's open glee warmed his heart, and he knew he needed to start spending more time with him before it was too late to be of influence. Talen's father had been a no-good piece of crap, but at least Johnny had had the decency to die in prison before Talen was born. Miranda had done an admirable job of being a single mother, but Trace was glad that she had Jeremiah now to help out because there were some things that women simply did not understand, no matter how cool they were.

Such as armpit farts.

"Have you been practicing?" he asked his nephew solemnly, and Talen broke into a delighted grin before proceeding to make all sorts of disgusting noises with his cupped hand and armpit. He laughed and high-fived the boy. "Excellent. Your mom never could master that skill," he said conspiratorially with a sideways glance at Miranda, who rolled her eyes.

"That's because I never wanted to," she retorted, ruffling Talen's hair and sending him off to bathe before bed. "It's way past his bedtime, but he wanted to see Uncle Trace. So if he has a hard time getting up in the morning, I will squarely blame you."

Trace made a mock salute to Miranda and then realized Jeremiah wasn't home. "Where's the squeeze?" he asked, teasing his sister because of her former staunch refusal to date in any way. She changed her tune when Jeremiah came around—thank God. He was tired of bloodying people's noses for making unkind remarks about her, ahem, activities.

"Jeremiah had to go to Anchorage for a training summit. He'll be back tomorrow."

"Good. Doesn't he know you're not trustworthy on your own for too long?"

Miranda swatted at Trace but otherwise let the snarky comment slide. That was the thing with brothers and sisters—they knew too much about each other's lives and never failed to tease you with the information later. Delainey came around the corner and leaned against the wall, regarding him with a wariness that he mirrored. "Are you ready to go?" he asked. He wasn't going to waste time asking if she wanted to stay with him because they both knew she would.

"I'll get my purse," she murmured and disappeared.

He exhaled a short breath and Miranda chuckled. "It's not actually funny," he said, scowling.

"From this side of the argument it is."

"Yeah, well, keep your chuckles to yourself," he said.

"Such a grouch. Don't be so hard on her. She's trying to make something you both can be proud of."

He shook his head, not wanting to get into it. He didn't agree that Delainey's motivation was purely grounded in such magnanimous soil, but he wasn't about to defend his feelings to his sister, particularly when she regarded the whole thing as one big chuckle-fest. "Thanks for picking her up," he said.

"Sure. You're lucky Delainey isn't more like me," she said.

Trace frowned. "Why's that?"

"Because I'd have taken the truck and left your sorry ass walking home." She grinned. Funny thing was, Trace believed her. He supposed he *was* lucky. Delainey reappeared and she hugged Miranda briefly. "Don't let this big lug get under your skin. You do what you think is right. You always have, and you know what? Who's to say you were wrong?"

Trace glowered at his sister for her asinine advice and ushered Delainey into the truck. Delainey had plenty of sidewise thoughts in her head. He didn't need Miranda adding more.

"I'm sorry I stormed off," he said, once they'd returned to the house. The ride home had been excruciatingly silent, and by the time they'd arrived at the house, Trace had realized the conversation needed to start on his end with an apology. "I don't know what came over me, but I reacted badly. I just want you to know I'm sorry."

She nodded and folded her clothes before climbing into bed. He waited but she flipped on her side and gave him her back. He frowned. "Don't you feel compelled to add something of your own?" he asked.

She turned. "Did you offer a legitimate apology or did you make a strategic apology in the hopes that I would offer one, as well?"

"Well, yeah, I guess I hoped you would feel sorry, too."

"I don't." She returned to her side, adding over her shoulder, "Good night."

He stared at her slim back and fought the urge to start yelling all over again. *Delainey Clarke, you are the most aggravating, singularly stubborn woman I've ever known.* He grabbed his pillow and muttered, "I'm taking the couch."

She muttered, "Good idea."

And he realized that's exactly what she'd wanted all along. He shook his head, realizing he'd just been manipulated. He sighed and got settled, preparing for a long and restless night. *Well played, you little vixen. Well played.*

DELAINEY WAS LIVID. And hurt. But mostly livid. How dare he try to manipulate her into some half-baked apology when he was the one who'd stormed off like a teenage boy who'd been scolded. Miranda was right—she didn't need Trace chastising her for chasing her dreams and being protective of her ambition.

The fact that he never—not once—had ever supported her ambition was something that stuck in her side like a thorn. She didn't need his approval for anything she did in her life. He was bananas if he thought just because she enjoyed sex with him she would be willing to sacrifice everything she'd ever wanted.

If he had any idea how hard she'd worked for this opportunity to shine, he'd never dream of asking her to put it on the back burner for anything or anyone. Had she ever asked him to walk away from his dream just because it didn't gel with her idea of what a boyfriend or partner should be? His job took him away for weeks at a time. How was that conducive to a stable relationship by his standards? Simply put, because he expected her to stay in the home and tend the hearth like a good little woman should.

She gritted her teeth and suffered a red-hot streak of pissed-off ire. Who did he think he was? She'd actually bought into his little scolding tirade, and that made her doubly angry. So angry in fact that she couldn't lie there and quietly simmer. She threw the blankets off and stalked into the living room, where Trace was tossing and fidgeting on the uncomfortable sofa. "Where do you get off judging me for my choices when you've never once taken responsibility for your part in my leaving?" she demanded, crossing her arms with a glare.

"Me? What the hell are you talking about? *I asked you to marry me!* How was I supposed to know that was some kind of unforgivable sin in your book? I wanted to spend the rest of my life with you!" he shouted while flinging aside his blankets to stand. "You want me to take responsibility for you bailing on every single person who ever cared about you so you don't have to take the heat? Forget it, honey. Deal with it. You bailed. Not the other way around."

"I bailed because you never took me seriously and I knew if I had stayed, I was looking at eating everything I'd ever wanted! Yes, my first thought was of the production when you told me about your parents, because that's my life you're messing with, too. I already told you everything is on the line for me, but somehow that seems to fade into the ether with you because you don't value what I do and you *never have.*"

"Why does your dream have to come at the expense of everyone else in your life? For crying out loud, Laney, you even cut off your friggin' brother when you split. You didn't have to burn every bridge just to make your dreams come true, but somehow you thought you had to set fire to everything in order to succeed. And yet you refuse to apologize for hurting people when you went."

She blinked back tears of frustration. "You don't understand and you never will. I know I hurt people, but if I'd left a path open to myself I would've known in the back of my mind that I had a plan B. I didn't want a plan B! I wanted to make sure that I had no option but to succeed at what I wanted to do. You couldn't possibly understand what it's like to fear failure so much that you would literally force yourself into cutting off your support system so that you had to rely only on yourself, because you've never been plagued by insecurity. You've always enjoyed the freedom of knowing that you were the best at what you do. I've never had that luxury."

"Being the best at what you do for your career doesn't guarantee happiness," Trace said. "Being the best didn't help me find Simone in time, did it? Sometimes being the best brings its own pitfalls, and I would never want to face them alone. You say I never faced insecurity? Wrong. When you left, I'd never been so insecure in my life. And for the first time ever, I felt completely alone and abandoned. You didn't give me a chance to support you in your dreams. You assumed a hell of a lot when you split. You could've given me the courtesy of failing you on my own before assuming I would."

She swallowed. "I…" She didn't know what to say to that. She had made assumptions and she hadn't given him a fair shot because her fear had eclipsed any good sense or reason she might've had.

Trace jerked the blanket back over him and turned away from her, finished with the conversation.

"Trace—"

"Just go to bed."

Left with only the ash of her anger, she returned to the bedroom and climbed beneath the blankets. It killed her to realize that Trace had been right in one respect. An explanation and an apology were way overdue. He wasn't asking her to apologize for chasing her dreams, only for the method in which she'd done it. To that end, she probably owed quite a few people apologies.

A tear squeezed out of the corner of her eye and she buried her face in the pillow, but there was no escaping the emptiness echoing in her heart.

CHAPTER TWENTY-SEVEN

MORNING CAME BUT no resolution to the turmoil between Trace and Delainey seemed forthcoming. Both were still stiff with resentment and hurt feelings, so much so that neither said a word to the other as they went through the motions of getting ready for the morning call.

Trace hadn't slept well. His old sofa wasn't meant for sleeping. Hell, it was barely suitable for sitting. But he'd be damned if he was going to be crawling into the bed beside Delainey after everything that had been said. But even as he was still angry and hurt, he couldn't help but think of everything that she'd proclaimed. She accused him of never believing in her dreams and for discounting her ambition. Had he done that? If he were being brutally honest, he would have to admit that there might've been some truth to that accusation. It wasn't that he didn't want her to chase her dreams. He just didn't understand why her dreams had to take her so far away. He couldn't understand how she could so easily leave him if she loved him as she professed. Maybe she had a different idea of love than he did, because he couldn't have imagined a life without Delainey by his side.

He wanted to see her succeed, but did it have to come at the expense of everyone else? He didn't understand why she was so driven to return to a place that she claimed was not a nice place. Warm weather filled with crappy people wasn't a big draw for him. But for whatever reasons, she was dead set on returning. That meant he was in the same place he was eight years ago—left behind.

Trace walked into the bedroom and found Delainey exiting the shower. Her skin glistened from the moisture as she wrapped a towel around her and his groin immediately tightened with awareness in spite of the tension between them. She cut him a short glance but otherwise ignored him. Even as angry as he was, the sight of her near-nude body had an effect on him. He forced himself to look away. The worst thing he could do right now was to confuse the situation with more sex. "I didn't mean to squelch your dreams," he started. She regarded him warily, and he said, "I just didn't understand how much they meant to you. If I'd known, I would have stood by you."

"Don't you think it means something that it didn't even occur to you?" she asked. "The fact is, you are who you are and I am who I am. And as much as we are attracted to one another, we're not meant to be together."

"Maybe." He hated the possibility, but he had to admit there was some truth to it. "But if we're not meant to be together, why are we so attracted to one another? And I'm not just talking about a physical attraction, Delainey. When I'm around you I feel whole, and when you're gone I feel half a man. You know I don't necessarily believe in all that 'soul mate' stuff, but all I can go off of is how I feel when I'm with you. I know when you leave it will hurt as much as it hurt the first time, and I should cut you loose now. But I can't bring myself to do that. I want to squeeze every last moment with you until there are none left. But how do you feel? Am I alone in this? Are you just doing time with me while you're here?"

"No, of course not," she cried, clearly distressed. "Everything in my life is complicated—except how I feel about you. You are the one thing in my life that always made sense. I love you, Trace, and I always will." Her eyes filled with tears. "But I guess my dream is bigger than the love I feel, because I can't imagine giving it up, not even for you. I just can't. And I might grow to regret this and I might end up hating the decision I'm making right now, but I can't bring myself to give up."

"I don't want you to give up. One of the things that I've always loved about you is your determination. You are one of the fiercest people I've ever known. I would never ask you to sacrifice that quality in yourself for me. But I can't change who I am in the hopes of keeping your love, because in the end it would destroy the very things you love about me."

The corners of her mouth lifted in a sad smile as she said, "We're a pair to draw to, aren't we? I wish it were simple and I wish the answer were neat and tidy. If I were another kind of person, I would gladly spend my life with you. You're good and kind and solid. Any woman would be lucky to have you by her side."

"If you were another kind of person, I wouldn't want you. You've always been perfect for me. So, what's the answer? Do we carry an undying flame for one another for the rest of our lives but move on with other people? Or do we try to squelch our feelings and try to forget what we once had?"

She grimaced and he knew that she found the idea as distasteful as he did, but what choice did they have? "I don't know what the answer is," she admitted, feeling trapped by their circumstances. "Do we have to figure it out today?"

she implored. "Can't we just keep doing what we're doing until it's time for me to leave?"

"We can, but how much damage are we going to do to each other in the meantime?"

She closed her eyes as if trying to hold back tears, and he went to her without hesitation. "I want to be the kind of woman you deserve," she said against his chest. "Dreams of you and our time together was all that kept me going for the longest time. At my lowest point, I imagined you by my side, cheering me on, and it gave me the strength to climb back to my feet even if you were never actually there."

"You are always in my heart, no matter how many miles are between us."

They held each other for a long moment, allowing the silence to fill the space between them until they ran out of time and needed to get ready. Trace's heart felt heavy in his chest and he knew it would only get worse, but he couldn't let her go, not yet. There was no help for it. He was, and likely would always remain, helplessly in love with Delainey Clarke.

DELAINEY NEEDED the distraction of work to keep her from weeping. Why couldn't she have been a different kind of person, the kind of woman who could happily be a wife and mother as so many of her friends from school had? It wasn't that she didn't want to be a wife or mother. It was that she couldn't fathom being any of those things without reaching that pinnacle of success first. What kind of example would she be to her children if she could not follow her dreams? How could she teach them to reach for the stars when she had been content with only staring at them? She used to daydream about what she and Trace's children might look like, until she realized she couldn't stay and he wouldn't go. Now the thought of children was like a sharp pain to her heart. She quickly realized the best way to prevent heartache was to avoid the fancies of her youth.

They had only a few more days of shooting left before she could leave Alaska. She needed to focus on the production because there was no money in the budget for pickup shots later. Today they would spend most of the day shooting with the little girl, and Delainey welcomed the break from Trace's footage. She would go with Trevor to shoot the reenactment scenes while Scott would shoot the remaining footage with Trace. The break would give Delainey some breathing room. Right now her head and her heart were competing for her attention, and she couldn't think straight any longer.

Seconds before they were ready to walk out the front door, she turned to Trace and said,

"I'm sorry for putting the production's concerns ahead of yours with your parents. You do what is right and I'll deal with whatever aftermath might happen. Your mom's safety is most important, and I'm sorry that I didn't see that first."

The warmth in his slow smile told her he appreciated her gesture, and he bent down to seal his mouth to hers in a searing kiss that made her knees wobble. She clung to him as if afraid to let go, and for a long moment it was only her and him in the entire world. But soon enough reality intruded and he reluctantly let go. "Thank you," he said and slipped his hand into hers.

Nothing felt more natural than the two of them leaving for work together.

She purposefully ignored the knowledge that it was an illusion.

When they arrived on location, the crew was already there, sipping coffee to warm up as well as wake up, and the little girl hired to play Clarissa Errington was laughing with Scott as he showed her coin tricks while they waited. If any of the crew noticed that Trace and Delainey always arrived and left together, they wisely kept their opinions and their ribbing to themselves. Delainey spent ten minutes going over the shot list with Scott, and then after a brief introduction to the little girl, whose real name was Molly, Delainey and her crew set off to start shooting the reenactment scenes.

They'd managed an hour into shooting when Trevor started giving her a hard time during a short break so Molly could use the bathroom. "Are you going to pack your man-toy into your suitcase on the flight home?" he asked, and Delainey cast him an irritated glance.

"I'm just saying, you seem attached at the hip. Didn't know if you'd be able to leave him behind."

"First, it's none of your business, and second, refer to the first. How's the light?" she asked, redirecting the conversation. "I was a little worried that her face would be in shadow with all the trees."

"Suddenly you don't trust me to adjust for lighting?" Trevor asked, tsking. Then he said, "You know, he's really not your type."

She stopped writing notes to herself for the editing later and glared at him. "And what do you know about my type?" she asked.

"He's too rugged and manly. You need a man you can push around. Strong women don't need a strong man. It creates a power conflict. You need someone who doesn't care about the power but is turned on by strong women. Like me," he added, shocking her. She stared, unsure of what to say. How'd she miss the signs that Trevor had a thing for her?

"Trevor…I don't know what to say…"

He mistook her awkwardness for something else and grinned. "Baby, you and me are a natural foregone conclusion, and don't say you didn't think of it, too. Why else do you always pick me for your projects?" he pointed out.

Oh, good grief. The reason she always picked him was because he was the best. Definitely not because she was attracted to him. "Listen, hold up. Before you start spouting poetry and bringing me flowers, I have to set you straight. You and I are not a foregone conclusion no matter what signs you thought I was throwing out. We work together and that's it. Sorry."

"Oh." He actually looked dejected, and Delainey felt compelled to pat him awkwardly on the shoulder.

"You're a good camera guy and I appreciate the quality of your work. I hope this doesn't change our working relationship."

"Yeah, sure. It's cool," Trevor said stiffly, recovering some of his swagger. "There are plenty of fish in the sea, you know? It's not going to ruin my day that you're not digging me in the same way."

"Glad to hear it," she said, happy to be done with that conversation. But as she thought about it, she couldn't help but ask, "Out of curiosity, why do you think that I would want a man weaker than me?" That just went against her entire upbringing. Men were supposed to be the strong ones. "Just because a woman is strong doesn't mean she has to have a weak man to balance out the dynamic."

"Wrong. It's like having two magnets of the same polarity—they repel each other."

"No. People aren't magnets," she said firmly. "Besides, your theory as it applies to me is flawed. Weak men disgust me. I need a strong man who can be my equal, not some weakling who will let me push him around."

"Maybe *weak* wasn't the right word, because I'm not a weak guy. But you need someone who isn't threatened by the idea of a woman running the show. I like when a woman takes control. It's sexy as hell. This is why I date older women in power positions. They know what they want and they take it. Especially in the bedroom." He waggled his eyebrows suggestively and Delainey grimaced. "C'mon, don't tell me that you don't like to take control for a little cowgirl action? I bet you're—"

"Stop," Delainey said, instantly covering her ears with her hands. "This conversation just got really inappropriate. Thank you for answering my question, but I'm your boss and I don't want to get busted for sexual harassment." She saw Molly and realized with relief they could get back to shooting. "Molly's ready. Set up for shot fourteen and please watch the shadows. I can't come back to Alaska for pickups."

And then she practically ran away from Trevor, feeling as if she needed a shower.

How could he think that she would be attracted to a weak pushover? Not even close. The idea was so abhorrent and sexually repulsive. No, she was dead certain that Trace was her sexual equal, and if that was true, she was attracted to a man who was possibly stronger than she was. Trace always took control in the bedroom, and it thrilled her senseless. Just thinking of Trace in a sexual manner revved her engine unlike anyone else ever had. She pressed her palms to her cheeks to see if they felt hot.

What a morning. Why hadn't she and Trace spent more time getting sweaty and less time arguing? A slow, private smile curved her lips. Tonight she'd have to rectify that little error in judgment. Tickled by the idea, she set about the rest of the day's shooting with a renewed vigor and dedication.

CHAPTER TWENTY-EIGHT

TRACE AND DELAINEY finished their day of shooting and, after a quick bite with the crew, headed back to Trace's house. While initially the acting thing had been totally foreign, he was starting to fall into a rhythm that he could understand. It wasn't rocket science and it was a lot easier than tracking. All in all, it was the easiest cash he'd ever made.

"I'm going to take a bath," Delainey announced, her voice trailing suggestively as she added, "Feel free to join me...."

He didn't need further encouragement and began stripping before he'd even reached the bathroom. The room was filled with steam as she adjusted the temperature in the antique claw-foot tub he'd purchased at a swap meet with Delainey in mind. She'd always loved baths and he'd planned to surprise her with it on their wedding night as a gift. He'd spent hours restoring it to its former glory, and he was humbled by the open appreciation in her eyes as she sat on the edge in nothing but a towel. "I love this bathtub," she said, smiling. "But then, something tells me you knew I would."

"I bought it for you. For us," he amended, clearing his throat, wondering if they shouldn't talk about the past again. He didn't want anything to upset the mood that was building. After last night, he needed her so badly his hands trembled with the desire to touch her smooth, silky skin, and his mouth went dry at the memory of sinking into her wet heat. Satisfied with the water level, she turned off the faucet and stood, dropping her towel. Her body never failed to incite him to a fever pitch, but he watched with open hunger as she pinned her hair up, exposing her nape, and then gingerly climbed into the steaming water. Her eyes fluttered shut on a groan, and he couldn't wait another moment.

When her gaze landed on his straining erection, she smiled with appreciation and beckoned with her crooked finger. "What are you waiting for?" she teased, and he climbed into the tub so quickly, water sloshed over the sides. She laughed and moved to settle into the cove created by his body, laughing when he couldn't help but prod her backside with his insistent erection.

"Sorry, sometimes I have no control over what happens downstairs...especially with you."

"I like that I drive you crazy," she replied in a husky murmur. "Makes me feel sexy."

"You are the epitome of sexy," he growled against the moist skin at her nape. Her scent, unique to her, filled his senses, and he closed his eyes against the surge of primal possessiveness that followed. His mouth traveled a soft line up to the shell of her ear and nibbled until she moaned and cocked her neck farther to the side to give him better access. He whispered sexy little phrases that he knew pushed her buttons, and when his hand strayed south, she whimpered softly as he teased her flesh with a gentle touch. "You're so beautiful," he said, loving the way her breath caught and her breasts rose and fell with each gasp. Her hardened nipples broke the water like two peaks in the ocean, proudly jutting from her chest and tempting him to rise from the tub, to carry her to the bed, but he wanted to draw out her pleasure first.

He pinched her swollen clitoris with enough pressure to cause her to gasp but not enough to hurt, and she groaned as her hand covered his, encouraging him to apply more pressure. "Yes," she nodded, sliding her tongue along the seam of her lips. "Harder…"

Trace slipped his middle finger deep inside her channel and pushed up, meeting the soft, spongy area behind her pubic bone, and she shuddered against him. He could spend a lifetime listening to her soft cries and sharp gasps of pleasure. His penis was hard as stone, but he paid it no heed, so intent on wringing every ounce of pleasure from Delainey's lips until she was shaking and crying from his efforts.

"I can't take any more," she admitted in a tight, raspy voice. He pressed harder and she melted against him as another shudder passed through her. The little nub pulsed, and he responded by pinching it again. This time Delainey jerked and water sloshed over the sides of the tub. She turned in his arms and launched herself at his mouth, rubbing her breasts against his chest as her tongue slid against his in a wild dance of abandon.

They were breathless by the time Trace lifted them from the cooling water and, after a quick towel-down, they fell onto the bed, entwined with one another. Delainey surprised him when she pushed him down to take his length into her mouth. His eyes rolled in his head as her lovely mouth did terrible, wonderfully wicked things to him until he wasn't sure he could hold back the need to explode. Afraid he might do just that, he pulled her to him and plunged his tongue deep, rolling her to her back. He fumbled for the condom package—their second— and pulled the last condom from the box. "Last one," he said with a grin, and she laughed heartily as she distracted him with plenty of kisses so that he struggled to get the condom on. "You're going to pay for that," he promised after he'd managed to roll the latex on and pounced on her. Her high-pitched squeals quickly turned to breathy moans as he wasted little time in pushing himself as far as he could go inside her willing body. She clasped her arms around his back and urged him to make love to her faster, harder, and he was only too happy to oblige.

His last thought before he tumbled into sweet bliss—he could live and die a lifetime in her arms.

DELAINEY LAY NAKED against Trace's chest with her fingers interlaced with his. The darkness their only cover, she was thankful for the cheerfully glowing woodstove in the other room throwing off plenty of heat to keep them warm. She was sated beyond words to the point of bone-deep lethargy. She could gladly lie in Trace's arms for an eternity. Delainey closed her eyes on a happy sigh, and she would've fallen right to sleep if Trevor's words hadn't come sneaking into her consciousness, robbing her of her well-earned rest. She frowned and Trace must've sensed her disquiet, because he shifted and asked, "What's on your mind?"

Should she share what Trevor had said? Would it make things weird? She didn't want anything to ruin the serenity of the moment, but something about Trevor's assessment of her kept coming back to poke at her.

And not in a good way.

"Someone," she hedged, not wishing to use Trevor's name, "recently told me that a woman like me needs a man who's willing to let me run things. Do you think that's true?"

She could hear the frown in Trace's voice as he asked, "Who said this? Is this someone who knows you?"

"The *who* doesn't matter, but are they right? They said I needed a weaker man than myself if I wanted to be happy. They said you and I weren't right for each other because you and I were both strong individuals."

"That person is plainly an idiot. Who was it, so I can punch him in the face?"

She smiled. "How do you know it was a man?"

"Because that's something a man would say if he were trying to make a move on someone he couldn't have. It's the oldest trick in the book—divide and conquer."

"So you don't believe that I need a weaker man to make me happy?"

"Hell, no. You'd devour a weaker man. You need someone who isn't afraid to stand up to you and tell you when you're being a stubborn brat," he answered gruffly. "But I really don't like talking about this hypothetical perfect man for you when you're lying in my arms naked. Okay?"

"Of course," she agreed, secretly happy with his answer. Trevor was an idiot and he had been hitting on her, which laid credence to Trace's answer. Not to mention, it was exactly how she'd felt about the situation, as well. They were so well-matched in so many ways, except the one that kept them apart. She exhaled softly and snuggled into Trace's side, determined to stop thinking and just enjoy the moment. Delainey was a firm believer in that refusing the gift of happiness was an invitation to misery.

She drifted into a deep sleep where she dreamed of green meadows and snow-capped mountains, butterflies and laughter. And she dreamed of babies. Beautiful, utterly charming babies with eyes of summer blue and blond hair that curled in a wild array of tousled waves and made her want to bury her nose against their sweet scalps. She dreamed of deep, soulful kisses that awakened her spirit and made her feel alive for the first time in years.

And she dreamed of Trace, his handsome face crinkling in laughter and pride as he swung the children in the air, catching them with ease,

mouthing to her "I love you" as their babies
smothered his cheeks with sloppy kisses. Her
heart felt ready to burst with such emotion that
could not be contained. This was joy. This was
happiness in its purest form. But as she started
to walk toward them, ready to join her family
and be included in the happiness, dark clouds
rumbled from an unknown direction and she
stared at the rapidly changing skyline, knowing a storm was on its way. She called to Trace
and the babies, but they didn't seem to hear
her or the thunder that boomed from behind
the roiling, ominous clouds, and she began to
run, stumbling on hidden rocks on the meadow
floor. No matter how fast she ran, Trace and the
babies got farther away. She screamed Trace's
name but he climbed to his feet and, shouldering each child, began to walk away from her.
"No!" she screamed, running after them. "No!
Please don't go!"

She awoke, drenched in sweat and panicked
as Trace tried to calm her. Delainey clung to
him, so relieved that it was just a dream and
that Trace hadn't left her and taken her babies
with him. But it was then she realized he was
trying to tell her something.

"Your stepmother just called."

"What?" Delainey asked, still a bit disoriented. "What do you mean?"

"I thought the phone ringing had woken you up, but then I realized you were having a nightmare. She left a voice mail." He handed her the cell phone and Delainey accepted it with trembling fingers. She looked to Trace, feeling sick inside. There was only one reason Brenda would be calling this late, and it was not good news. She pressed Play and listened to the message.

"Hi, honey, I know it's terrible late, but I wanted you to find out right away. Your daddy passed about five minutes ago. He didn't suffer none and he's at peace. Call me tomorrow when you can."

Delainey dropped the cell phone to the bed and stared at nothing in particular. Her father was dead. Trace was waiting but she couldn't quite get the words out. When they did finally break free from her mouth, her voice was strangled. "He's dead. He died five minutes ago."

"I'm so sorry, Laney. Do you want to go to your family? It'll just take me a minute to get dressed." He started to climb from the bed, but she stopped him with a desperate shake of her head, tears already starting to flow.

"Don't go. Please stay here with me. I…I'll go tomorrow."

He nodded in understanding and quickly gathered her in his arms. She sobbed against his chest, unable to fathom that her father was dead. Trace had been right. She should've made her peace with him before this moment, but a part of her never truly believed he would die. Her father was stronger than death, meaner than death for sure. But he hadn't been and he was gone.

And now she could do nothing but cry because she hadn't said goodbye or done a single proper thing as his daughter. In fact, their last words to one another had been terse and angry—that's what she had to keep as her lasting memory.

The knowledge made her sob harder.

Trace held her until she passed out from sheer exhaustion.

CHAPTER TWENTY-NINE

DELAINEY CALLED HER CREW and let them know the situation, and everyone agreed she ought to take the day off. Scott, bless his heart, promised to get more B-roll footage so that they were assured of having enough when they returned to Los Angeles. Trevor, surprisingly, made himself scarce and didn't offer anything aside from a short condolence, and Delainey was grateful. She didn't have the stamina to deal with one of his petulant fits today.

Delainey and Trace arrived at her father's house and Delainey walked in, unsure of her reception given how she'd avoided her father's hospital room. But Brenda gathered her in a tearful hug, shocking Delainey with her kindness. "He didn't suffer none," Brenda said, patting Delainey softly. "He just went to sleep and never came back. Wherever he is, he's not in pain no more, and that's what matters."

She nodded, unsure of how to handle Brenda's lack of judgment. Shouldn't she be mad at her for avoiding Harlan when he needed her the most?

She pulled away and realized her brother wasn't there. "Where's Thad?" she asked, wiping at the stray tears that had escaped. "I thought he'd be here."

"He's down at the funeral home making the final arrangements for me. I was plain tuckered out and he offered to do it, bless his heart."

"Oh," she said, feeling small for not helping one bit. If her father knew he was sick, he probably made arrangements for the funeral and whatnot, but Delainey didn't know a thing about what needed to happen next. She didn't even know if her father had made a will. He probably had but the fact that she knew absolutely nothing about her father's final days made her heartsick and ashamed. Delainey glanced at Trace and he, sensing that she was under water, came to stand by her side. She immediately leaned on him for support as she offered a tremulous smile of gratitude.

"Is there anything you need?" Trace asked solicitously, and Brenda shook her head as she wiped her nose with a tissue. "You'd be surprised but my Harlan did everything ahead of time. He wanted to make sure everything was taken care of when he went. But I appreciate the offer. We're planning to have a small get-together here tomorrow for his friends and crew. He wasn't much for social gathering but he was known for being fair and honest, and that carries a lot of weight around here."

"I'll help," Delainey offered, swallowing the lump in her throat. "Whatever you need."

"That's good of you, sweetie. I appreciate it. I know you're going through your own pain, too. Your daddy told me that you had a rough time of it growing up. I just wished you could've worked that out before he went. He was real proud of you."

Delainey fought the violent urge to run from anything that resembled praise from her father, even secondhand, but she jerked a short nod of acknowledgment, not trusting her voice. Trace put his arm around her and she leaned into him, so grateful he was there. Brenda's red-rimmed eyes cleared as she found a purpose, saying, "Can't think on an empty stomach. How about you join me in the kitchen?"

Trace looked to Delainey for the okay, and she nodded and said, "Would you mind checking on Thad and making sure he's got everything under control? I know he probably does, but maybe the moral support would be nice."

"Are you sure?" he asked.

"Yes, I'll be fine. Thank you," she said, rising on her tiptoes to press a soft kiss on his lips. "Call me if you need anything."

Delainey watched Trace go and took a deep

breath as she joined Brenda in the kitchen. She could tell Brenda was the kind of woman who equated food with love, and she was going to make sure Delainey felt loved, judging by everything she was getting ready. Brenda pulled out leftover lasagna and started reheating it while directing Delainey to make a salad. "I'm not really all that hungry, actually," Delainey said, but Brenda waved away her comment, clearly intent on putting some more meat on her bones.

"Honey, if you're going to stick around any much longer, you're going to have to fatten up or you're going to freeze in the middle of the night," Brenda said, clucking at her. "Besides, I need to do something to keep my heart from breaking in two, so please let me feed you something."

"Okay," Delainey said, smiling. "Although I won't be staying for long. I have to head back to California soon."

"Oh, that's a shame," Brenda said. "I'd hoped that you and that young fellow of yours had worked things out."

Delainey quieted. She realized Brenda had probably made assumptions from the obvious way Delainey had been leaning on him for support, but she sensed that Brenda knew more about her history with Trace than what she'd just seen. "How do you know about me and Trace?" she asked.

"Oh, honey, your daddy told me, of course. We didn't have any secrets. I know it's hard to believe, but your daddy had changed. It's just a shame you never got to see it."

"If he'd changed so much, why was he so terse with me?" she asked, unable to mask the bitterness leaching out.

"Sometimes, even when we want to, it's hard to break free from the roles we play in our lives. Your daddy didn't know how to be anything but what you remembered of him. But I know that if he'd had more time, he would've been able to show you."

Was that true? She had no way of knowing. It already felt as if she'd tumbled down a rabbit's hole. What was one more thing to add to the incredulous nature of her life right now? She focused on shredding the lettuce, but a tear fell from her eye. She wiped at it and rinsed her hand, trying not to get tears in the salad. "What did he tell you about Trace?" she asked, curious.

"He said he was a good man and that if you were smart you'd find your way back to him," Brenda said. "Nothing harder to find than a good man. I spent twenty years married to a no-good, rotten—pardon my language—SOB, and I was glad to be rid of him. I used to cry myself to sleep because I never had any children, but I realized later it was a blessing in disguise. When Bart died, I near cried myself silly with joy because I hadn't had the courage to leave him like I should've. I found Harlan a few years later."

"You weren't married for long," Delainey said. "You must feel cheated to have spent all that time with your ex only to lose your new husband after a few years."

Brenda shook her head resolutely. "Absolutely not. Any time with Harlan was a blessing and I was grateful. He was a good man."

"I have to admit, it throws me when you say things like that. You do realize he used to beat me and my brother? He was a terrible father."

"All in the past, love. There's so much that we do in our youth that provides the wisdom for our later years. Your daddy was very sorry for all that."

"I'm sorry. I have a hard time believing that. You didn't know him like I did."

"No, I knew him better. He shared with me things a parent couldn't possibly share with their child."

"Such as?" Delainey bristled a little.

"Such as the toll it took on him to have a wife who was clinically depressed."

"My mother was depressed because she had

my father for a husband," Delainey snorted, irritated. "She probably died to get away from him. Their life was no picnic, I can promise you that."

"Love, you remember things as would a child who is loyal to the memory of their mother. I have no allegiances that cloud my judgment. Your mother was sick and beyond your daddy's ability to help or understand. In the end, her death was surely a blessing to them both. That's harsh, I know, but life is filled with harsh twists and turns, and you of all people should understand that." She sighed. "My aunt Dee was sick like your mama. She ended up killing herself one fine summer day. I can still hear the echo of the shotgun in the sweltering Kentucky stillness and the dogs barking like crazy." Brenda lost the far-off look in her gaze and grabbed a few plates. "The thing is, sometimes there's nothing we can do for those who are determined to leave this earth. Wherever they go, they're happier than they were. At least that's how I like to think of it."

"I'm sorry about your aunt, but my mother didn't kill herself," Delainey said quietly, not quite sure what to think of what Brenda had shared. Ordinarily, her first reaction would've been to tell her to mind her own business and leave, but Brenda's matter-of-fact kindness stopped her. The truth was, she hadn't known much about her mother, only that she'd always seemed sad. Delainey had attributed her sadness to the fact that she was in a miserable marriage. She didn't know what to think about the possibility that her mother had been mentally ill.

Brenda noticed her disquiet and said, "Honey, don't waste your life thinking about what was when you have an opportunity to create new memories. Do you love this man, Trace?"

"Yes," she answered cautiously. "Unfortunately, there are bigger things to consider."

"Not true," Brenda disagreed. "Having been a person who lived without love for too long, I can tell you it's the only thing that matters. Your daddy showed me how a man is supposed to treat a woman, and he treated me right." How was she supposed to argue that point? Delainey swallowed a sigh and focused on the salad, but Brenda wasn't finished. "The first time you walked through that door, you had a chip on your shoulder as big as a boulder. It was written all over your face how unhappy you were to be there. But I don't think your unhappiness was solely because of your issues with your daddy. I think you have unfinished business with your man."

"He's not really my man," Delainey corrected

Brenda with a flush in her cheeks. "He's his own man."

Brenda chuckled. "Oh, I know it's not politically correct to call a man yours, but honey, when you've lived a life like mine, when you have a man worth holding on to, you take pride in calling him your own. And if you love him, you'd better do what you can to hold on to him before he finds someone smarter than you." Delainey drew back, hating the idea of Trace moving on to someone else. But wasn't that the natural order of things? If she was planning to leave, how could she expect him to sit and wait on the shelf like a forgotten toy?

Brenda chuckled knowingly as she ladled steaming portions onto two plates. "Darlin', you've got to stop listening to that head of yours and just go with your heart. Your head carries all sorts of angry memories, but your heart just holds on to the love."

Delainey was tempted to roll her eyes if only to dispel the feeling that Brenda knew what she was talking about, but she reined the impulse before she ended up insulting the kind woman. She wanted to retort that the older woman didn't understand the rigors of a career in television and film, but she knew Brenda would call her out for making excuses, so she remained silent.

"Time to eat," Brenda announced, carrying

both plates to the scarred table in the dining room. Delainey dutifully followed, carrying napkins and utensils, but her mind was moving in dizzying circles. Had her father changed so much for Brenda? Had he become a man worth knowing? Did it matter? No matter how he'd changed for Brenda, he hadn't changed for her, and he'd been a miserable human being to live with.

"This is good," she said around a hot bite, but she didn't actually taste anything. She was too twisted in knots to truly enjoy her stepmother's Southern cooking. She just hoped Trace came back soon. She'd had just about all she could handle of this episode of *This Is Your Life in a Parallel Universe* before she completely broke down and lost it.

If only she could simply change the channel and move on.

"Your daddy loved my cooking, said I put all the good stuff he wasn't supposed to have into everything I made. Secret is I cooked everything with butter and plenty of cream. I tried to stop on account of his doctor making stern faces at me when I took him to his appointments, but he said to me, 'Baby, you and your cooking is about the only thing keeping me going these days. Don't deny an old man his luxuries.' And so I just kept on cooking him his favorites because that's what my man wanted," Brenda said, choking up for the first time. But with obvious effort she recovered and put up a soft smile. Must've been that Southern hospitality ingrained in her to never let a guest feel unwelcome or uncomfortable. Unbidden, Delainey grasped Brenda's hand and squeezed. She wasn't a hugger but she could do this. Brenda seemed to sense this and smiled gratefully, a moment of understanding passing between them, and Delainey realized no matter what kind of man her father was to her, he'd been a good husband to Brenda and it wasn't her place to say otherwise.

CHAPTER THIRTY

IT WAS DIFFICULT not to think of his own parents as he watched Delainey go through the motions of grief in preparing for her father's funeral. He knew she was struggling with the realization that her father had changed and also that he hadn't done so in time for her to reap the benefit. Trace remembered all the times Delainey had cried on his shoulder when they were young and how helpless he'd felt to protect her. Each time she'd come to him with a new bruise, his young heart had beat frantically as his fists had curled. But his own father had cautioned him to keep his distance.

"We don't know all the facts," Zed had warned, rushing to calm a hotheaded seventeen-year-old Trace.

"What's there to know, Dad? He beat her! Didn't you see the bruises on her arms and legs? We have to do something!"

"No one likes to be told how to parent their kids. Harlan is a rough man, but he's fair and honest."

"In business, but not with his kids," Trace had shot back. "How am I supposed to just stand by and watch her get abused and do nothing? What kind of man would I be?"

"You're not a man yet," Zed had reminded him, placing a hand on his shoulder. "To Harlan, you're still a boy, and he won't respect a thing you have to say. I'm not saying I agree with his methods, but Delainey is a tough girl. She'll come out fine."

Trace had fought childish tears, hating that his father wasn't charging down Harlan's door with him to rescue Delainey, but what could he do? "She's hurting, Dad," he said, his voice breaking. "And I can't do anything about it."

"I'm proud that you want to protect your girl, but this isn't a fight you can win right now." Zed held his son's gaze for a long moment, and Trace saw his father falter in his own advice. Zed didn't like the bruises he was seeing, either. Finally, Zed said, "If it makes you feel better, I'll have a word with Harlan. Maybe it'll help. But maybe it'll make it worse," he warned Trace. "Like I said, no man likes when another man oversteps his bounds when it comes down to parenting or running their household."

"Yeah, well, maybe if he wasn't an abusive asshole, no one else would feel compelled to step in," Trace said, not even caring that he'd just cursed in front of his father. In this case, it was warranted. Zed must've agreed because he didn't say a word.

Zed had never shared what he'd said to Harlan, but the beatings had stopped, according to Delainey. Shortly after, Delainey had relocated to Anchorage to go to college, and after graduation she had moved in with Trace.

Trace wasn't sure why that particular memory had returned to him at this moment, but it'd left behind sadness in its wake. Where was that man who'd quietly championed Trace's girlfriend— going against his own counsel because his son's heart was breaking?

God, things were a mess. His father was no longer that man. And Trace missed that man. He rubbed at his eyes, wiping away the moisture that gathered in the corners. Was there any way to repair the damage from the past? It wasn't Simone's fault for dying. But the wreckage caused by the aftermath had really done in the Sinclair family, and it seemed they'd all been guilty of simply watching it happen. Things had to change before it was too late. Miranda had been right about their mom and dad. But the most pressing problem was their mom's hoarding. There had to be a way to get through to her, or else Trace was sure they were going to lose their mom just as Delainey had lost her dad.

He could take some of the money given to

him for participating in the pilot to pay for a professional organizer to come in and help straighten things out, but according to Miranda, she'd already tried that. What was he supposed to do in this kind of situation? He didn't know, and worse, he didn't even know where to start. He needed Wade here. It was time to rally the troops, circle the wagons and whatever other saying that worked, because the situation had just gone critical. He supposed he should've called Wade before now, but a part of him wanted to see if he and Miranda could handle this situation on their own. It was time to admit that he needed his older brother, too.

Wade wasn't going to be happy. They'd all taken Simone's death hard, but Wade couldn't handle staying in Alaska after it was all said and done. He understood the need for distance, but Wade had taken it to a new level. Ironic, that Wade and Delainey had fled to the same state. What was so damn great about California? As if on cue, his phone rang, and it was his sister. The phone call he'd been dreading had finally happened with impeccable timing.

"Trace, I need you to come out to Mom and Dad's.… The cops are there and he's being arrested. Mom called me in a panic. We need to be there to calm her down before she has a stroke. Can you meet me there? I'm on my way."

"Yeah," he answered, knowing this was how it was going to go down. He knew Delainey would understand, but he hated leaving her. "I'll be there in fifteen minutes. Hold down the fort in the meantime."

"Okay," Miranda said. Even though his sister was strong, Trace knew this was hard on her. Hell, it was hard on him, too. "See you then."

Trace clicked off and quickly texted Delainey the situation. She texted back "k" then added "good luck" a second later. A rueful smile followed. Luck was exactly what he'd need.

JENNELLE STARED IN HORROR as Zed was hauled out of the garage in handcuffs, bellowing about his rights and threatening to sue every single one of the officers involved in this humiliation and blatant abuse of authority. What was happening? There were three squad cars with lights blazing and officers combing their property, traipsing over their land as if she and Zed were common criminals, crushing her plants and poking their noses where they didn't belong. She rushed over to where an officer was trying to stuff Zed into the patrol car, and another officer fended her off with a terse, "Please stay back, ma'am."

"What is going on?" she demanded, her gaze

darting from one officer to the other. "I want to know what is going on right this instant!"

"Don't say a word," Zed yelled from the back of the squad car, handcuffed and looking like a wild man. "You hear me? Not a damn word!"

Jennelle nodded, but she wasn't sure how to handle this invasion. Never in her life had she ever been so shocked, to the point of speechlessness. Another car rolled up and it was Miranda. Relief flooded her. Miranda would sort this out. This had to be some sort of mistake. They obviously had the wrong person. "Miranda! Oh, my God, thank goodness. They've arrested your father!"

But instead of outrage, Miranda looked resigned and Jennelle felt punched in the stomach. "You knew about this?" Jennelle could barely manage the words. The betrayal by her own daughter was too much to absorb at once. "How could you?"

"I had to," Miranda answered with a fair amount of sadness in her eyes. "You gave me no choice."

"Me?" Jennelle blinked back bewildered tears. "How did I do this?"

"You have a problem, Mom. We're trying to help."

"By having your father arrested? By having strangers violate our privacy? Have you lost your mind?" Her voice had become shrill, but she didn't care. She was screaming mad and humiliated at the same time. Then she noticed two more vehicles pulling up, Trace's and a township car. She looked to Miranda with withering anger. "Your brother was in on this, too? Of all the rotten moves, Miranda…this has to be the top."

"Mom—"

"No. This is unforgivable," Jennelle whispered harshly, too angry to see straight. She turned on her heel, determined to lock them all away from her, but as she approached the house, an officer stepped forward and prevented her from entering. "Sorry, ma'am. Not until we've determined if the dwelling is safe to enter."

She gaped. "Safe?" Jennelle returned her stare to Miranda, and the true ramifications of the day became clear. She pressed her hands to her heart in utter despair. *Oh, Simone…if only you were here. You would've been on my side. You and Wade would never betray me like this….*

The township worker stepped forward with a business card and a perfunctory smile. "Hello, Mrs. Sinclair. My name is Stella Rogers and I'm with Social Services. We're here to help you," she said, speaking slowly as if Jennelle were a child. "We need you to stay out here with your daughter while we assess the home, okay?"

"No, it's not okay," she snapped, causing the woman to pull back in alarm. "My privacy has been violated and I will not tolerate any more. Do you hear me? I will sue and take every single one of you to court for committing this abomination—and that includes you two Judases!" She stabbed a finger toward Trace and Miranda.

Miranda looked ready to cry, but Jennelle didn't believe her tears, not for one second. The girl had always hated her, and this was simply a new and creative way to hurt her. Trace's mouth firmed in a disapproving line but he said nothing to Jennelle, instead motioning for the officer and the horrid Social Services woman to go ahead.

Embarrassment heated Jennelle's cheeks as she watched strangers push their way into her home, armed with masks and clipboards and a camera. Rigid with anger, she turned to her children and said, "I hope you're happy."

"Mom—" Miranda started, but Jennelle put her hand up to silence her. There was nothing her daughter could say to fix what she'd done. Nothing.

Several minutes later, the group emerged from Jennelle's home, some coughing and gasping for air as if they'd just emerged from the sewers. Jennelle glared at what she believed were theatrics. "Are you finished?" she asked stridently.

"Yes, Mrs. Sinclair," Ms. Rogers answered, pulling her mask free and drawing deep breaths of air. She seemed relieved to be outside again, and it was a long moment before she'd gathered herself to speak again. "Your daughter was absolutely correct—that home is no longer habitable." She ripped a notice free from her clipboard and handed one copy to Jennelle and one to the awaiting officer, who then tacked it to the front door. The word "Condemned" stood out in angry red letters. "Until this home is inspected and cleared, no one is to return. Am I clear, Mrs. Sinclair?"

"This is my home. Bought and paid for. You can't tell me where to live."

"She can if your safety is at risk," Trace said firmly. "And she has just told you that this house is a safety risk."

"And where, pray tell, am I supposed to live?" she asked.

"You can stay with me and Talen," Miranda offered, and Jennelle was astounded she would even suggest such a thing after the stunt she'd pulled.

"I would rather sleep outside," she answered.

"You brought this on yourself! How many

times did I try to help you get things cleaned up and you refused? If you had taken control of your own situation, we wouldn't have had to step in. Do you think we like being the bad guys? You're our parents, for crying out loud! Try acting like it! Do you have any idea what it's like to have parents who are acting so shamefully? It's embarrassing!"

"Don't you talk to me about embarrassment when you've spent the last few years whoring around like a common floozy!"

The social worker and police officer shifted in discomfort at the private conversation, but Jennelle didn't care. She was beyond caring what others thought of her and her life, but if Miranda wanted to throw stones, Jennelle could throw them right back.

"Well, it seems you have a lot to talk about," Ms. Rogers said, pulling a hasty exit and taking the officer with her.

"If Simone were here—"

"She'd never step foot in that house," Miranda cut in with exasperation.

"This isn't helping," Trace said sternly. "What's done is done. Stop being stubborn and let Miranda take you in temporarily. You need a place to sleep at night, and you're not staying here."

"I'd rather stay in a hotel."

"Everything is booked because of moose season," Trace said.

"Then I'll stay with a friend," Jennelle said.

"Who?" Miranda asked caustically. "I don't believe you have friends anymore."

"Miranda," Trace warned, shooting her a look. "That's not helpful." To Jennelle, he asked, "Who will you be staying with?"

"None of your business."

"Mom, here's what I think is going to happen. We'll leave and you'll go right back into that house, not caring that you're prohibited from doing so."

That's exactly what she was going to do. "I've been living in that house for longer than you've been alive. It's my house and I won't be ousted from it!"

Miranda looked to Trace, frustrated. "What are we going to do? Hog-tie her and throw her in the backseat?"

"You wouldn't dare," Jennelle gasped, outraged that Miranda would speak so casually about doing something so horrendous to her own mother. But then why was she surprised? Miranda had always been rough around the edges, just like her damn father. But as mad as Miranda was, Jennelle didn't know if she wouldn't try to do just that. She wouldn't put it past Miranda to do a late-night check and then haul her out by her hair. Jennelle forced herself to appear as if she were settling down, when in fact she was still so angry. But she'd do anything to get away from her rotten children. "I will stay with Florence. I'm sure she'll take me in for the night until I can get this mess settled," she said stiffly.

"Florence would be a good choice," Miranda agreed, then added under her breath, "If she'll take you."

"She is a good friend. Once she hears that I've been kicked out of my house by my own children, I'm sure I'll get the assistance I need."

"Great," Trace said, glad to have a solution and completely ignoring the sarcasm in Jennelle's voice. "We'll get this figured out and then you'll see that we're doing this for your own good."

"Not likely," Jennelle disagreed, not interested in discussing the merits of their actions. Her gaze followed the officers removing the many plants Zed had so carefully tended, and although she wasn't sorry to see them go, she was mortified for her husband's treatment. "Now, Trace, you will need to take me to the police station so I can bail out your father."

"Okay," he said, sharing a glance with Miranda—the two conspirators. "Do you need to grab anything from the house?"

Jennelle paused, indeed wishing she had some personal items, but when she realized how much effort it would take to procure those belongings, she lifted her chin and proclaimed she needed only a toothbrush, which she could buy in town. Then, she walked past Trace as if he were not her son but simply her driver.

Because in her heart, that's where he'd been relegated.

As for her daughter? She no longer had two daughters.

CHAPTER THIRTY-ONE

THE FOLLOWING MORNING, as Trace and Delainey prepared for Harlan's funeral and wake, the silence between them was fraught with personal troubles as each privately processed the most recent events. Trace had more than enough to keep him preoccupied, and yet with everything that had happened, in the back of his mind he struggled with the knowledge that Delainey's time in Alaska was rapidly drawing to a close. The shoot was nearly finished, and all that remained were a few last-minute add-on shots that Trevor had suggested and Delainey had agreed on. He wasn't sure if she'd agreed because she truly believed they needed the footage or if she was trying to stay a little longer. He hoped it was the latter. He hated to think he was the only one struggling with saying goodbye.

Delainey came over and helped him with his tie, straightening it gently before pressing a sweet kiss on his lips. "Your mom can't stay mad at you forever, right?" she asked.

"I'm not sure. According to Miranda, she's a

hell of a grudge-keeper. I've never seen her so mad. I felt like shit doing that to her, but that house…it's beyond belief."

"You know she needs professional help. It's not going to get better just because you say it will. She doesn't believe there's a problem. And your dad, well, he's going to face criminal charges. How much was the bail?"

"Five thousand," he answered grimly.

"Did your mom pay it?"

"No. She didn't have the money and I told her I didn't, either."

"Why'd you lie?" she asked.

"Because I wasn't about to spend good money on a man who'd already given up on life. If I need to spend that kind of money on my parents, it'll be to help my mom get better. Besides, he's safe in jail and he doesn't have access to his pot. Maybe he'll start thinking clearly for the first time in eight years."

Delainey nodded with understanding. "I always remember your parents being so nice. Your mom taught me how to make strawberry freezer jam. I still use her recipe to this day. And your dad…he may well have changed my life all those years ago. I don't know what he said to my dad, but he stopped beating me after that one visit from Zed. I'll always be grateful for that, and you know what? I think my dad, in his own way, was thankful someone else had called him on the carpet for his behavior, because he respected your dad and never said a word against him. It's hard to reconcile the reality of your parents today with who I remember them to be."

"You and me both. We never could've imagined that Simone's death was going to rip us all apart."

She quieted, slowly smoothing his tie before stopping to regard him with tears in her eyes. "I shouldn't have abandoned you like I did when Simone died. I was a stupid, naive girl who didn't realize the damage that was being done. Can you ever forgive me?"

He traced her jawline, loving her so much it hurt. "I forgave you a long time ago. I didn't realize how selfish I was being when I assumed you wanted a life here with me. I didn't understand how it wasn't enough for you."

"Oh, Trace…I wish it had been enough. I really do. Sometimes I close my eyes and imagine my life with you and I feel stuffed with happiness. But then I think of my career and how I would have to give up everything I ever dreamed of, and that happiness drains away. I don't want to resent you and I don't want to hate myself. I wish there was another way, but I don't see how it all works out."

"I know," he agreed, knowing there were no easy answers for either of them. He kissed her forehead and exhaled a long breath. "What time is the funeral?" he asked, putting an end to the conversation before they both fell into a morose quagmire.

She wiped at her nose. "Ten. We need to leave in about fifteen minutes."

"Are you okay?" he asked.

She nodded bravely. "I think I am. Because of you."

"No, you're a strong woman. You'd have been fine without me."

She shook her head resolutely. "No. Without you I wouldn't have made it. You're my strength, Trace Sinclair, and it's high time I admit that. Your love makes me strong. Even if you're not with me. Thank you for being you. Always."

His eyes stung and he had to look away before he embarrassed himself by bawling. How had fate dealt them such an unfair hand? To know that they were meant for one another and yet fated to live apart? How was he supposed to move on? Meet someone else? His heart was permanently branded with Delainey's ownership, and it felt right.

It was the only thing that felt right these days. So why was it ultimately wrong?

THE NEXT FEW HOURS Delainey floated through her father's funeral and wake in a surreal fog. It hardly seemed possible her father was dead. How many times as a teenager had she wished for his boat to sink so she'd never have to see him again? Too many to count.

She smiled and murmured her thanks and appreciation as a multitude of people offered their condolences for her and Thad's loss, but she was on autopilot, smiling when appropriate and accepting well-meaning hugs and handshakes from strangers and a few people she remembered from her distant past. It was so odd to her to hear the stories of her father that directly contradicted everything she'd known of him when she was a child. Hearing what a good man he was struck a discordant chord, one that she had difficulty hiding.

"It's a good thing you work behind the camera," Trace murmured against her ear. "Because you are a terrible actress."

She supposed that was accurate. "It's hard," she said, moving over to a private spot ostensibly to grab a few bites to eat. "It's as if they're talking about a man I never knew."

"I'd say that's probably true. The man they're mourning isn't the man who raised you," he said. "But I guess you need to get to the point where you can accept that he'd changed and let that be your new reality."

"And I'd say that's impossible."

A tiny smile curved his lips that made her want to kiss him...or slap him. She did neither. "It's unfair of me to begrudge them their memory even if it doesn't jibe with mine, right?"

"Something like that."

How had Trace become so wise when she'd somehow remained stagnant? "I really appreciate you being here with me right now. I can only imagine what you're going through with your own parents. It sucks all the way around."

"Yeah, it does," he agreed. "But you can't fix a problem by ignoring it."

"So they say," she quipped drily. "But maybe the people who said that little nugget of advice weren't doing it correctly."

He chuckled. "Perhaps." He popped a cherry tomato in his mouth. "About that strawberry jam... If I bought the strawberries, would you make me some? I haven't had my mom's jam in years. I was plain addicted to it."

"Why do you think I learned how to make it?" she answered back with a coy smile. The venue was inappropriate for anything but mourning, but why was he becoming even more handsome than before? Dressed in his Sunday best, he looked sharp and clean, which made her want to get dirty right that second. "I wish I could kiss you right now," she said.

His gaze darkened and an awareness stole across her body. "There isn't a moment that goes by that I don't want to do wicked things to you," he said for her ears only. She bit her lip and grinned, her heartbeat quickening. "Later," he promised, and she followed him with her gaze as he returned to the gathered people, talking with folks he knew and otherwise playing the host so she could collect herself.

Thad joined her, grabbing a plate and loading up before the food was all gone. Her boyishly good-looking brother seemed more grown-up than he had before. When she'd left, he'd been a kid. Now, he was in charge of their father's fishing operation. "You did a good job with the arrangements," she said to her brother.

He shrugged off her compliment, saying, "Pops did all the work, and I just put it into play. He knew this was coming and didn't want anyone, especially Brenda, to be stressed over it."

"He really loved her, didn't he?" she mused. Thad nodded. Delainey wished she'd seen them together in better times just once. Maybe that would've helped her to see how he'd changed. "She's a good woman."

"Brenda is…a very good woman. I wasn't sure about her at first, but to know Brenda is to love her. I think Pops never realized how to live until Brenda came around to show him. She brightened his life. I wish you could've known her sooner."

"Me, too."

Silence followed for a long moment until Thad asked, "So, after everything…you still planning to go back to California?"

It was a loaded question and the answer brought a lot of pain, but she wasn't going to lie. "My life is in California now. My career… everything I care about…" No, that part wasn't true. *Most* of everything she cared about was here. She looked away, buffeted by recent events. "I don't know, Thad. Seems much simpler to go back to the way things were. People won't get hurt that way."

"Who won't get hurt?" he asked but didn't give her a chance to answer. "I think you're running away again because *you* don't want to get hurt. It's all right, Laney. Just fess up. Own it. You're afraid of what being here might mean, not to your career but to your heart. You left behind a lot when you split. I think you want to run away because it hurts to be reminded."

"Thad, you don't understand. It's complicated," she said but then stopped. Who was she trying to convince? Her brother could plainly see through her excuses, and she was doing them both a disservice by continuing to blather on about nothing that mattered. She barked a short, embarrassed laugh. "You caught me. I *am* scared. What if Trace and I weren't meant to be together and I throw everything away on something that isn't built to last? I have a lot to lose, and there are no do-overs."

"Seems to me you have more to gain if it works out," Thad pointed out. "I'm just saying...you love him. Shouldn't that make things pretty simple? It would for me."

Something in Thad's voice caused her to regard him with surprise. "Are you dating anyone special?" she asked, embarrassed that she knew so little of her brother's personal life.

"No," he answered, shaking his head. "But I know if there were someone who loved me the way Trace loves you...nothing would stand in my way. Nothing."

She stared, unable to believe the words coming from her baby brother. "How'd you get so smart?" she asked.

A small grin crooked his mouth and he shrugged. "I may not have been a great student in school, but I pay attention to what matters."

That you do, little brother. She pulled him into a fierce hug. "I love you, Thad."

"I love you, too, Laney."

As they broke apart and Thad returned to

mingle with the guests, Delainey hung back and closed her eyes. She wished she could follow Thad's advice. But there was a part of her that stubbornly refused to yield—a spark of fire that burned dangerously hot to the touch and resisted any attempts to put it out. And it was that part of herself that knew as much as she wanted to stay and build a life with Trace, she would board that plane back to California, no matter how much it hurt.

Because her ambition was like a hungry beast and it would devour Trace if he stood in its way. She could never hurt him like that—it's one of the reasons she'd left in the first place. And nothing had really changed.

CHAPTER THIRTY-TWO

"SORRY, ZED, seems like no one is bailing you out," Eddie Polk, a longtime officer, said with an expression of chagrin.

He'd been hauled in kicking and screaming, outrage outstripping good sense, but sitting in a cell for a few hours had managed to cool his rage, leaving behind regret and the knowledge that he'd let things spiral out of control for too long. Zed had known Eddie for near thirty years, and it was an embarrassment to be sitting on the other side of the bars. But what was done, was done. He supposed he had it coming, but it was a sour pill to swallow just the same.

"You need anything? We have extra blankets if you need," Eddie asked.

"I'm good," Zed said, settling against the wall on his narrow bed. "Thanks for asking."

"No problem, Zed. You holler if you need anything. I'm sure you're going to be let out soon enough."

Zed nodded and closed his eyes. He could feel the last trace of THC leaving his body, and total sobriety wouldn't be far behind. How long had it been since he'd been completely sober? He couldn't remember. He'd always enjoyed a little recreational marijuana use, which Jennelle had tolerated. But after Simone had died, he'd gone from using recreationally to using it to get through the day. And once he was stoned all the time, he couldn't carve for shit and needed a new source of income. He rubbed at his eyes, wondering how things had gotten so sidewise so quickly. Shame and regret flooded his old bones, and he felt older than his actual years.

He must've dozed off because he awoke with a start when a familiar voice started insulting him.

"Look at you…you look like hell. Wake up, you sorry drug addict." Rhett Fowler, a man he'd once considered his best friend, stood glaring at him from the other side of the bars, plainly disgusted with what he saw.

"What do you want?" Zed asked, not interested in hearing Rhett's opinion of the situation. "Come to gloat?"

"Oh, get over yourself. I've come to bail your ass out."

Zed stared at his old friend. "What for?"

"Damn if I know," Rhett grumbled. "But I've come to bail you out just the same. Unless you're enjoying your stay at the Homer Community Jail. If that's the case, I'll just collect my five grand and leave you be." Rhett's gaze swept the small jail cell, resting on the toilet, and he shuddered. "Make your choice."

A part of him was resigned to sitting in his cell as a penance for letting his family down, but another part of him was anxious to see just how bad the damage was to his pot garden. It was the latter that scared him. "I think I'll stay," he answered slowly, realizing it was the best, if not desirable, choice.

Rhett narrowed his stare at his old friend. "Why?"

"Because this is where I need to be right now."

"You don't trust yourself, do you?" Rhett said with a sad shake of his head. "Zed, you've got yourself a real bad addiction. What are you going to do about it? You can't stay locked in this cell forever. Your family needs you. Your wife needs you most."

"Jennelle ask you to bail me out?"

"She did. What's this about her getting kicked out of the house?"

"I don't know…something about the house being condemned until further notice," Zed answered, shifting with guilt. He'd known how bad the conditions were, and yet he'd allowed his wife to continue living in it. "Jennelle has a problem with keeping stuff," he admitted evasively, not wanting to go into detail. "I moved out of the main house several months ago, and I've been staying in the garage. I made a makeshift living quarters inside the garage."

"That's not the only thing you made in your garage," Rhett said, whistling. "Word is that the cops collected a pretty big pot garden from your garage."

What was the sense in lying? He nodded. "It's true."

"What happened to you, Zed? We used to enjoy a toke now and then, but this? This is out of control. You know that, right?"

"Yes, I know it," he shot back, irritated. "I don't need you to tell me how I've screwed up."

"Don't be taking my head off. You're the one sitting on the wrong side of the bars, my friend."

"I know."

"Jennelle's in a tizzy. Never seen the old gal so worked up. She's right mad at Miranda and Trace. The way I see it, Jennelle's got an even bigger problem than you right now. You need to man up and help your woman. There ain't no cause to be hammering on the kids she's got left. Simone died, and it was a damn shame, but you all got three kids still living. Try to remember that, all right?"

Zed felt the burn of anger starting to build

again, but everything Rhett was saying was right. Didn't make it any easier to hear, though. "You finished?" Zed asked.

"I figure I am, if you're done listening."

Rhett exhaled with an expression of frustration at Zed's stubbornness and turned to leave. Zed called after him with a reluctant thanks. "Means a lot that you'd come down and bail me out, even though we haven't been tight for a few years now. Means even more that you're looking out for my family still. You're a good man, Rhett Fowler."

"Yeah, well don't let too many people know that. I have a reputation to protect." Rhett's weathered face crinkled in a brief smile before he sobered and said, "You know, I've always envied you your family. I've never made it a secret that I thought Jennelle deserved better than you, but she didn't never see no one but Zedediah Sinclair. Had stars in her eyes over you. And now, it's up to you to get your family back on track. They need you. Be the man you used to be—the man who used to be my best friend."

"I don't even know where to start looking for that man," Zed answered, sinking a little deeper into morose self-pity. "Maybe there's no going back to what was."

"You can't go backward but you can move

forward instead of sitting on your ass watching the world go by while stoned out of your gourd."

"I never meant for any of this to happen," Zed said in his defense. "I certainly never imagined my baby girl would be taken and killed. Talk to me when you've suffered a loss like that. It changes you."

Rhett's expression softened at the mention of Simone. "It was hell," he acknowledged. "I loved her like a daughter, but I know that's not the same. But she's gone and you're all still here. That ought to account for something. Your kids are practically begging you to snap out of it. You're going to have an easier time of it than Jennelle. I fear that gal is lost and fighting the way back home, if you know what I mean."

He did. Jennelle's favorite place to be was in that godforsaken room of Simone's that was done up like a shrine. It was creepy and he hated it, but Jennelle screeched like a banshee when he suggested that they turn it into a sewing room or something. In the end, it'd been easier to let her have her way. "What am I supposed to do if she doesn't want the help?" he asked.

"Sometimes you have to take the reins away from a runaway coach, you know? I know Jennelle has a wicked temper, but I've never known you to be afraid of your wife's sharp tongue. You could always handle Jennelle just fine. And she respected you for it. Stop tiptoeing around the situation and just start doing something to fix it before it's too late." Rhett let that sink in for a moment before adding, "You've been hiding for far too long, and maybe I should've said something earlier—not that you would've listened, but that's no excuse—but things gotta change. While you were too busy shutting out the world, the world changed. You've left your kids and wife to twist in the wind, and that's plain selfish. You know I always thought of your kids like my own, but the truth of the matter is there was no cause for me to step into your job when you're still around. They need you, Zed. You've been putting a lot on Miranda's shoulders, and it's not fair. She's got a boy of her own to tend and a new man in her life. All her free time shouldn't be used up tending to your mess."

What could Zed say? It was all true. "I didn't mean to put it all on Miranda's shoulders. And besides, no one asked her to take on the world for me."

"That's a chicken-shit response. Take responsibility, Zed. No more excuses. Man up, for crying out loud, and stop whining and hiding like a little girl behind her mama's skirts."

The disgust in Rhett's voice caused Zed to wince privately, but in a strange way he felt he needed it. He needed to feel the shame and the anger. The shame made him take stock, and the anger gave him the power to do something about it. Miranda had accused him of being apathetic; she'd been right.

"I don't know where to start," he admitted.

Rhett shrugged. "Start with 'I'm sorry.' I'm sure Miranda and Trace would be there for you if you showed an effort. You screwed up. That's all. You can still fix this. I know you can."

Tears stung his eyes but he held back the tears. Rhett was a good friend and an even better man. Zed missed their friendship. "Thanks," Zed said, knowing the word would convey much more than simple gratitude. Rhett smiled and waved goodbye as the awaiting officer let him out.

Zed sighed. He used to have so much pride, so much zest for life. Now, he lived like a hermit, tending his garden, selling enough to get by and getting stoned the rest of the time. He never saw his kids. Never saw his grandson. Hell, by this time, he should've been teaching Talen how to track just as he had all his kids. Could've been teaching the boy some carving tricks. He remembered Miranda saying something about the boy having some talent in that area. As far as his wife? He'd let her down worst. There was so much damage between them that he didn't know if he had what it took to fix what'd been broken.

What a mess.

Well, his court date was in a week and a half. He'd better have things figured out by then, because things had to change. They just had to.

JENNELLE'S HANDS SHOOK with anger as she tried to sip her tea. It took two tries to lift the dainty cup to her lips before she could do so without spilling.

"The nerve," she muttered, unable to stop herself. Florence, a good friend with a sweet disposition, had seemed appalled and unsure of how to help, which was why she'd rushed to put on a pot of tea. In her opinion, tea helped everything. "I never imagined my children to be so wretched and self-absorbed. Where'd I go wrong, Flo?"

"Oh, dear, I don't know that you did anything wrong, Jenny," Flo said, sitting in her floral-backed chair with a frown. "Maybe this is all a misunderstanding?"

Jennelle snorted. "A misunderstanding? I've been kicked out of my home and my husband was arrested like a common criminal. How could that be a misunderstanding?"

Florence fluttered her hands in a helpless gesture. "I don't know. But why would Zed be arrested if he hadn't done anything wrong?" she asked timidly, as if she were afraid to point out the obvious.

Jennelle sniffed and sipped her tea. "It was an overreaction. Zed grows some herbs for medicinal purposes…" she started, but then her throat choked up as if her own body were trying to prevent her from uttering a blatant lie. Her cheeks heated as she took another sip to clear her throat. When she could safely speak again, she said, "Well, in any case, kicking me from my home was unforgivable."

"I don't understand what happened. How could they kick you from your home?" Flo asked, confused. "How bad could it have been?"

Jennelle hadn't let any of her friends visit in years. No one knew just how things had changed. Jennelle tried for a variation of the truth. "Over the years, I've been collecting a few things. It helps to keep me occupied. Zed is so busy with his own thing, and for reasons that I cannot fathom Miranda refuses to let me have a real relationship with my grandson. And my sons never visit. So I found my own hobbies. Now I'm being penalized for my interest in collections. What was I supposed to do? Sit in a corner and twiddle my thumbs? Would that have been acceptable?"

"Of course not," Flo said, disagreeing. "Surely,

that's not what they were thinking. You have the right to your own life. And there's nothing wrong with a collection or two. I collect *Gone with the Wind* plates, and I cherish them. I'd be appalled if someone came along and told me what I could and couldn't purchase with my own money."

"Exactly," Jennelle said, feeling somewhat validated. Of course, she left out the part where she'd not only started collecting but she'd discovered an odd aversion to throwing anything away, too. "Miranda has always found fault with everything I do. She has since she was a child, and now she's found the perfect way to get back at me for some imagined faults. As for Trace, I cannot believe he would betray me this way." She exhaled a shaky breath before finishing her tea. "I don't know what to think anymore. If only Simone were here," she added with a watery sniff.

"Maybe things will look better in the morning," Flo suggested with a kind expression. "Right now, you're angry and hurt…"

"Tomorrow will look the same as today. A new dawn isn't going to change the fact that two of my children betrayed me. Do you realize Trace wouldn't even put up the five thousand for bail? His own father! Tell me again how I didn't go wrong in raising them?"

"Five thousand is a lot of money. Maybe he didn't have it to give," Flo offered, to which Jennelle waved away her suggestion.

"Oh, he had it. Trace has plenty of money to spare. He didn't offer it up because he's angry with his father and siding with Miranda. It's practically a coup."

"That sounds terribly harsh," Flo said, shaking her head and sipping her own tea. "I've never known your children to be that sort of people. I think perhaps you're looking at things through a clouded lens."

"If Simone were here, she wouldn't have let them do this to me," Jennelle said, placing her cup in her lap so she could wipe at the tears gathering in the corners of her eyes. "If Simone were here…she'd be appalled at what her siblings have done. Simply shameful."

"Simone was a dear girl and you were so close. Her death was such a tragedy," Flo murmured.

Jennelle often wondered if people said those things only because they felt it was appropriate given the circumstance and not because they felt any true emotion. How could they possibly understand the pain of losing a child unless they'd gone through it themselves?

"But I do wonder… Simone and Miranda had

been very close as I recall," Flo added. "I don't know that she would've sided with Miranda."

Jennelle stared at her friend, irritated at her recollection at such an inopportune moment. "Yes, well be that as it may, Simone would've been outraged at everything that's happened."

"Something tells me that if Simone were here, none of it would've happened," Flo said quietly.

Jennelle struggled with that small bit of wisdom. So much had changed the day Simone was taken from their lives. What would life have been like if that incident hadn't happened? She blinked at the pain in her heart. Simone had been such a bright, happy girl, and she'd adored her older sister and brothers. They'd all been so happy. Why had fate been so cruel to the Sinclairs? "Yes, you're probably right," she admitted against the anguish building in her chest. "Everything changed when she died."

Jennelle couldn't hold back any longer and sobbed into her hands. Everything was ruined. Life would never be the same, and it had nothing to do with a messy house. She longed for the safety of her special room; it was the closest she came to happiness these days—and Miranda and Trace had taken it from her.

CHAPTER THIRTY-THREE

DELAINEY SETTLED INTO her plane seat and closed her eyes, shutting out the murmurs of the passengers around her. It felt hard to breathe, but she knew why and didn't fight it. This too shall pass, she reminded herself, steeling her nerves against the overwhelming urge to jump from her seat and run back to Trace before he left the terminal. She knew it'd been risky to have Trace drive her to the airport, but he'd insisted and she hadn't had the willpower to refuse him.

Besides, it was good closure, she'd told herself. But now as she sat, rigid and feeling sick for leaving him, she realized it'd been a mistake. She should've taken a cab. Goodbyes weren't good for anyone, much less someone who was fairly certain she was saying goodbye to the one person who was her other half. She signaled the stewardess and ordered a vodka tonic, not caring about the expense of a watered-down alcoholic beverage, just desperate for something to settle her thoughts.

"We haven't even been in the air for fifteen minutes and you're already tossing them back?"

The irritation of Trevor's voice caused her to open her eyes and stare crossly. "Excuse me?" she asked. "Is it any business of yours?"

"Not a bit. Just sharing an observation."

"Well, unless you're sharing information about a camera that I will care about, please keep your observations private."

Trevor shrugged, her curt reply bouncing from his shoulders as he tossed a peanut into his mouth. "I can see why you wouldn't want to stay. Alaska is *b-o-r-i-n-g*," he said by way of conversation, and she wondered why she hadn't switched around the seating to avoid sharing proximity with Trevor. He was such an obnoxious ass. "Nothing like the excitement of L.A."

"That's not a glowing endorsement," she muttered before she could censor herself.

"Not a fan? That's a surprise."

"Why is that surprising?" she asked, grudgingly curious.

"Because it's the opposite of Alaska and you seem to hate Alaska."

"I don't hate Alaska," she corrected him irritably. "I just couldn't follow my dreams there."

"Why not?"

"Because the film industry is in Los Angeles,"

she answered. "And why are we having this conversation?"

"Seems someone ought to have it with you."

"And that person should be you?"

"I guess."

"Why? We're not close."

"That's exactly why I should be the one. Everyone who is close to you has probably already given you loads of good advice that you've promptly ignored. Maybe hearing it from someone you're not close to might make a difference."

"That's some curious logic," she grumbled. "But let's just say for the sake of argument you have a mild point…. What's in it for you? What do you care about my personal life?"

"Everyone deserves to be happy," he said. "Even you."

"Thanks," she said drily, finishing off her drink and signaling for another. She might need to be drunk to listen to Trevor play armchair shrink, but what the hell, maybe it'd make the time go by faster. "So what's this advice you're offering?"

"You say I'm not your type," he said, pointing out the obvious. "And you know what, I'm glad."

"And why is that?"

"Because the guy who is your type, you left

behind without blinking an eye. Lady, that's harsh. Even by L.A. standards."

"I didn't just leave him behind. It's complicated."

"Not really."

"Yes, it is." She glared.

"Only as complicated as you make it. Look, if you spent half the time looking for a solution that you do making excuses, I'll bet you'd have something figured out by now."

"Okay, genius, you seem like you've got it all figured out—what's the solution?"

"Depends…you want to stay in California or Alaska? You have to choose."

"*Duh.* That's been the problem all along," she said, annoyed that Trevor had sucked her into a dead-end conversation. "While I appreciate—sort of—your attempt at helping me with my personal life—"

"Did you know that Alaska has the largest commercial halibut fishing outfits?" he interrupted.

"Of course I know that," she snapped. "My father and brother are longline fishermen. Your point?"

"So if you know that, then you also know that longline fishing is very controversial for snagging unintended fish and fowl."

"Yeah," she agreed slowly, wondering where he was going with this information.

"Seems like a good hook for a series…kind of like *The Deadliest Catch,* but with halibut instead of crab. If I were you, I'd be using the momentum of your pilot success to springboard to a new project—one that doesn't put you at odds with the main star. Doesn't take a rocket scientist to see that your guy isn't one for the limelight."

"No, he hates it," she said, staring at Trevor with newfound appreciation. "So you're saying, pitch the new series while I might still have a chance to open some doors?"

"That's what I'd do, but hey, I'm just a camera guy."

She immediately thought of her brother—handsome, sweet, yet hardworking—and the camera would love him. Except for one thing… She frowned. "It's a good idea but it hinges on one thing—the network has to love Trace's pilot for me to get the green light for the new project."

"Not necessarily," Trevor added with a crafty smile. "You really need to get more cutthroat if you're going to make it. You and I both know that Trace's pilot, no matter how good, is a dead-end street because he's not interested in doing a full series. However, the network doesn't know that. And, even better…neither does the competition.

You polish that pilot until it shines and then when you gain momentum, you pitch that new idea to a competitor and see what happens."

"I'd lose my job," she said, her stomach trembling at the idea.

"Who cares if you're moving on to bigger and better things? Besides, in case you haven't noticed, Hannah's out to get you canned. Unlike you, she's been actively campaigning to put you out on your ass."

"Yeah, I noticed," she said. "It's a huge risk, though."

"Life's all about taking risks, baby. If you're not willing to take big risks, you don't deserve the big reward. There's no room for a Pollyanna in our line of work. Either go after what you want or step aside so you're not in the way of those who will."

She nodded, knowing Trevor was right. She'd long ago figured out that sooner or later Hannah was going to get her fired for something. And she wasn't likely to gain much respect from the network at this point, no matter how well the pilot did. The incentive to stay with her current employer was pretty weak. She could lose her condo if this all went sideways, a voice reminded her. Screw the condo. Why did she care about a building? A building wouldn't love her back. And she certainly didn't suffer any illusions that Los Angeles was the place of stardust and magic that she'd believed when she'd first moved there. What was she holding on to? Fear—that's what she was holding on to, and she was ready to let it go. She regarded Trevor with a growing spark of excitement. "You wouldn't have suggested it if you hadn't already known who would be open to it. Tell me who's in the market."

"On one condition," Trevor said.

"Which is?"

"You take me with you."

Delainey did a double take. "What?"

"I'm not getting anywhere where I'm at. Besides, Alaska could grow on me."

"You said Alaska is boring," she reminded him.

"I just said that to get your goat. Alaska is cool. Besides, with me there, it would cease to be boring," he said with a grin.

She laughed ruefully, not quite sure if she was making a devil's bargain. "Okay, deal. Give me the skinny on who's buying what."

For the next hour Trevor shared everything he'd gleaned from his contacts out there in the field, and by the time they landed at LAX, Delainey was anxious to put their plan into action.

For the first time in a long time, Delainey couldn't wait to get to work.

TRACE CLIMBED THE short steps to where his mother was staying and knocked. Florence, a short, stout woman with a frizz of gray hair, opened the door, and a tremulous smile followed when she recognized him. "Oh, Trace, it's you," she breathed with relief. "Come in, come in. Your mother is in the den." She gestured for him to lean down, and she whispered in his ear, "She's been crying off and on all night. Go easy on her, dear. She's taking things pretty hard."

Trace nodded and followed Florence into the den. Jennelle sat in a chair with a box of tissue, her eyes swollen and her nose red. When she saw Trace, her expression became pinched and she looked away. "Come to oust me from my friend's house, too?" she asked.

"Florence, would you mind giving my mother and I a moment to talk?" he asked, and Florence bobbed a short nod before disappearing.

Trace took a seat opposite his mother and wondered where to begin. He decided to start with the facts. "I thought you'd want to know that dad opted to stay in jail until his court date," he said.

"What are you talking about? Why would he do such a thing?" she asked, wiping her nose with a glare. "That's nonsense. Your father would never choose to stay behind bars."

"Well, he did. Rhett Fowler went to bail him out and he refused. That's straight from Rhett's mouth."

She stared, her mouth trembling. "He wants to stay in jail?"

"I don't think it's that he wants to stay in jail, per se, but I think he knows it's the best place for him right now." He gentled his voice. "He's admitting that he has a problem, and he's using this time to sort things out. The way I see it, this is a good thing."

Her stare withered. "You would."

"Okay, come on, now. Don't you think you're being a little childish here?" he asked gently. "You need to admit that Dad has a problem. The fact that he can admit it and you can't says you have a bigger problem than he does."

"Of course, blame me some more. That seems to be the thing to do these days."

"Mom, I'm not blaming you. I'm being honest. It's high time we all start being honest with each other."

"I've never lied to any of my children, or my husband for that matter."

"Tell me about the room."

She balked, as if chagrined that he'd brought it up. If he'd caught her with her pants around her ankles, she'd likely look no less mortified. "What are you talking about?"

"Miranda said there's something about Simone's old room. You won't let anyone go near it. Why?"

"I don't know what you're talking about."

"Mom."

"What?"

"Tell me about the room."

"That's none of your business."

He sighed. "Mom, you realize we're going to see what's in that room when the cleaners come."

"What cleaners?" she asked, startled. Her voice rose a level. "What are you talking about?"

"Mom, let's not play games. What are you afraid of? That I'll judge you? I promise I won't."

"There's nothing to tell."

He sighed. Whatever she was hiding in that room would become evident soon enough, but it killed him to see her act like this. She was so far from the woman he remembered from his childhood. And he had to take responsibility for his part in the change. "Mom, I know I haven't been there for you, but I promise that's going to change. I think we've all been pushing our heads into the snow, afraid to acknowledge what's happening right in front of our faces, which is that Simone's death took a lot more from this family than just her presence in our lives."

"I don't want to talk about Simone, and I

won't have you blaming your dead sister for the problems in this family," Jennelle said. "If that's all you have to say, you can take yourself off and go."

"Mom," he said, frustrated. "Will you stop and listen for a minute?"

"I'm done listening. You didn't try to talk to me before you ousted me from my home. Why should I listen to a word you and your sister have to say? Don't you understand how betrayed I feel?"

"I can only imagine and I know you're mad, but think of this as a temporary thing. We don't want you out of your home permanently, but if we don't work together, that's exactly what's going to happen—and it won't be by our hand. Your house has been condemned." At the word *condemned,* Jennelle winced and looked away, but Trace couldn't mince words if he was going to get his point across. "We have a certain amount of time to get it cleaned up and approved by Social Services. Do you want to go home?" he asked.

"That's a silly question, not even worth answering," she said sullenly, crossing her arms tightly. "What are you saying?"

"I'm saying, if you want to go home, you're going to have to work with us to make it happen. And that means no more of this attitude."

"Fine. I'll start cleaning it myself."

"No. That's not happening," he said. "You had your chance. It's gotten beyond what you can handle. I've hired a professional cleaning and organizing crew to come out and help."

"Strangers going through my things?" She looked appalled. "I don't think so."

"Then say goodbye to your house," he said, shaking his head. "You can't have it your way. It's going to be this way or no way." She clenched her fists and looked ready to scream, but she held it in. He hated being so firm with her, but he knew there was no backing down. He pressed a bit harder, knowing he was likely going to be the bad guy, but it was time he shouldered the responsibility instead of letting Miranda take the load. "I also want you to see a professional who specializes in hoarding."

"I'm not a hoarder," she spat, her eyes watering. "Was this Miranda's doing?"

"No. It's not Miranda's fault, and you need to stop blaming her," he answered sharply, protective of his sister. "You're unwell, Mom, and I'm going to see that you get the help that you need."

"What does your father say about all this?" she asked, the bitterness in her voice killing him. "Does he agree to this ambush, too?"

"I haven't talked to Dad about it yet. My concern is with you. I have talked to Wade, though. He's coming out to help."

Her lips trembled and she stared at Trace. "Wade is coming?" she asked, her voice barely a whisper. "He's coming home?"

"Yes," he lied. He hadn't actually convinced Wade to come home yet, but if he had to fly to California and drag him back to Alaska by his ears, he'd do it. Wade was as guilty as anyone in leaving to escape the pain of Simone's loss. It was time for Wade to man up and be the oldest brother. "In the meantime, we need to get you ready for the cleanup."

She seemed lost for a moment, and Trace realized it'd been a long time since their mother had had all her children home. The impact of that realization made him feel like a wretch. He'd always blamed his job for his frequent disappearances, but that wasn't entirely truthful. He'd eagerly accepted every job that took him far away because being home had been too filled with memories, both good and bad. And they weren't all of Simone. Truth was, he'd been stuck in the past for a variety of reasons.

But not any longer.

"Whether you like it or not, we're all going to be here for you, Mom," he said in earnest. "And I know you don't believe it right now, but we love you and we care about your welfare. I hope someday you'll come to realize this and forgive us for the hard line we're taking now."

She didn't answer but the wounded look spoke volumes. Lord, grant him patience. If Miranda were to be believed, his mother could hold a grudge like no one's business.

Well, he was about to put that belief to the test.

He just wished Delainey were here to brave the battle lines with him, because this war was going to be hell.

Just the thought of Delainey brought a sharp pain that was difficult to hide. A part of him wished he could follow her, no matter where she went, just to be with her. But he knew that wasn't possible. He loved her desperately, but he knew himself well enough to know that following her to Los Angeles would've ended badly for them both.

And so, he pushed that pain of loss deeper inside him so he could function with everyday life as well as focus on the situation with his parents.

But it wasn't easy.

And it hurt like hell no matter how deep he buried it.

CHAPTER THIRTY-FOUR

DELAINEY HAD JUST finished packing her office when Hannah walked in, her pinched expression as sour as if she'd just been informed her skinny mocha latte had been made with whole milk rather than skim. "Aren't you clever," she said, not waiting for an invitation. "Can't say I'm surprised. I tried to warn Mr. Pilcher that you were a Judas, but he thought better of you. Can't say why. All you ever did was bring this network down, and frankly I'm glad you're leaving."

"Don't hold back, Hannah," Delainey said, chuckling. Oddly, it was refreshing to hear Hannah openly insulting her rather than hiding her jabs behind the thin veneer of concern or support. "There's no need to hold back now."

"Oh, I've waited a long time to get this off my chest, and I can't wait to tell you exactly what I think of you." But instead of launching into a tirade, Hannah swallowed whatever she'd been planning to say and said, "Karma will be your reward for screwing over the very network that gave you a chance in the first place."

"Not that I have anything to worry about in the karma department, but if I did, and karma were an actual thing in the cosmos, my guess is that everyone in the film and television industry would have cause to worry…especially you."

"Oh, is that so? And what puts you above the rest?"

"Because even though I tried really hard to fit in with the sharks, I never truly did because I never wanted to lie, cheat or steal my way to the top. Now, I don't have to. The Discovery Channel is very happy to add my new show to their lineup, and I am more than happy to go." Delainey paused before adding, "By the way, sorry to hear about that impending lawsuit against *Hubba Hubba*. Who knew filming drunken college coeds during spring break could end so badly? I hope that poor kid recovers from his fall. Good thing you caught it all on camera. I'll bet that will help in court."

Hannah's perfect lips compressed to a tight, angry line, and Delainey wanted to laugh and point out that when she did that, all the wrinkles and fine creases she'd been trying to squelch through chemistry returned with a vengeance. But for reasons unknown, Delainey didn't. Maybe she didn't see the point in trading barbs with someone who was plainly unhappy and likely to become even more so as life wore on.

In the past two months since returning from Alaska, she'd had a series of epiphanies that had left her giddy with the newfound knowledge and understanding of not only herself, but her driving ambition. After she'd put together a rough cut of Trace's pilot, the head of the network, Frank Pilcher, had nearly wet himself with glee because he knew it was going to be a hit. But when she'd tried to explain to him that Trace wasn't interested in pursuing a whole season, Pilcher's glee had turned to anger pretty quickly.

"You'll secure this man or else it's your job," the mean old man had threatened as he jabbed a finger at her. "Do whatever you did to get him to agree to the pilot. That seemed to work well enough. I don't need to know details. I just want results."

And it was then that Delainey realized this would be her future—constantly sacrificing her morals and ethics to cater to someone else's vision. Her next decision had been laughably easy.

"Trace Sinclair has too much integrity to have anything to do with you or this network," she said, shocking Pilcher into speechlessness. "He did the pilot because I strong-armed him into doing it. I manipulated him into doing something he hated because I thought I needed this for my career. But I was wrong. And you were wrong. The only one who was right was Trace."

"You're out of line, girl," Pilcher warned, spittle appearing on his bottom lip as his anger built. "You're out of line and I won't tolerate it!"

She laughed. "It's okay. You won't need to tolerate me or my ideas any longer. I've accepted a job elsewhere."

Pilcher gaped. "You ungrateful little bitch!"

"On the contrary, I'm very grateful. You helped me realize who I don't want to be and whom I don't want to be associated with. I quit."

She hadn't waited for his response and had gone to her office to pack, a smile on her lips, a song in her heart, and as she passed the breakfast cart, she'd snatched a double chocolate doughnut that she would've been too terrified to eat four short months ago for fear of it landing on her hips and thighs.

It'd been the best damn doughnut she'd ever eaten.

She'd been given a glimpse into a future that she wanted, and she was about to grab it with both hands. She wasn't sure if she believed in fate or what have you, but she had to wonder if something else was at play with the circumstances that had unfolded in her favor.

The Discovery Channel had been more than

ready and willing to listen to her pitch without even seeing the rough cut of Trace's pilot, thanks to the bold and loud bragging of one particular cameraman who happened to know whom to share the information with over cold beers and nachos. And once she'd pitched the halibut fishing idea, they'd been immediately sold, happy to cash in on the recent rash of public interest in all things natural or blue collar.

She'd been welcomed into the Discovery Channel family with open arms. The best part? They'd been eager to hear her other pitches, as well. For the first time in her professional life, doors were flying open instead of slamming shut.

But the best part had been the biggest and most unexpected blessing.

"You may think you're the cat's meow today, but tomorrow may be a different story. You're crazy for relocating to Alaska for a new job that you don't even know is going to work out in the long run. I hope you crash and burn."

With that Hannah turned on her Louboutin heels and left, her steps rigid and brisk until she disappeared around the corner. Delainey laughed, leaning back in her chair, amazed at how different everything felt.

Hannah was right; she was taking a huge risk

in relocating to head up the halibut show, but she wasn't worried. She knew Thad would test well in the demographics they were shooting for, and she had plenty of other ideas in the wings, all of them focused on Alaska in some way or another. But aside from all that, she no longer suffered that desperate hunger that threatened to chew on her soul if it wasn't appeased. Instead of that awful nothingness, she was filled with a glow that radiated from her heart and spilled over into her entire being.

She no longer had to choose—she could have Trace *and* her career.

And she was going to grab on to the opportunity with both hands.

Trevor had been right—good gravy, she'd never admit that to him in person—but if she'd spent more time figuring out how to succeed, rather than running scared in the other direction, she wouldn't have spent the past eight years limping from one desperate attempt to another to fit into a world she despised, living apart from the one man who was her life.

Delainey hefted the box that contained the sum of her work for the past eight years and gladly walked away.

She had a life to live.

And a plane to catch.

TRACE LIFTED THE SPOON to his mouth for some stew, courtesy of Miranda, when there came a knock at his door. He glanced at the clock and frowned at the time. Who was bothering him at this hour? Dropping the spoon back into his bowl, he climbed to his feet and went to the door, prepared to skewer whoever was on the other side. But he wasn't prepared for whom he saw.

"Delainey?" he started, shocked. "What are you doing here?"

Before she could answer and before she could playfully remind him of the last time she'd shown up at his door unannounced, he grabbed her by the jacket and hauled her forcibly across the threshold to seal his lips against hers. He didn't care why she was there. The fact that she *was* there was all that mattered.

He kissed her long and deep, all of the pent-up longing and heartache coalescing into a giant ball of need, and before she could catch her breath, he hefted her across his shoulder and carried her as she laughed and squealed straight to the bedroom. "I hope this is what you had in mind, because I'm not about to stop," he warned, giving her behind a good squeeze. She shrieked in open delight, and he grinned as he threw her to the bed, ripping his clothes free as he stalked toward her.

"Don't you want to know what I'm doing here?" she asked, breathless, as her fingers made quick work of her clothes. Within seconds, she was naked and his vision crossed. He fell on her like a beast, so desperate to touch and feel her again, to make sure that he wasn't dreaming and she was, in fact, there with him. She held his face tenderly as she kissed him deeply, her breasts rubbing against his chest with beautiful friction.

"I've missed you," he said with a hoarse groan as her deft fingers found his erection. "God, I've missed you so much…."

"Ask me why I'm here," she whispered against the shell of his ear, and he pulled away, staring down at her with open curiosity. She grinned. "Go ahead…ask me."

"Why are you here?" he asked, almost afraid.

"Because I've finally come to my senses and I'm saying yes to the question you asked eight years ago."

He stared into her eyes, his heart tripping a beat, afraid to hope. "Yes?" he repeated, almost unable to breathe. "Are you saying…yes to what I think…you're saying?" The words caught in his throat and he blinked back tears.

"Ask me again," she murmured, tucking the errant wisps of hair behind his ears.

Trace shook as he stared into her eyes. "Delainey Clarke...will you marry me?"

"Yes," she said, nodding with tears. "Yes, you beautiful man. I will marry you. I will gladly spend the rest of my life with you. And," she added with a twinkle in her eye, "I think we've had a long enough engagement. Are you busy tomorrow? My calendar is free if you are...."

"Tomorrow?" he repeated, astonished. "You mean, going to the courthouse and just getting it done?"

"That's exactly what I'm talking about."

The fact that she couldn't wait another second to be his wife filled him with such joy that words escaped him. He'd resigned himself to living without her, determined to watch her soar without him if need be. But she'd come back to him on her own, and he wasn't about to let her go again. He didn't know what had changed, but he didn't care. Whatever it was, they'd make it work. "We can be at the courthouse by 9:00 a.m."

She grinned and pulled him close. "Perfect. Gives us just enough time to sleep in a little, because you're not going to get a lick of sleep tonight."

"That's my girl," he growled, pressing another deep and lusty kiss against her lips, nearly delirious with the need to feel her against him.

"Your girl…always and forever," she said on a sigh.

And then they took turns showing each other exactly how much they'd missed one another— over and over and over.

Come morning, they were both bleary-eyed and sore in muscles they hadn't even known they possessed, but they didn't mind.

They were about to spend the rest of their lives together and couldn't wait to get on with it.

Come what may, they were a team and forever more always would be.

EPILOGUE

TRACE AND DELAINEY were married at the court-house with Miranda, her guy, Jeremiah, and Talen as witnesses, both eager to start making up for what they believed as lost time. But even as they shared a wondrous bond and their future together seemed rosy, Trace worried about the future. For one, the situation with his parents was likely to get worse before it got better, and he didn't want to scare away his new bride.

"You're not allowed to fall into a funk a day after our wedding," Delainey teased, tapping at the frown gathering on his forehead. "What's wrong?"

"I'm worried about the situation with my parents and how it might affect us. And I'm worried about your new job with the Discovery Channel," he admitted, not willing to start their new life together with a veneer of half-truths. "We're taking on a lot, and right now I'm thinking selfishly. I don't want anything to come between our happiness."

She smiled and wrapped her arms around his torso. "I love how protective you are. That's a wonderful quality in a husband, in my opinion. But you need to stop worrying. I'm not going anywhere. Not this time. I'm not that same naive girl who expects wine and roses every day. I know times might get tough, but I'm not scared because I know whatever comes our way, we'll handle it."

Her quiet trust floored and humbled him. "I love you," he said. "Not in the easy way most people say the words. I mean, I love you more than I love anything else in this world. I love you more than a cold beer on a hot summer day. Or the thrill of tracking a lost hiker and finding them alive and well. I love you so much, Delainey Sinclair. Would it be completely corny if I said, you complete me?"

"Yes," she answered, but followed with a grin. "And I love it." They shared a kiss, and when they pulled away, she sobered and said, "I know things are going to get hard with your parents. But I love your parents, too. They were there for me when I had no one. I want to be there for you *and* them. Plus, I don't know why, but I'm not worried about my career anymore. I know I'll always be okay. Especially now that

I've found my niche. Who knew that I'd have to leave and come back to realize that what I'd needed all along was right here to begin with? It's going to be okay."

Her confident assurance filled him with such intense emotion, he started to tear up. "Gahh," he said, wiping at his eyes with embarrassment. "You've turned me into a blubbering baby."

"Not hardly," she retorted, laughing. "You're the most manly man I've ever known. And you're going to make an amazing father someday."

"Someday?" he repeated, his heart leaping with the possibility. "Someday..."

She smiled coyly. "Someday soon, I wager. I figure...we've waited long enough."

He cradled her to his chest, unable to believe what an incredible gift he had in his wife.

No matter the pain he suffered all those years without her, she'd been worth the wait.

And since she'd pretty much given him the green light...he grasped her hand and pulled her to the bedroom.

"What are you doing?" she asked, laughing.

"Like you said, we've waited long enough... and practice makes perfect, right? Time to get naked, Mrs. Sinclair...and make some babies!"

Her delighted laughter turned to gasping moans, and Trace realized he'd never tire of either sound. Life wasn't perfect—but it was damn near close.

* * * * *

Be sure to look for the last book in THE SINCLAIRS OF ALASKA *trilogy by Kimberly Van Meter—available from Harlequin Superromance in July 2014!*

LARGER-PRINT BOOKS!
GET 2 FREE LARGER-PRINT NOVELS PLUS
2 FREE GIFTS!

HARLEQUIN®

super romance®

More Story...More Romance

HSRLP13R

LARGER-PRINT
BOOKS!

HARLEQUIN *Presents*

PASSION GUARANTEED SEDUCTION

GET 2 FREE LARGER-PRINT
NOVELS PLUS 2 FREE GIFTS!

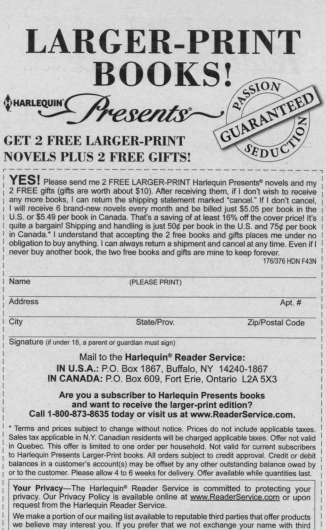

YES! Please send me 2 FREE LARGER-PRINT Harlequin Presents® novels and my 2 FREE gifts (gifts are worth about $10). After receiving them, if I don't wish to receive any more books, I can return the shipping statement marked "cancel." If I don't cancel, I will receive 6 brand-new novels every month and be billed just $5.05 per book in the U.S. or $5.49 per book in Canada. That's a saving of at least 16% off the cover price! It's quite a bargain! Shipping and handling is just 50¢ per book in the U.S. and 75¢ per book in Canada.* I understand that accepting the 2 free books and gifts places me under no obligation to buy anything. I can always return a shipment and cancel at any time. Even if I never buy another book, the two free books and gifts are mine to keep forever.

176/376 HDN F43N

Name	(PLEASE PRINT)	

Address		Apt. #

City	State/Prov.	Zip/Postal Code

Signature (if under 18, a parent or guardian must sign)

Mail to the **Harlequin® Reader Service:**
IN U.S.A.: P.O. Box 1867, Buffalo, NY 14240-1867
IN CANADA: P.O. Box 609, Fort Erie, Ontario L2A 5X3

**Are you a subscriber to Harlequin Presents books
and want to receive the larger-print edition?
Call 1-800-873-8635 today or visit us at www.ReaderService.com.**

* Terms and prices subject to change without notice. Prices do not include applicable taxes. Sales tax applicable in N.Y. Canadian residents will be charged applicable taxes. Offer not valid in Quebec. This offer is limited to one order per household. Not valid for current subscribers to Harlequin Presents Larger-Print books. All orders subject to credit approval. Credit or debit balances in a customer's account(s) may be offset by any other outstanding balance owed by or to the customer. Please allow 4 to 6 weeks for delivery. Offer available while quantities last.

Your Privacy—The Harlequin® Reader Service is committed to protecting your privacy. Our Privacy Policy is available online at www.ReaderService.com or upon request from the Harlequin Reader Service.

We make a portion of our mailing list available to reputable third parties that offer products we believe may interest you. If you prefer that we not exchange your name with third parties, or if you wish to clarify or modify your communication preferences, please visit us at www.ReaderService.com/consumerschoice or write to us at Harlequin Reader Service Preference Service, P.O. Box 9062, Buffalo, NY 14269. Include your complete name and address.

ReaderService.com

Manage your account online!

- Review your order history
- Manage your payments
- Update your address

*We've designed
the Harlequin® Reader Service
website just for you.*

Enjoy all the features!

- Reader excerpts from any series
- Respond to mailings and
  special monthly offers
- Discover new series available to you
- Browse the Bonus Bucks catalog
- Share your feedback

Visit us at:
ReaderService.com